THE BULLYING OF
NATALIE CORDOVA

KENNON KEITH

Copyright © 2022 Kennon Keith

All rights reserved. No part of this book may be reproduced, stored, or transmitted by any means—whether auditory, graphic, mechanical, or electronic—without written permission of both publisher and author, except in the case of brief excerpts used in critical articles and reviews. Unauthorized reproduction of any part of this work is illegal and is punishable by law.

ISBN: 979-8-88640-076-2 (sc)
ISBN: 979-8-88640-077-9 (hc)
ISBN: 979-8-88640-078-6 (e)

Because of the dynamic nature of the Internet, any web addresses or links contained in this book may have changed since publication and may no longer be valid. The views expressed in this work are solely those of the author and do not necessarily reflect the views of the publisher, and the publisher hereby disclaims any responsibility for them.

The Ewings Publishing LLC
One Galleria Blvd., Suite 1900, Metairie, LA 70001
1-888-421-2397

Six-thirty in the morning, and a new day begins. An alarm clock activates, sending out a loud, repeated beep throughout the dark room. Natalie Cordova rolls over in bed, hits the snooze, and stares at the clock. 6:30a.m. She has two hours to get out of bed, shower and dress, eat breakfast, and get to school before the first bell. This is her normal routine, yet she moves very slowly, and reluctantly. Why should she go to school? She already has an idea of how the day will progress.

She will start her day by taking off the earrings, bracelets and necklace that her grandmother requires her to wear, and store them in her purse. As she walks to her first class in the back of campus, she will pass the quad where Heather Long hangs out with her best friend Ashley Tyler. She will rush briskly through the area in order to avoid them, yet they will find her anyway. Heather will call her a whore, fucking bitch or some other derogatory slur, while Ashley will just stand there and watch. Natalie will try to walk away quickly, but Heather will trip her into a nearby puddle, ruining her clothes. Dirty again, showering would have been a wasted task.

After her first few classes, the lunch bell would sound, and Natalie will head to the library to study. On her way there, she will go to the bathroom to urinate. While in the restroom, she will run into Heather again, as well as her friend, Lynn Bennett. Natalie will try to mind her own business and ignore the many insults they hurl at her. After washing her hands, Lynn will bump her down to the dirty floor. The school only cleans the restrooms in the morning; so by mid-day, the floor will be filthy and disgusting. The feeling of being on the dirty, gritty, grimy bathroom floor that smells like urine will make her nauseous and want to vomit, so breakfast is out of the question.

Towards the end of the lunch break, she will head to her locker and exchange her math and history books for her economics and science books. Something will fall out her locker and she will squat down to pick it up. While kneeling, Marco Ruiz and Howard Haynesworth will walk by. Marco will reach out and slam her locker door shut, catching her hand. She will clutch her hand in obvious pain and attempt to hold back her tears. Marco will walk away, giving a sarcastic "Oops" for his transgression. Howard will feign concern and search her purse for anything he can find to help her. When finished, he will toss it down to the ground, stating he could not find a first-aid kit or an ice pack, and advise her to be more prepared for emergencies and walk off. Natalie will then inspect her purse and discover that her jewelry is missing. Her clothes are ruined, her jewelry is gone and her hand hurts like hell. Dressing nicely makes no sense.

In her final class of the day, she will have an economics test. She is a very smart girl, so the test is easy for her. The teacher will grade the exams in class as he always does and give them back the same day. She will pass, tied with Monica Bynes for the best grade in the class. After the class ends, Monica will move in and ask, "How long did you have to suck his dick for that grade?" Natalie will continue to walk away, trying to ignore the last remark. While walking off campus, she will see Howard and Lynn making out under the marquee. Lynn will thank Howard for the beautiful new jewelry he just gave her.

Upon arriving home, Natalie will walk in and see her grandmother. Rebecca will see the dirty clothes, missing jewelry, the injured hand,

and curse under her breath. She will reprimand Natalie for not gaining the respect of her peers that day and send her back into her basement bedroom. Natalie will then change her clothes, do her homework and climb into bed. In bed, she will cry herself to sleep. She will wake up he next mooring feeling as miserable as she does now, thus continuing the vicious cycle.

At 6:37 a.m., the alarm clock sounds again. Natalie turns it off and sits up in bed. She reaches over to her nightstand and turns on the lamp. Her bedroom is a converted basement. A thin carpet covers the concrete floor. The walls were painted white years ago and the paint is starting to flake off. Her twin size bed rests against the north wall facing the furnace room. On cold winter nights, the roar of the furnace will keep her awake, unable to sleep. In the southwestern corner of the room, a small table stands with a simple chair and an old laptop computer and printer. The lamp on her nightstand is a relic of the 1940's. It emits a soft amber glow that barely lights the room. A small bathroom with a toilet, sink, and shower rests in the northeast corner. The bathroom has no light, so Natalie has to shower with the door open. Her clothes hang on a laundry rack against the east wall. She is not allowed access to the laundry room. She must wash her clothes outside by hand and let them hang dry. Natalie was accustomed to these deplorable conditions. She has lived in this basement since she was 12 years old. She is now 18 and about to graduate high school.

Natalie closes her eyes and breathes steadily. She takes a few minutes to focus and try to gain enough strength to face the day. The usual checklist runs through her mind. Avoid Heather and her friends at all cost. Keep to herself, speak only when spoken to, and only when she must. She opens her eyes and heads to the bathroom. She grabs the towel off the rack and turns on the shower. She gets very little hot water in her shower, so she must bathe quickly.

The shower is one of Natalie's few avenues of relaxation. She closes her eyes and tries to enjoy the sensation of the warm water running down her naked body. Relaxing is not without its struggles. The sound of the water hitting the shower floor reminds her of that day six years ago, when she lost her mother.

That day was rainy and cold. Natalie was sitting silently in the passenger seat of her mother's car. Her mother, Raylene Cordova was traveling at 70 miles per hour on the highway. Natalie stared out the window, watching the cars go by. She wondered where they were going, but she did not dare ask. She learned at a young age that when she spoke out of turn, her mother quickly and harshly put her in her place. Sometimes she would use a hard stare and a tongue-lashing, other times she would hit Natalie across her backside or her face. Therefore, she was not a talkative child. As they approached the Carter Street exit, Natalie figured they were headed to another glamour photo shoot. Raylene loved having pretty photos of herself and her daughter all over the house. Natalie however, hated these shoots. Her mother would always yell at her to get her poses right and to smile at the camera. She remembered one instance when the photographer called in a security guard after her mother started screaming and made her cry. Once Raylene threatened to call off the shoot, the guard was sent away and the session completed.

Raylene parked the car at a house Natalie had never seen before. The house was not far from her home, only 15 minutes away and just down the street from the school she attended. Raylene unbuckled Natalie's seat belt.

"Out of the car," Raylene said, "now."

Natalie did not talk back. She got out of the car and waited as her mother got out and came over to her. Taking her hand, Raylene led the girl up the porch steps and rang the doorbell. An older woman answered the door and opened the screen. She was an elegant woman with a slim build, shiny black hair hanging down past her shoulders and radiant skin. She stood in the open door, smoking a cigarette. She took one long puff of her cancer stick and looked at Raylene.

"About time you showed up." She spoke with low, serious tone.

"I know, and I'm sorry I'm late." Raylene's voice was shaky and timid. "It's good to see you again mother."

This statement surprised Natalie. She had always wondered about her grandmother. Raylene told Natalie stories of how her grandmother grew up in Deep South Decatur, Georgia. She was a true southern belle and a lifelong pageant winner. She was the one that taught Raylene how to use her beauty to get what she wanted out of life. Natalie had so many questions she wanted to ask, but she kept quiet.

"Good to see me? Oh really?" The grandmother's voice hardened. "You avoid me for 12 years and now it's good to see me?"

Raylene's head hung low and ashamed. "I'm sorry mother."

"Rebecca!" the grandmother shot back. "Call me by my name. You lost the right to call me mother when you left." Raylene kept her head down.

Rebecca gazed down at Natalie. The girl looked up and smiled, wanting to make a good impression. Rebecca puffed on her cigarette and kept her gaze on Natalie.

"What's your name kiddo?" She asked.

"Natalie Renee." Natalie replied. She was giddy on the inside. She finally met her grandmother.

Rebecca quipped, "You're adorable. Got some real potential. Tell me kiddo; do you know who I am?"

Natalie answered carefully, "I think you're my grandmother."

Rebecca grinned slightly. "Do me a favor kid. Never call me grandmother. It's title for wrinkled has-beens who don't give a shit about life anymore."

"MOTHER!" Raylene shot back. "Is that language really appropriate?"

"What did you call me?" Rebecca asked.

"I'm sorry Rebecca, but she's only 12 years old." Raylene lowered her head again.

"And from what you told me, she needs to grow up." Rebecca responded. "Better she hears it from me than from some random prick on the street." Rebecca flicked her cigarette to the ground and stepped on it to put it out. She opened the door wider and motioned for her family to come inside.

Natalie and her mother walked inside the entree hall. This was the biggest house that she had ever seen. As she gazed around the foyer, she admired the antique furniture and light fixtures. The walls were wallpapered gold and adorned with pictures of a younger Rebecca and her friends and family. The high ceilings and hardwood floors were adorned with white crown moldings. French doors separated the foyer from the living room on the left and a spiral staircase lead to the second story on the right. This exemplified the kind of house that Natalie had always wanted to live in.

Rebecca walked next to Natalie a placed her hand on her shoulder.

"Natalie, there is a room in the back with a T.V." She said. "Why don't you go and watch, so your mom and I can talk?"

"Yes ma'am." Natalie replied.

"Don't call my ma'am either." Rebecca said. "Call me Nana."

"Ok, Nana." Natalie scurried off to the back room.

That was the last time Natalie saw her mother. Rebecca and Raylene worked out an arrangement for Natalie to stay and live there. Raylene wanted to pursue an acting career and did not want a child to weigh her down. She also grew tired of trying to mold her daughter into an idol of beauty. Natalie wanted to be a kid and Raylene would have not of that. Natalie was sent to school in expensive designer clothes, with hair styled and makeup perfected. This caused her to be picked on and bullied by the other students. When Natalie tried to tell her mother, she was punished for not winning her peers over. Natalie figured, if her mother would not help her, then neither would the teachers and principal. She endured the treatment everyday at school since kindergarten.

Raylene reached out to her mother for help. Rebecca's first reaction was to shun her daughter. She felt if she could not raise Natalie to be beautiful, then she was an unfit mother. Raylene believed that Rebecca could do what she could not. After warming to the idea, she agreed on the condition that Raylene could not interfere. Raylene agreed.

Natalie was devastated when Rebecca told her the situation and she cried uncontrollably. She thought she was such a horrible daughter; her own mother wanted nothing to do with her. Despite her fear, Natalie always thought of her mother as her friend, but now she was gone. Rebecca provided no comfort to her weeping granddaughter. Instead, she left her in the backroom to cry alone in the dark. When Natalie did emerge, Rebecca laid out the ground rules.

Natalie was to live in the downstairs bedroom in the basement. Until she learned to fit in socially, she would live like an outcast. With the exception of school, meals, and emergencies, she was to remain in the basement for all hours of the day. She would not have any friends over nor have telephone access. If Rebecca were entertaining company, Natalie would remain in the basement and not emerge under any circumstances. Natalie would be inspected every morning before school for proper color coordination, hair, and makeup. Natalie would not be coddled or assisted in anyway; she would achieve her beauty on her own. Any harassment she encountered at school was entirely her own fault and she would receive no remorse or comfort from her Nana.

Natalie did not have the will to protest these rules. She accepted the conditions and moved her belongings into the basement.

The shock of cold water brings Natalie back to reality. She steps out of the shower and dries off. Walking out of her bathroom, she checks the time. 6:57 a.m. She walks to her clothing rack to pick out her clothes for the day. She chooses a crimson top, a low cut blouse with sleeves barely below the shoulder; and a white, knee length skirt. Simple white Keds, no socks, completes the look. She runs a comb through her still damp blonde hair and gets dressed.

At 7:22 a.m., Natalie gathers her backpack and heads upstairs. She needs to find something to eat and pass her Nana's inspection before she leaves for school. Once on the main floor, she heads to the kitchen. She eats a Nutra-Grain bar and drinks a small glass of milk; her usual breakfast. She enters the dining room and inspects the table. This is where her Nana leaves the jewelry for her to wear. She finds a thin silver necklace with a butterfly pendant and small hoop earrings. After she puts them on, she looks up from the table and sees her Nana in the living room watching the morning news. Natalie heads over to her, ready for her inspection.

Rebecca sees Natalie enter the living room. She looks up from the T.V. and inspects her granddaughter. She casually looks Natalie up and down, checking the fit of the blouse and the rise of the skirt. She goes through her mental checklist half-heartedly, making sure the clothes conform to Natalie's body and accentuate her features. She looks away, shaking her head in disappointment. She waves her hand, shooing Natalie away. "Go."

At 7:34 a.m., Natalie grabs her backpack and heads for the front door. She does not look back at her Nana. When she opens the door, Rebecca calls out to her.

"Natalie." Her voice is firm. "When are you going to learn? How you look on the outside is nothing when you carry yourself like shit. Until you gain some confidence in yourself, you'll always be the fucking outcast."

Harsh words, but Natalie was numb to them. She heard similar speeches every morning.

"Natalie," Rebecca continues, "we have done this routine everyday for the past six years, and I'm tired of it. I can't do anything more to help you, and the main problem is your refusal to help yourself. Therefore, you leave me no choice. This will be you last chance."

This was a new development. Natalie had no idea she had a limited number of chances. This became cause for concern.

"My last chance?" she asks softly.

"I'm leaving this afternoon." Nana answers. "I'm going to Italy with Etienne. We will be spending the summer there."

Etienne is Rebecca's young lover, almost 24 years her junior. They met on one of Rebecca's many summer trips to Paris. Rebecca felt that by dating a younger man, she was justifying her high maintenance lifestyle.

"I've made the same provisions," she continues, "so you have my credit cards available to you for bills and emergencies. However, this will be the last time I leave you unattended. I have taught you everything I can, but you refuse to put that knowledge to work. Therefore, you have this final summer to gain confidence, improve your look, carry yourself like a lady, and break down the shell you have built around yourself. Show me you have learned something!" Rebecca sounds very determined. "If you do, we will be fine. You will move out of the basement and life will be good. If not, I'm putting you out!"

"Out?" Natalie is confused. "What do you mean?"

"Simply," she answers, "I'm throwing you out on your ass!" Natalie is taken aback. She and Nana have had there disagreements, but never had she thought that she would be thrown on out on the street.

"But, how can you do that?" Natalie asks. She is alert, and very distressed.

"Easily!" Rebecca shoots back. "You obviously do not appreciate this good life that I'm trying to give you. The expensive clothes, the fine jewelry, this big beautiful house, all this can be yours! Yet instead of claiming them; you leave here every morning looking like a piss rat; you don't defend yourself when you are treated like a doormat; and you have no friends from which to draw envy. Maybe it's time for the cold, cruel world to take a stab at you, because I've had it!" Rebecca storms off.

The shock of this latest confrontation leaves Natalie almost speechless. She calls after Rebecca.

"What am I supposed to do on the streets?!" She yells.

"Not my problem." Rebecca's tone is dismissive and she continues to walk away.

Natalie is shocked. She cannot believe her grandmother would kick her out of her home. Tears stream down her face as she runs out of the house. She slams the door on her way out. The impact of the door causes some of the pictures to fall off the wall.

Natalie walks down the street. She can barely breathe, nor can she clear her mind. She stops walking, attempting to catch her breath. Her eyes are red and puffy from crying, her knees feel weak, her head is dizzy, and her stomach wants to vomit. She sits down on the curb to gather her thoughts. She has felt this way before.

She was 13 years old. During her physical education class, she was hit in the face by a tennis ball, causing a massive nosebleed. As she lay on the ground bleeding, she saw Howard Haynesworth running over to her. She liked Howard. He was tall and athletic with a mocha skin tone. She thought he was very cute and thought, *"Maybe this is the moment I have been waiting for. My prince will come and rescue me."* No such luck. Instead, he stopped short and turned to Lynn Bennett, the girl who had served the ball. He was laughing hysterically. She saw him whisper something to her, and before Natalie could realize what was happening, she was hit in the face again. This time, both Lynn and Howard were in a hysterical fervor. She picked herself up and ran away as fast as she could. She was crying so hard, she could barely see ahead of her. Somehow, she made it home.

When she got home, she ran downstairs and threw herself on the bed in a fit of sorrow and rage. She was saddened about bleeding all over herself, but she was more angry than sad. She was angry that Howard, the boy for whom she carried a flame, found humor in her pain. She was angry that Lynn made her look like a fool in front of him, twice. Finally, she was pissed that she did nothing about it. She did not know what she could have done. Her first reaction was to run away, and flee the ridicule. In her bed, she wished she had the courage to defend herself; but she did not.

Rebecca came down to check about the commotion. When she reached the bedroom, she saw Natalie and was horrified. Her face was swollen under her right eye and on the bridge of her nose, black and purple. Dried blood covered her mouth and chin. Additionally, she was wearing sweaty gym clothes and sneakers, instead of her sundress and designer sandals. Blood had dripped onto her shirt and soaked in. After surveying her granddaughter, Rebecca's emotions shifted from horror to anger.

"What the hell happened to you?" she demanded.

"In gym….a tennis ball….my nose…" Natalie sobbed, fighting hard to control the tears, but failing.

"Where are your clothes?" Rebecca cut her off.

"In my gym locker, at school." Natalie answered

"You left your dress in a sweaty locker?" Rebecca demanded. "Do you know how much that shit cost me?"

Natalie was shocked. Here she was, face swollen and bleeding, and all her grandmother could worry about was the dress.

"I'll get it tomorrow when I…" She began.

"No!" Rebecca grabbed Natalie's arm and pulled her hard. "You will march back to that school and change into your dress this instant!"

Natalie became very upset at hearing this.

"I can't go back. They'll all laugh at me." Natalie pleaded, "I won't go back."

"I don't give a shit what they do! You will go to that scho…"

"NO!" Natalie screamed. She pulled her arm hard and ripped it out of her Nana's grasp. The force of her pull sent her arm crashing into the wall mirror, shattering it. A larger piece of glass fell onto her arm and sliced it open, causing a large gash to open on her forearm.

She fell to the ground, holding her arm. The cut was bleeding badly, but she did not cry and she did not scream. She kept her eyes closed and controlled her breathing. She had never had this kind of control over her emotions before. The pain of the gash caused her emotions, her fear and anger, melt away. All she could do was focus on the pain.

Rebecca was stunned. Never had Natalie lashed out in such a way. She stood and watched her grand daughter lay on the floor bleeding. She wanted to do something, but she could not move. She did not know what to do.

After being still for what seemed like an eternity, she walked over to her fallen kin and placed a hand on her shoulder. Slowly, Natalie began to stir. She held her arm as she sat up. She opened her eyes and looked at Rebecca. No tears, no anger, she was in complete control of herself.

"I'm sorry Nana," she says quietly. "I'll go back and get the dress" She tries to stand up when Rebecca stops her.

"No, no child. It's alright." Her tone was calm as well. "That cut looks pretty bad. Let me wrap it for you and I'll get you to the hospital."

Despite the heated exchange of only minutes ago, both Rebecca and Natalie had calmed dramatically. Natalie's injury caused both women to reshift their focus and calm their nerves. Natalie never forgot this lesson and became a cutter. When she felt those feeling of anger and rage, she would take out a razor blade and slice her forearm, not deeply, but just enough to hurt and allow her blood to trickle. She learned how to dress her wounds and hide them from her grandmother. Over time, Natalie gained a better grasp on her anger, and stopped cutting after her 15th birthday.

The blaring of a honking horn brings Natalie out of her flashback. She realizes she is sitting on the curb outside of her school. She collects her thoughts, gathers her book bag and heads for the campus. The school security guard is directing student traffic outside of the quad. Natalie stops and watches him for a moment.

He is a tall, muscular man. Natalie guesses, at least six feet, 5 inches tall, black, with a deep voice, very intimidating. She admires how he has the respect of the students. Some students stop by and have a quick chat with him before they head to class. He is always kind to the students and very good at his job. Natalie watches as he shows a male freshmen student how to whistle by using two fingers.

Natalie begins to think to herself. *Okay, Nana said you need confidence.* She takes a deep breath. *This guy seems kind and easy going. Just ask him to show you how to whistle.* Her heart begins to race. She has not approached anyone in any social way since she was eight years old. She takes another relaxing breath and walks towards the guard.

The young freshman boy blows hard on his fingers. He is rewarded with a whimpering whistle-like sound.

"That's it? Dude, that sucks!" he blurts out.

The guard throws his head back in laughter.

"Just practice little man." the guard answers back. "You'll get it in no time." The freshman turns around and walks off, still blowing on his fingers.

As Natalie approaches, she notices that the guard is older than she originally thought. He is probably in his mid to late 40's or early 50's. Natalie puts the thought out of her mind. She is going in to make contact and gain some confidence.

"Hey!" she calls out. The guard turns around, flashes a warm smile and replies, "Can I help you young lady?"

"Yeah, you think you could show me how to do that?" She asks with a smile.

"Show you what? I am a man of many talents after all." He responds.

Natalie cannot help but chuckle. He is being very sweet. This is new to her.

"You know," she says. "The finger whistle thing."

"Oh, you mean this." The guard turns his head and blows the loudest whistle she had ever heard.

"Wow. Yes that." She laughs. She maintains her smile, this is going better than she imagined.

"Sure kid." He raises his right hand. "First, you make your hand like you're giving an 'A-OK' sign." He demonstrates and she mimics his movements. "Be sure to pinch your thumb and index together." She does.

"Alright. Next, you lift your tongue and place it behind your front teeth, like this." He opens his mouth wide so she can see. She observes and does the same.

"Good. Now you gotta be quick with the next step. You shove those two fingers in your mouth, press them against your tongue, and blow." He shows her. Again, he makes a loud noise.

Natalie tries it. She does not move as quickly as he did, but she does manage a soft whistle. Not loud at all, yet it is better than the freshman from earlier.

"Hey." the guard replies. "That's not bad for a rookie."

"Really?" she exclaims. "It wasn't bad?"

"Bad? No." He answers. "You're a natural."

"Cool." she replies. "Thank you, Mike, is it?"

"Close," he answers, "Micah. Officer Micah Purvis."

"Officer huh?" She asks.

"Well, retired Officer Micah Purvis." He sighs and chuckles to himself.

Natalie gives him a big smile. "No matter." She reaches out and gives his arm a gentle squeeze. "Thank you, Micah." She turns and begins to leave.

"Oh, Miss?" He calls after her. She turns around.

"Don't you know it's rude to not return an introduction?" he asks jovially.

She blushes and smiles. "I'm sorry. Where are my manners? My name's Natalie. Natalie Cordova."

"Alright. Well, you have a good day Natalie." He waves goodbye.

"You too Micah." She waves back and walks away.

Natalie heads for the quad. She feels energized and excited. Her heart races, but now the beats are of relief and excitement. The smile on her face is as large as she has carried in years. She just held a friendly conversation with a stranger. Never before had she the courage to do such a simple task, but on this morning, she did; and that small gesture did wonders for her self-esteem.

She arrives at the quad and heads for a nearby table. She has to sit down for a minute to collect her thoughts. The feeling of euphoria is a little overwhelming, and she does not want to stand out. She reaches the closest table and has a seat. She checks the time on the school clock tower. 8:19 a.m. She still has eleven minutes to spare before class. She takes a deep breath, and closes her eyes. She just wants a minute or two in order to get composed. She hears the footsteps of the students walking past her; hears some birds singing in the background; she feels at peace. Today, she believes, is going to be a great day.

"What the fuck are you doing here?"

Startled, Natalie snaps her head around and her eyes grow large. She stares face to face with the bane of her existence, Heather Long.

Heather and Natalie have a history together; one that is very one sided. Heather's parents are Halem and Cerise Long, amongst the first to invest in Microsoft Corporation on the ground floor. Today, they are worth hundreds of millions of dollars. She grew up a spoiled daughter of privilege. Every toy, every piece of trendy fashion, every popular gadget and such, she was the first to have it. She is a socialite, appearing in local tabloids as the "it" girl. To be able to say that Heather Long is a good friend, is a privilege that most kids her age desire. Almost every person in her age group seeks her public approval. Everyone, except Natalie.

As youngsters, Natalie and Heather had quite a lot in common. Both girls were sent to school looking like little heiresses, both were born into upper class families, and both were being raised to use what they had to take advantage of those around them and get what they wanted. Natalie had beauty, and Heather had money. Heather also had something Natalie did not; a very bad attitude. Heather was scornful, and very aggressive. While Natalie was taught to let things come to her, Heather was taught to get them at all cost.

In grade school, classmates were initially drawn to Natalie. Although she was socially upper class, other kids thought she looked friendly and likeable. She welcomed their nice words and funny comments. To witness the interaction, was to assume that Natalie would grow up to be the popular girl, just as her mother wanted. However, Heather would not be denied. She approached Natalie as well, but for different reasons. She never learned about friendly competition, and she viewed Natalie as the enemy. When other kids told Natalie she looked nice, Heather would call her gutter trash. Whenever any kid would compliment Natalie, Heather would find a way to retaliate. Actions included knocking Natalie into mud puddles, pouring glue in her hair, or even throwing sand in her face and eyes. Natalie was not prepared for such attacks and did not know what to do about them.

Heather inspired fear in the other children, and fear created power. She would threaten her classmates with physical harm if they befriended Natalie. To back up her words, she physically made examples out of girls that openly defied her. Her behavior did carry disciplinary repercussions; however, her parents were often able to make these problems go away, either through a donation to the school district or the threat of legal action. As years went by, Natalie lost more and more friends. By her fourth grade year, she was a schoolyard pariah.

This treatment continued through Junior High and into High School, and Heather was quite proud of her accomplishments. Not only had she crushed her rival, she had managed to keep her at the bottom rung of the social ladder. In the process, Heather became one of the most popular girls in the city. In her pursuit of social domination, she even turned Natalie's best friend, Monica Bynes, against her. All it took was an invite to her birthday party and a small taste of high society. By her first year of high school, she successfully alienated Natalie from all social events and gatherings of children their age. Natalie believes that

Heather is responsible for her current social standing, but she does not have the necessary courage to change any of it.

"Answer me! What the fuck, are you are doing here?" Heather demands.

Natalie cannot think straight and quietly utters, "Shit!"

"Shit? You calling a piece of shit?" Heather asks. She swats Natalie across her head, just above her left eye.

"No." Natalie stammers "I...uhh...wrong table. I'm leaving now." She gets up to leave. Before she can step away, she runs into Marco Ruiz, Heather's boyfriend and personal enforcer. She falls back on the seat.

"Naw, baby." Marco looks over at Heather. "I think she did call you a piece of shit"

"No, I didn't" Natalie interjects. "Just a slip up. I promise."

"You know what Cordova," Heather says smuggly, "I've been waiting a very long time for you to slip up."

She grabs a fist full of Natalie's blouse and pulls her hard. She is mere inches from Natalie's face.

"Maybe I should say thank you." She continues.

"Please, don't..." Natalie pleads as her eyes well with fearful tears.

"Don't what?" Heather interrupts. "Do you know what I'm gonna do? I sure as hell don't; but if I do do, what you what you think I'm gonna do, who would stop me?" She stares hard into Natalie's eyes, getting high off the fear she sees.

"Nobody." She says. "That's who. I've worked too damn hard to make sure of that."

"No, please, don't." Natalie pleads again. Her tears are visibly running down the side of her face.

Heather looks up at Marco.

"What do you think I should do papi?" She asks.

Marco loves every second of the scene in front of him.

"I think you should beat that sweet ass chica." He answers.

Natalie panics. She is choked up, and can barely speak as she pleas for mercy.

"Sorry hun," Heather replies, "but my man has spoken."

Heather cannot wait and is on the verge of drooling. Physically beating Natalie is one goal she still has yet to accomplish, and this is her golden moment.

Natalie cannot think and her mind is racing. She knows that Heather is right, and no one will help her. All she can do is try to block the blows with her arms. She does not have the will to fight back. She looks around one last time in a desperate search for help; and she finds it. Out of the corner of her eye, she sees the security guard, Officer Micah Purvis, strolling across the quad heading to the main office building. She does not think and moves quickly. Natalie jams two fingers in her mouth, presses against her tongue, and blows as hard as she can. She is rewarded with a loud reverberating siren of a whistle that echoes though the quad. Micah stops and looks toward the whistle.

Heather lets Natalie go. She looks up and sees the guard looking in her direction. She stands up and motions for Marco. She quickly stares at Natalie and flips her off.

"Fuck you bitch." She blurts. "Let's go Marco."

She grabs Marco's arm and they hurry off in the opposite direction.

Natalie places her arms on the table and lowers her head. She breathes very hard, torn between two emotions, fear and relief. She knows how close she came to getting beaten by Heather, but she is also relieved that it did not happen. Just two minutes ago, she was so sure her day would different, but at this moment, she doe not know what to think.

"Hey, I knew you were a natural." A voice speaks.

Natalie looks and sees Micah's friendly face. She already forgot she signaled for him, but is glad to see him. As Micah gets closer, he sees that Natalie's face is red and her eyes are puffy. He sees the tears still on her face and grows concerned.

"Hey, hey, hey." He sits down next to her. "What happened?"

"Nothing." She replies. "Nothing happened. It's over now" She looks at Micah and tries to flash a smile, but Micah is not fooled.

"Miss Cordova," he begins, "you're a good whistler, but a bad liar."

Natalie gives a quick chuckle under her breath. She knows he is right.

"It's okay," she says in a quiet tone. "The year is almost over, and I'll never have to worry about nothing ever again."

The five-minute warning bell rings at 8:25 a.m. Natalie has five minutes to get to class or else she will have a tardy on her record. She stands up, grabs her backpack, bids farewell to Micah, and turns to leave.

"Hey, Nat!" Micah calls out. She turns to him in response. He gets up and walks over to her.

"Nothing doesn't end when you graduate." He says. "Nothing is a lifestyle choice, and it thrives in an environment of self-doubt. Nothing doesn't stop on its own. It doesn't want to. You have to stop it. Because if you don't, nothing follows you for the rest of your life."

Natalie looks down at the ground, knowing his words were true, and they hurt. She wants the torment to end, but does not know how. She knows she has to find some way to do it. She looks up at Micah.

"How do I make it end?" she asks

"Only you can figure that out," he answers, "but if you need any help at all, I'm here for you. Just holler."

The words feel good to hear. She never had anyone be around for her. Not her mother, not her Nana, not anyone. She feels like she found a friend in Micah, and she is grateful. She reaches out and gives Micah another squeeze on the arm.

"Thank you, Micah," A tear runs down her face, a tear of joy.

"I'll see you around kid." He answers, and flashes a quick smile. Natalie turns and quickly walks towards her first class. She barely makes it in time.

Her first class is a math class, College Calculus. She enjoys this class. Not only is she proficient in math, many of the students pay no attention to her. This allows her to feel comfortable and secure. She begins to think to herself.

This would be a great change to take another step, to make up for the Heather incident.

She puts on her best smile and enters the class. After taking her seat, the bell rings and the class begins. The instructor, Mrs. Schoval, issues a surprise pop quiz, much to the dismay of all the students. Natalie reaches into her backpack to get a number two pencil. She feels and looks around, but she cannot find one. She is unprepared for class. This is a first for Natalie and she does not know what to do.

"I ain't got a pencil." shoots out a random voice next to her.

Natalie glances to her right and finds the source of the voice, Zachary Flood. They have sat next to each other all year, but never spoke. Zack was a starter on the school's basketball team and just received a scholarship to Duke University. He is one of the most popular kids in school; therefore, Natalie consideres him, "out of her league."

"Zack, I thought athletes were always prepared." Mrs. Schoval replies. "You know, always gotta stay up for the big game."

"The big game is always scheduled." He responds.

Those two always got into playful verbal sparring. Natalie typically ignored these sideshows, but today she decides she would watch and react with the rest of the class.

Mrs. Schoval smiles and chuckles a bit.

"Mr. Flood, life is not always scheduled and you must be prepared to face it." She says. "Let me prove it to you"

She flips through her grade book.

"Aha! I knew it!" She continues. "The student with the highest grade in the class is, Natalie Cordova."

Natalie stops smiling. Her eyes get big and fear sets in. She is being put in the spotlight, and she does not like it.

"Miss Cordova is always in class on time," the teacher goes on, "and has never come unprepared. Isn't that right Natalie?"

All eyes in the room turn to Natalie. Her heart begins to race and she feels sweat running down her brow. She has to respond quickly. She takes a deep breathe and thinks to herself,

"Okay girl, round two."

"Miss Cordova, isn't that correct?" Mrs. Schoval asks again.

Natalie gives a little smile and replies coyly, "Actually, I don't have a pencil either."

The classroom erupts in oh's and ah's. Mrs. Schoval's mouth goes agape in feigned shock. Zack jumps out of his seat and points to Natalie.

"Yeah!" He shouts. "You see? The big game is always scheduled."

He turns to his new ally and puts his hand up.

"That's my girl!" He states.

Natalie puts her own hand up and before she can realize what he was doing, he slaps her palm. She draws her hand back down to her desk. She was not ready for a high-five but is happy to receive one. Her smile returns and she laughs with the rest of the class.

Mrs. Schoval stares at the hooting class with a smile on her face and a tear running down her cheek. She takes off her glasses and wipes her eyes.

"I'm really going to miss you guys after graduation." She cries.

The class gives a collective "ah."

"We love you too Mrs. Schoval!" shouts a young man from the back.

More chuckles and laughter come from the class. Natalie tries to keep a low profile, but the atmosphere of happy students' makes her join in and she begins to blush.

The laughter dies after a moment and Mrs. Schoval returns her stare to Natalie.

"Well well little Miss unprepared," she begins, "I have to give you kids one last quiz before the final next Friday. What do you think we should do about this?"

Natalie does not think. She just blurts out the first thing that comes to her mind.

"Postpone the quiz until the Friday before the final."

"Yeah." Zack agrees. "Give us some practice before game. Don't leave us unprepared coach."

"Coach?!" The impromptu title catches Mrs. Schoval off guard.

"Coach! Coach! Coach! Coach!" The class starts chanting and Natalie joins in.

Mrs. Schoval playfully flails her arms and begs for quiet. After the ruckus calms, Mrs. Schoval takes a deep breath and addresses the class.

"Alright, we'll have the quiz this coming Friday." She states.

Once again, the classroom erupts in cheers and hollers. Natalie surprises herself when she too jumps out of her chair in celebration. Zack turns to Natalie and again puts his hand up. This time, she knows how to react and slaps his palm first. Suddenly, other students converge on Natalie, hands in the air. She spends the next couple of minutes giving high fives and cavorting with her classmates. At 9:15am, the bell rings and the students march to the door. Zack gets to the door right before Natalie and holds it open for her.

"After you, Mademoiselle." He gestures to the door.

"Thank you, kind sir." She walks out to the hallway.

As she heads towards her next class, she feels exuberance. Not only had she interacted with the other students, her classmates had rallied around her. She has completely forgotten about her run in with Heather earlier that morning. Once again, her heart is racing with the sweet beat of elation. To her amazement, she looks forward to the rest of the day.

"Wait up baby!" It's Zack's voice; and it is right behind her! Natalie freezes and ponders the possibilities.

Is he following behind me? Does he want to talk to me; possibly carry a conversation?

She cannot wait to find out. She excitedly whips her head around to greet her potential suitor.

She sees Zack; however, he is headed in the opposite direction, towards the science building, and into the waiting arms of Ashley Tyler.

Ashley Tyler is the campus social butterfly and Heather Long's best friend. No matter where Heather was, Ashley was always in tow. Both girls came from wealthy families, but that is where the similarities seem to end. Ashley was the Yin to Heather's Yang. Where Heather was aggressive and domineering, Ashley was calm, cool and collective. They even differed in their treatment of Natalie. Heather viewed Natalie as her arch-nemesis, yet Ashley took the more diplomatic approach. One incident occurred during a school pep rally. Natalie stayed after school to study in the chemistry lab until the late afternoon. On her way out, she saw some students cheering the football team in a pre-homecoming pep rally. Away from the crowd, she saw Heather, Ashley, and a few other students in a small huddle smoking marijuana and giggling. Ashley looked up and saw Natalie staring at them. Natalie broke the stare and quickly went off in the other direction. The next day, she heard that Heather and some of the other students were suspended from school. During the lunch break, Ashley confronted her. Natalie swore she did not snitch on there smoking and Ashley believed her. It was at that moment Natalie made a bold move.

Natalie made a plea for peace between herself and Heather, and believed Ashley could placate such an arraignment. Ashley was always civil to Natalie, never tormenting her, yet never helping her either. Natalie felt this was her chance to lay out how she felt and hoped that Ashley would be an ally. She poured her heart out and cried when she pleaded her case. Ashley felt remorseful and even some guilt, but refused to help. She understood the power Heather had around the city, and had she helped Natalie, then she would have become the target of Heather's wrath. Natalie continued to beg her for her help, but Ashely finalized her answer when said, "Better you, than me."

Natalie watches for a few seconds more as Zack and Ashley make kissy faces at each other. Seeing enough, she turns and walks in the other direction. She is little depressed, but is able to talk herself out of it.

"I've made too much progress today." She tells herself. *"It's okay, just expected a little too much. Just keep pushing."*

She continues to encourage herself. *"You're doing great. Just keep it up and Nana won't be able to throw you out."*

Natalie is able to manage the day from her first class until her last, stress free. She walks from class to class with a smile on her face. Some friendly students even return her pleasantries. To avoid trouble during lunch, she switched her books early and uses a different restroom then her usual one. Except for the incident earlier in the day, she has avoided Heather and all her cohorts. All she has left is her final class of the day, economics.

Natalie walks into the classroom and takes her seat. She scans the room briefly, and finds who she is looking for, her former best friend Monica Bynes.

Natalie and Monica connected early in life. In kindergarten, they sat next to each other and became friends immediately. When Heather did something mean to Natalie, Monica was the first one to run over and help her. She even acted as Natalie's protector for a time, standing up to Heather when she felt she had to protect her friend. That all changed in the third grade. Heather wanted to step up her intimidation of Natalie, but she could not as long as Monica was around. She had tried fighting her, but Monica fought back, so she devised a different plan. On her birthday, Monica came to school and found a wrapped present on her desk. She excitedly unwrapped it and squealed with glee. Inside was the latest California Tara doll, with roller skates. Monica had been begging her dad for that exact doll all year, but he could not get one for her; stores were always sold out. She held up the box and hugged it tight. Attached to the box was an envelope. She opened the envelope and found a card inside. She read the card and could not believe what she saw.

Dear Monica,

I'm sorry for being a meanie to you. I don't want to be, but I get scared around people that I like. I think we should be friends. Please come to my party next week. It's for California Tara fans only. I know you will have a great time. Please say that you will come.

Heather Long

Monica had never thought about her and Heather being friends. She wanted to ask Natalie about it, but she could not at the moment. Natalie was out of school with chickenpox, and the party was this weekend. She had heard that Heather's parents let their daughter have big parties, with many other girls, some boys, and lots of food. She wanted to experience it just once, but she did want to betray her best friend either. She did not know what to do.

At that very moment, Heather came by and sat next to Monica in Natalie's chair. She looked at Monica and gave a big smile.

"Do you like the doll?" she asked.

"I've wanted one for so long!" Monica replied. She held up the card. "Is this true, you really want us to be friends?"

"Yes I do." Heather answered.

"Then why are you so mean to me and Natalie?" Monica shot back.

"I don't mean to." Heather replied. "Monica, you are such a cool person, but you don't hang out with the other cool kids in school." Heather kept her smile. "You know, all the other kids are talking about you."

"What other kids?" Monica inquired.

"You know, the popular girls in the fifth grade. They say that you seem cool, but you hang out such dorks." She may have only been nine years old, but Heather was very manipulative, and she knew it.

"I don't hang out with dorks. I play with Natalie." Monica defended.

"The fifth graders say that she's the biggest nerd in school." Heather responded.

Monica was not dumb, but she was gullible. She knew that to be popular in middle and high school, she had to be a popular fifth grader. She did not want to be considered a nerd.

"I think you're really awesome," Heather continued, "and I want to show them that you are. Some of them will be at my party. Once they meet you, I know they'll love you."

Monica thought long and hard about the option being presented to her. She decided that maybe if she went, she could let them know about her best friend, and then they could all be friends.

"Okay. If my dad says I can go, I will." She smiled when she replied.

"Great!" Heather giggled. She pulled out a piece of paper. "Here is my number. Call me when your dad says you can go." She gave Monica the paper and went back to her desk.

Monica went to the party and had a great time. She met many different girls from school and they all loved their dolls. Heather hung around Monica the entire time and the two girls became close friends.

Natalie returned to school the following week and looked for Monica on the playground before class started. When she saw her, she headed towards her, but stopped just short. She saw her talking and laughing with a group of girls that included Heather. Natalie was confused, so she walked over there to try to talk to her. She tapped Monica lightly on the shoulder.

"Natalie!" Monica seemed surprised to see her. "What are you doing here?"

"Can I talk to you for a second?" Natalie asked.

Monica looked around, feeling uneasy. She knew what she had to do, but it would not be easy.

"No, Natalie." Monica's voice was timid. "We cannot talk now, or ever." Heather smiled a wide grin.

"What?" Natalie was stunned. "Why not?"

Heather stepped in, "Because she just graduated from Dork University." She stepped up and pushed Natalie hard, sending her to the ground on her backside.

"Heather! Stop!" Monica jumped between Heather and Natalie.

Heather leaned in close to Monica. She put her mouth close to Monica's ear and started to speak.

"Think about his Monica. All the girls love you and want to hang around you. The way you felt at the party, you could feel that way everyday. All you have to do is get rid of the little baby Natalie."

Monica felt terrible. She and Natalie had been best friends since kindergarten, but she could not pass up a chance to be one of the most popular girls around. She felt the tears start to run down her face. She looked at Natalie.

"I'm sorry Nat." She cried, then hurriedly turned and walked away.

Natalie was torn apart emotionally. She had just lost her best friend and she did not know why. The two girls continued to sit next to each other for the rest of the year, but did not say one word to one another. As the years went by, Monica joined Heather and her friends in Natalie's daily torment.

The bell rings and the economics class began. The instructor, Mr. Tolliver, gives the class the topic of the day, Brand-Word association. He will pick a student from the class and have that person close his or her eyes. Then he will say a brand name and the student should blurt out the first word that comes to mind. Each response will be recorded on the board. Afterwards, the class will discuss what they said and think of ways that companies use this technique for advertising. He picks his first student, James Curtis.

James walks to the front of the class, sits in the chair and closes his eyes.

"You ready?" Mr. Tolliver asks.

"Yeah. Hit me." The student responds.

"Alright. Coke."

"Sugar."

"Nike."

"Ballin."

"Def Jam."

"Ghetto." Some in the class chuckle.

"Nestle."

"Cocoa."

"Alright, thank you Mr. Curtis." Mr. Tolliver excuses the student to his seat.

"Let's get a female this time." Mr. Tolliver continues. "Natalie how about you?"

"Um…sure." She replies. She gets out of her seat and goes to the front of the class. She sits in the chair and closes her eyes.

"You ready."

"I'm ready."

"Alright. Toyota."

"Small." That was easy.

"Levis."

"Tight." Another easy one. She started to relax.

"Sony."

"Music." She relaxed completely.

"Speedo."

"Wet."

A cell phone chimes, interrupting the session. It was Monica's phone. She scrambles to turn it off and Mr. Tolliver looks up.

"Monica." he says.

"Harlot." Natalie blurts out.

The class erupts in giggles and laughter. Monica sits with a shocked look on her face. Mr. Tolliver looks bewildered, and Natalie, realizing what she just said, quickly sits up in the chair and puts her hand over her mouth. She is human after all.

Monica stands up and heads for the front of the class. She is pissed-off and her face is beet red. She has long since developed Heather's bad attitude.

"What the hell did you call me?!" she asks.

"Take it easy Miss Bynes." Mr. Tolliver steps in between the two girls. "I'm sure it was an accident. Right, Natalie?"

"Yes, an accident." Natalie responds. "I'm sorry. Really." She becomes very worried. Monica looks as if she is about to snap.

Monica steps back, heads toward her seat, and then reconsiders.

"You know what?" She asks. "Forget this. I'm outta here."

"Miss Bynes, if you leave it will count as an inexcusable truant." The instructor tries to reason with her.

"I don't care!" she shoots back and points toward Natalie. "I'm not staying here any longer with that cocksucking whore!"

The class is now worked up into a frenzied state. Mr. Tolliver stands at the front of the class stunned, but before he can respond, a random voice sounds from the back of the room.

"She must have learned it from you bitch!"

The students are out of control at this point. The instructor raises his voice and makes a plea for order. Monica scans the room; demanding to know who would dare say such a thing. No one claims responsibility.

A minute passes and the class finally calms down. Most of the students take their seat, yet Monica remains standing in the middle of the room. Her face is deep red, her jaw is tight, her eyes are wide open and tears stream down her face. Her anger transformed into all out rage.

"Monica," the teacher speaks softly, "please take your seat. Let's put this behind us."

Monica looks around the classroom. She had never been so embarrassed in her life. She opens her mouth to speak, but has difficulty getting any words out. She turns her head and stares directly at Natalie.

"Fuck you." she says tearfully. She turns to face the whole class and shouts, "Fuck all of you!" She heads towards the door and storms out of the classroom.

The students become uproarious after Monica's comments and they let her hear it as she runs out. While all this is going on, Natalie, very quietly, gets up from the chair and slinks back to her seat. She does not know how to feel. The whole scenario left her startled, because she knows exactly how Monica feels. She knows the feeling of embarrassment beyond comprehension, when the only thing you know to do is run and flee the ridicule. She knows how it feels for others to bring her to tears with their taunts. She also knows Monica's anger. The anger is what drove Natalie to cutting all those years ago.

When class resumes, Mr. Tolliver alerts the class he would have to file an academic standards report on this incident and some of the students may be called into the office. Although dismayed, they all understand and focus back to their studies. As Natalie opens her book, the girl on her left slides a folded piece of paper in front of her. Natalie looks over at the young woman. The student just smiles and nods towards the paper. Natalie takes it, holds it under desk, unfolds it and reads the note scribed onto it.

Good job. I've wanted to tell that bitch off the whole damn year!

Natalie reads it in disbelief. She received a compliment on starting the incident that made Monica look and feel like a fool. She looks back at the young woman, who in turn just smiles and gives thumbs up. Natalie folds the note and slides it into her economics book. The bell rings at the conclusion of class and Natalie walks out, heading towards the library.

Over the next two hours, Natalie studies in the library. Finals are next week and she wants to be prepared. She has a 4.0 GPA for the year and wants to maintain her high academic standards. She applied to colleges all across the country, but due to her late submissions of these applications, she had not yet received any acceptance or rejection letters. She feels she is under the gun and wants to keep her grades sharp.

Overall, Natalie considers her day a success. She not only made a friend in Micah, she spoke to Zach and incited two separate classroom incidents; both in which she was the rallying point.

Not bad, Natalie. She thinks to herself. *Keep this up, and you'll be alright.*

Natalie gathers her schoolbooks and leaves the library. As she exits the building, she notices the lack of students around campus. The school is practically empty and rather eerie. She heads down the hall back towards her locker. She has to get her math book so she can study and complete her homework.

She reaches her locker, spins the combination on the lock, and opens the door. As she digs through her various supplies, she reflects on the events of the day. She cannot help but smile. She is in a wonderful mood. Suddenly, she hears a loud whistle from down the hall. Her eyes get big and she gets excited.

"That must be Micah." She tells herself. She could not wait to share the events of the day with him. She turns to her right to greet her new friend.

WHAM!

Natalie falls to the ground, landing hard on her side and smacking her face on the pavement. She holds her hand to her mouth, feels an intense pain in her lower jaw, and a warm taste spread over her tounge. Before she can realize what happened, she feels a swift and sudden blow to her stomach. The pain is unbearable. She coughs and wheezes as the air rushes out of her chest. She gasps repeatedly, but cannot get any air. She lay curled on the floor, unable to comprehend her situation.

When she looks up, she could barely see straight. She sees three figures standing over her, but cannot recognize whom they were.

"Make a fool of my friends will ya?" a random female voice shouts.

Another strike lands on her stomach. Natalie coughs hard and cries out in pain. Another kick lands square in her abdomen. She wants to scream, but two more kicks find their mark.

"Answer me dammit!" Natalie recognizes the voice. It is Heather, and she is enraged.

Heather squats down next to Natalie and slaps her face hard. She grabs Natalie by her the neck and chokes her for a few seconds. Next, she yanks on Natalie's collar and holds her face inches from her own.

"I warned you what I would do if you continue to fuck with me!" Heather screamed. Her face is hardened and her jaw clenched.

Natalie is breathing hard and fighting the urge to pass out. She feels dizzy and weak. She wants to run from the beating, but her body aches all over. Taking a quick glance around, she sees Howard standing to Heather's right and her boyfriend Marco at her left. Howard's visage is staring straight ahead and very hard; his arms crossed over his chest. Marco sports a big grin, his left arm is hanging at his side and his right hand is busy inside his pocket. She looks back at Heather through teary eyes.

"Beg me Natalie." Heather says softly. "Beg me to stop. Beg me to spare you. Accept your place in society, and beg me for mercy."

Natalie hears her words clearly. All she has to do is open her mouth and plea with Heather to stop the pain. She thinks briefly, "*Say you're sorry. Take fault, appease her, and do as she says.*" Her thoughts race around her mind, and she knows she has to make Heather happy. She slowly opens her mouth. She begins to form her lips. She is about to beg. Then, one final thought flashes in her mind.

"*You always do!*"

Natalie stops herself, before she can begin. That one thought repeats in her mind in different variations. "*Yeah, do it again. You always do. Because you're weak! She is your superior. Accept your place. Be a doormat your whole life!*" Natalie's head begins to spin. She cannot understand her thoughts. One final thought comes to her and she acts on reflex.

"*FUCK THIS BITCH!*"

PTOOEY!

Natalie purses her lips and spits right into Heather's face. Heather drops Natalie and recoils backwards. She wipes her face of the mixture of phlegm, saliva and blood, and looks back down at Natalie.

"So this is how you what it?" she asks.

Natalie does not respond. Her thoughts plea for her to beg and accept Heather's terms, yet her body reacts quite differently. She rolls off her side onto her hands and knees. She looks up at Heather and stares her dead in the eyes. Each movement is excruciating, but she does not stop.

"Your funeral!" Heather responds excitedly. "Let's do this."

Natalie reaches up to brace herself. She is still dizzy and wants to stop, but her body will not allow it. Her locker is still open, so she grabs the door jam to hoist herself up. She keeps her stare on Heather.

"Fuck you." She utters quietly.

Howard and Marco watch in stunned amazement. Natalie has never defended herself, and now here she is, acting as if she wants to go blow for blow with Heather. Howard sees Natalie's left hand grasping the door jam and acts quickly.

"On your knees!" he yells and kicks the locker door shut, catching Natalie's hand.

The young girl screams and collapses back to the ground. The locker door catches the lock and shuts completely. Her hand is stuck inside the door jam and her midsection is left exposed.

Heather wastes no time and lands repeated hard kicks to Natalie's side, stomach and chest. She drops to her knees and starts punching at Natalie's ribs and gut.

Natalie is helpless. She tries to curl up to guard her stomach, but Heather's body prevents it. She keeps her arm up and tries to guard her head. She cries and screams with each blow Heather lands. The assailant looks up at Marco.

"Move her hand!" she yells. "I want this bitch's face."

Marco reaches over, grabs Natalie's free arm and pins it to the ground. She is now completely exposed. Heather begins punching her face, blow after blow after blow. Natalie's bottom lip splits from being punched into her teeth, and she can feel her mouth fill with the taste of her blood.

After what seems like an eternity, the beating stops. Heather is out of breath, and smiling happily. She feels vindicated for the incident from that morning and for Monica, one of her best friends. She kneels beside Natalie for a minute, and tries to catch her breath. She then grabs two handfuls of Natalie's hair and pulls their faces together.

"Thank you." She says quietly. "Fuck around again, and I'll put your ass in the ground." She then slams Natalie's head against the lockers, knocking her unconscious.

"Let's go." Heather says. She gets up and rapidly walks away, Howard and Marco close in tow.

Bruised and bloodied, Natalie lays motionless on the ground. Her left eye is swollen shut and she bleeds heavily from her nose and mouth. Her left hand is still stuck in the locker door and her rubbing against the metal causes additional bleeding. She is barely breathing and her right eye is rolled upwards. Her body is beaten and nearly broken, but her mind is elsewhere.

As she lays, she dreams.

Natalie lifts her groggy head. She looks around lazily trying to remember what just happened. As she gauges her surroundings, she becomes worried. She is not at school as she should be. Instead, she is in a truck traveling down a lonely desert highway. She looks down at her left hand. No bruises, no cuts, and no blood. She studies her hand intensely and notices she can see out of her left eye. She reaches up and feels her face; no blood, no pain. She reaches down and feels her stomach; again, no pain.

"Was it all a dream?" She asks herself.

"Assuredly not!" is the answer she receives, as a voice shoots out from her left. It is a girl's voice, meek and high-pitched, yet assertive. She averts her gaze and sees the driver.

The driver is female, about Natalie's height and build with choice differences. Her hair is pitch black and untamed. It covers her face and hangs down to her lower back. Her clothes are dirty and drab, as if she does not give a damn about her appearance. She wears a dark, heavy sweater that covers her arms and a short black skirt, unraveling at the hem and stopping at her mid thigh. Natalie can see the driver's legs. They were dark and pale at the same time; deep and foreboding. She keeps both hands on the wheel and her foot pinned to the pedal.

Natalie is confused and frightened. She looks away from the driver and stares out the window. Nothing lingers, only sand on the ground and dark clouds in the sky. No sunlight breaks through, as they sped though the scenary.

"Where are we?" Natalie asks. The driver accelerates, but does not answer.

"Please," She asks again, "Where are we?" No answer still

"Who are you?" Another question ignored, and Natalie's fear only increases.

"Who are you?" she is more assertive time, but she is still ignored. Her fear increases and her anger builds.

"WHO ARE YOU?!" she shouts. "WHO THE FUCK ARE YOU?!"

The driver whips her head around and stares Natalie dead in the eyes. Her eyes are red as fire, and her teeth black. Dark purple veins stretch across her pale face. A dark saliva drips heavily from her lips. Natalie covers her mouth in horror and reels back in the seat. As she stares at the horrifying presence, she notices that save for the skin tone and eye color, she and the driver look exactly alike.

The driver's breathing becomes heavy and larbored as she burns that sinister grin into Natalie's mind.

"YOU!" she bellows, her voice changing from its assertive meekness to deep and threatening.

"I have been silient for far too long, but together, we will be silent no more!"

Natalie cannot bear to look. The sight of the driver terrifies her and the voice makes her want to scream.

"Ah," the driver exclaims, her voice returning to its original tone. She points down the road. "There she is."

Natalie looks down the road. She sees a woman stading in the middle of the street. She looks slightly familiar, but Natalie cannot make out who she is. The driver hits the gas and the truck charges faster down the road.

"Please stop." Natalie pleads. The request is disregarded.

The truck pulls closer to the woman. Natalie sees she is fairly tall, and slender, but she still cannot figure out who she is. The truck backfires and goes even faster.

"Please!" she begs. "You have to stop. You'll kill her!"

A response comes in the form of a sinister giggle and the truck increases speed. Natalie panics. The driver has no intention of slowing down. Natalie again stares down the road at the woman and has a moment of clarity.

Staring hard, she sees that woman has deep red hair and dark blue eyes. She is not smiling, nor does she seem worried about the truck bearing down on her. Natalie falls back into her seat, her jaw agape in shock.

"Heather." She whimpers.

"THAT'S HER NAME!" the driver roars, her voice once again deep and threatening.

Natalie sits still and stares forward. They are barreling towards Heather, and Natalie cannot think. She again wants to plea for her life, but she stops herself. She has mixed feelings.

"What's wrong Natalie?" the driver asks in her meek voice. Natalie remains silent.

"No pleas? No cries for mercy?" Natalie stays silent.

"Should I spare her? Would she spare you?" Natalie cannot answer and the driver smiles.

"REMEMBER WHAT SHE DID TO YOU!"

Natalie closes her eyes. Instantly she relives all the painful moments in her life caused by Heather. Losing her best friend; Heather caused it. Her alienation; Heather did it. Making her a social exile; Heather initiated it. Low self-esteem; Heather. Low self-worth; Heather. Suicidal thoughts; Heather. Self-mutalation; Heather. Physical beatdown; Heather. Natalie's mind is racing.

"Look at her!" the driver demands.

Natalie leans forward in her seat and props herself on the dashboard. She stares hard into Heather's eyes. She feels her anger build, and for the first time, she feels hate.

"I hate her." Her voice is weak, but Natalie is firm in her statement.

"Yes." The driver responds. "Hate her. With all your heart, hate her!"

Natalie keeps her gaze on Heather, her emotions hardening.

"I hate her!" Natalie is louder and more assertive. Heather remains defiant as the truck draws nearer.

The driver begins speaking in a hurried tone.

"What will it be? Make your choice!"

Natalie's breathing grows heavy, her jaw clinches, and her heart races.

"Freedom or fear!" The driver roars. "Life or death! Mercy or hate!"

Heather is so close now. Natalie feels the hate burn inside her and it consumes her soul. Her blood runs hot and her pulse is rapid with anticipation. Her defining moment is at hand. She has endured a lifetime of abuse and torment. This is Natalie's time, and this is the only way she could ever even the score.

"What will it be?!" the driver demands.

Natalie screams, "I HATE YOU!"

IMPACT.

The truck plows into Heather. Natalie sees it in almost slow motion. Heather's body bounds off the front end, onto the hood, and her face bounces off the windshield. Natalie sees every detail. She witnesses the point of impact when Heather's skull cracks open, exposing her brain; and marvels as her teeth explode from her mouth. Her body then rolls up the winshield and flys over the truck.

The driver slams on the brakes and the truck spins completely around facing the opposite direction. The truck comes to a complete stop. Natalie was still haunched on the dashboard. Her breathing is climatic, as if she had experienced the height of satisfaction. She slumps back into her seat, sweat pouring down her face, and looks at the driver. The driver stares, silently and blankly, at the scene in front of the truck.

"It is done." she exclaims in between heavy breaths. "Death."

"Death?" Natalie asks. She is slowly coming down from her emotional high. "We killed her?" Natalie's voice was meek. She puts her hand over her mouth and trembles with fear.

"Yes." The driver responses with a sinister smile. "Dead. Killed. Murdered. Just as we desire."

Natalie is stricken with shock. She resents the way Heather treats her, but she did not think she was capable of killing her.

"Oh my god" she cries. "We're murderers!"

"No!" the driver shoots back. "We are saviors! Your salvation!" She leans in close to Natalie and grabs her hard by the face.

"Don't you get it?" she asks. "We are your saviors. We have shown you how to gain your salvation. Through her death, you are free." She lets go of Natalie quickly jumps out of the truck. Natalie is soon behind her.

Natalie reaches the front of the truck and stops. What she sees horrifies her. The driver is standing over Heather's mangled corpse. Natalie runs over to witness first hand.

Heather landed on her back, her face slanted to the right, blood flowing from her mouth and back of her head. Her right eye is hanging out of its socket. Her torso is shattered and twisted in the opposite direction. Her right leg was folded underneath her body and bent the wrong way.

"Listen." The driver says. "Nothing. No abuse. No torment. How does it feel?"

Natalie listens to her words. To her surprise, she finds them very soothing. For the first time, she is face to face with Heather Long, the girl that considers her the enemy and abuses her at every turn, and she hears no hurtful words or snide remarks. Natalie closes her eyes and revels in the silence. She feels no remoarse or sorrow over Heather's death.

"If only it were this easy." The driver's words shatter Natalie's peacefully silence.

"What?" Natalie opens her eyes and stares at the driver.

"Nothing worth having, is ever easy." The driver motions for Natalie to look behind her.

Natalie does, and her horror returns. Standing at the back of the truck is Heather, alive and well, showing no effects of the impact. Natalie's jaw drops.

"But how?" she wonders.

"If you want to kill the hydra," the driver responds, "you have to get all the heads."

From the other side of the truck, shadows emerge. Out of those shadows appear Ashley Tyler, Monica Bynes, Lynn Bennett, Marco Ruiz, and Howard Haynesworth. The rest of Natalie's main tormentors come forth and stand beside Heather. Natalie grows very afraid and she wants to run away, but her legs will not move.

Without warning, all six of them vanish and reappear, surrounding Natalie. She looks at each one of them, horror filling inside her. She begins to plea for mercy, but they do not listen.

Instantaneously, insult and fists fly. All six begin to beat on and pummel Natalie. She drops to the ground and tries to shield herself from the blows, but they come from everywhere.

"STOP! PLEASE!" she screams but the beating continues. Natalie starts to cry, and she screams with every blow that lands. She does not know what to do.

"Only you can stop it!" she hears the driver's voice, but cannot see her.

"Hate them Natalie!" Natalie can feel her anger build. "Use your rage, and hate them. Strike them down, so they can never hurt you again!"

Natalie closes her eyes. She is struck with punches and kicks, but she no longer feels the pain. She lets her fear turn to anger, feels the anger give way to hate, and lets it consume her. Her heart races, her blood runs hot, and her emotions harden. Lightining strikes the ground and the driver roars.

"SHOW THEM WHO YOU ARE! KILL THEM ALL!"

Natalie jumps to her feet and screams an ear shattering shiek. She tackles the first person she sees, Monica. Natalie grabs her by the collar and repeatedly punchs her in the face. With every strike, Monica's head recoils off the pavement. Blood begins to pool underneath her head and her face is beaten raw. Natalie continues to wail until Monica's face is shattered. She then grabs her around the neck and digs her nails into her victim's throat. She presses hard until her fingers penetrate deep into the skin and wrap around the meat of her windpipe. She grips firmly and holds on tight.

"DIE YOU FUCKING HARLOT!" she screams triumphantly, then yanks with all her might and tears Monica's throat out.

Monica's blood erupts from her neck and splatters heavily on her assailant. Natalie, covered in Monica's blood, looks over at the remaining five. She locks stares with all five, hate raging in her soul. She squeezes and feels the texture of the warm, meaty mass still in her hand, and to her surprise, the texture changes. She looks down and sees that she no longer holds a throat, but a large hunting knife.

Again, she strikes quickly. She pounces off the ground and darts behind Lynn. She grabs her next target by the mouth, holds her face up and points the blade at her neck. Lynn tries to scream, but her cries are muffled. Natalie whispers softly into Lynn's ear.

"Bleed for me."

She thrusts the length of the blade into Lynn's neck. She presses it in deep and twists to cause maximum damage.

After one complete twist, she yanks the blade downward, slashing Lynn from throat to navel and spilling her insides onto the road.

She throws the dead girl to the ground, leaving the blade embedded inside her.

She turns her murderous gaze to Howard. He steps back from her, in an attempt to prevent the inevitable.

"C'mon now, wait!" he pleads. "You don't have to this! Think about this, please!"

"Yes I do!" She roars. "It must be done! No more thinking!"

She whips her head around and glares at Ashley.

"Ladies first!" She bellows.

Using her right hand, she swiftly jams two fingers, second knuckle deep, into Ashley's eye sockets.

Ashely screams in pain and horror. She tries to jerk her head back in reflex, but Natalie hooks her fingers inside the girl's head, effectively holding Ashley by her face. Keeping her hand in place, she throws the girl down, presses her knee onto her chest and pulls with her embedded fingers. Blood pours on of Ashley's eye holes and covers her face and Natalie's hand. Natalie pulls harder, causing more blood to gush and ooze. With one final tug, she rips the maxilla away from Ashley's skull and falls to the ground. Natalie looks at her hand and admires the upper jaw and haggard skin still clutched. She looks back down at Ashley and watches her damaged eyes and brain sloop out of her skull.

Natalie flings the jaw to the ground and makes her way towards Howard. He backs up and again tries to plead his case, this time to no avail.

"On your knees!" she screams and punts Howard square in his balls. He groans in agony, grabs his nuts and falls to the ground, propped on his kness and chest.

She does not stop there. She walks behind him and punts over and over again, landing multiply kicks to his groin, crushing his testicles. Howard tries to escape the punishment, rolling away to avoid her, but she would not be denied. She jumps on his back, reaches behind herself, between his legs, grabs a handful of manhood and squeezes with all her strength. Howard screams from the torment, but he was helpless. Natalie savours the terror and pain in his scream for a little while before letting go. After she lets go, she grabs his head and twists 180 degrees, snapping his neck, and killing him.

Natalie gets up, walks over to Lynn's corpse and retrieves her knife. She makes her way over to her next target, Marco. Heather begins to shout demanding that Natalie stay away from him, but the murderous vixen did not listen. Instead, she grabs Marco by the back of his neck, pulls him close to her and kisses him. She voraciously sucks on his bottom lip while sticking her tounge in his mouth. Then, she plunges the blade deep into his abdomen. Marco tries to scream, but his cried are filters by Natalie's mouth. Over and over, she withdraws the blade and stabs him again, alternating between stomach and chest. Marco begins to cough up blood and the fluid transfers into Natalie's mouth. She savours the taste of his life leaving his body as her chin is coated with his blood. She twists the blade on last time and dumps his carcass on the ground. Five down, one to go, saved the best for last.

Natalie slowly stalks the last of her prey. Heather turns from her and tries to run away, but her path is blocked by the reemergence of the driver. She is horrified by sight of the alternate version of Natalie.

"Time to die." The driver says meekly, and Heather screams.

Natalie comes up behind Heather and grabs a fistful of her hair. Heather screams as she is dragged away. Natalie stops when she reachs the truck. She then hoists Heather by her hair and slams her face first onto the pavement. Heather's forehead is badly scraped and her nose is shattered, bleeding profusely. She is dizzy and groggy. Natalie lifts one of Heather's legs and rams her knife through the back of her knee. She screams again, but has little time to comprehend.

Natalie grabs Heather's hair, picks her up and throws her against the truck. She wraps her hand around her neck to hold her up. She wants to look into her eyes and see her fear. Natalie stares hard and begins to torment Heather.

"Heather," she says through clenched teeth, "you must suffer! You must feel the most pain!" Natalie readjusts her grip so Heather cannot move.

"I hate you!" She continues. "I hate you with all my soul, and I'm really going to enjoy this!"

With that, she jams her knife into the top of Heather's right eyelid. She pushes the knife in, very slightly, and begins to cut around the edge of the eye socket.

Heather screams like a banshee as her eyeball is carved out of her head. Blood gushes as skin, muscle, nerves, and other tissue are sliced. Natalie takes a qick flick of her wrist and pops the eyeball clean out of Heather's head. She places the knife back at Heather's throat. The girl never stops screaming.

The driver appears behind Natalie.

"Do it!" She goads. "End her life and end your suffering!"

Natalie does not hesitate. She rips the length of the knife through Heather's gullet. Blood blasts like an explosion and covers Natalie's head and chest. She throws the bitch to the ground and looks at the driver. She smiles and cannot hide her pleasure from the kills.

"Do you desire freedom?" the driver asks.

"Yes." Natalie answers assertively.

"Will you make them suffer?"

"Yes!"

"Will you live in fear?"

"No!"

"What do you desire?"

"Vengence!"

Satisfied with Natalie's answers, the driver walks over to her and takes the knife from her hand.

"Good." The driver speaks meekly. "Your quest for redemption, begins now!"

Quickly, the driver grabs Natalie's left arm and holds it firm, then takes the knife and plunges it into Natalie's hand clear through. The girl screams in agony.

Natalie pops up off the ground screaming. She looks around and sees she is back at school. She also notices she can see only out of her right eye. Her left hand is still caught in the locker, and it hurts like hell. She has been laying there for only a few minutes, as the sky is still bright and the blood running from her hand is still moist. She reaches up with her right hand and tries to pry the locker door open. She just wants an inch or two of clearance to get her other hand free. She grunts as she pulls, feeling every millimeter of the locker door leave the gash on her palm. When she achieves a small gap of space, she yanks, and her hand comes free. She crumbles on the ground clutching her hand, as it is in terrible pain. She picks herself up and runs to the nearest restroom.

When she reaches the restroom, she turns on a sink and washes her left hand in warm water. She looks up in the mirror and freezes. She sees her face, but can barely recognize herself. She has been beaten black and blue. The left side of her face is swollen and she cannot open her left eye. Her lower lip is gashed open and her upper lip is plump. She remembers the driver from her dream and feels her anger build. Tears run down her face, but she is not sad, she is enraged.

Make them pay!

A random thought flashes through Natalie's mind. As she focuses on her image in the mirror, she can hear the voice of the driver.

Never again!

Natalie can feel her anger build.

They must suffer!

Her anger turns to hate.

Make your choice!

She lets her hate consume her.

Kill them all!

Natalie grunts hard and punches ther mirrior with her good hand, shattering it. The pain of the strike runs up her arm, but she does not care. She is infuriated and wants revenge. She wants her tormentors dead.

Patience.

Natalie hears the voice again. She knows it is right. She has to be patient and bide her time. If she rushes into it, she may only get to one before she is caught, or she could be overwhelmed and outnumbered. She needs to find the right opportunity to divide and conquer. Take them out one by one.

Natalie's shirt is torn. She rips off a piece of the fabric from her shirt, around her mid-drift and uses the cloth to dress her sliced hand. She quickly washes up, exits the restroom and leaves campus. She has to get home. She has to figure out how she will achieve her salvation.

Arriving home, Natalie goes downstairs and takes a shower. She needs to relax and her perfect refuge is the shower. As she let her stress melt away with the hot water, she closes her eyes and relives the visions of her dream. She relives the joy she felt as her targets were taken down one by one, and replays the moments again and again.

After her shower is complete, she turns on her laptop to surf the net. She needs a role model on which to base her plan of attack. She initially thinks of the gunmen of Columbine, but reconsiders. They were sloppy and desperate. Wildly shooting at random people, without specific targets in mind, just to kill themselves when it was over, is not the route Natalie wants to take. She wants to live and enjoy the fruits of her labor. She then turns her thoughts to Lorena Bobbit, but again changes her mind. Her husband lived, and her objective was to make a statement about spousal abuse. Natalie does not want to make a point; she just wants certain people dead.

In the midst of her research, her browser pings. She has an email wainting. She clicks the icon. Within the new window, she receives a message from the admissions counsel of Westin State University. She clicks the message and reads it.

Dear Miss Cordova,

Thank you for your interest in attending the State University of Westin. After review of your supplied documents and enrollment forms, we are pleased to announce the acceptance of your application.

Westin State University was founded in 1842 by former Senator Kellen Westin. His vision was to provide an institute of higher learning for young Americans seeking careers in the fields of law and medicine. Since its accreditation, WSU has maintained a graduation rate of 92.4%, near the top of the nation historically. WSU has been recognized internationally for its academic programs in Business Management, Business & Labor Law, Anthropoly, Theology, and Political Science; and is the premire university in the field of Gene Therapy and Genome Research.

As part of the WSU alumni, you will have unfettered access to all the academic and athletic facilities, so nothing can stand in your way of achieving your goals, dream and aspirations. You will also receive extraordinary discounts to all athletic events, so you can cheer on the nationally ranked Seraphs as they complete in Football, Basketball, Baseball, and our many other Division I-A sports.

The faculty and administrators of Westin State University welcome the opportunity of having you as a student, and we take pride in helping your dreams come true.

Welcome to the Seraph Family. We look forward to seeing you in Scalet and Gold.

Sharla Jackson
University President

Natalie marvels at the message, she has gained acceptance to her dream university. She stares at the screen and smiles brightly. She wants to cry and sceam for joy, but remains composed. She forgets about all previous thoughts and takes a momemt to bask in her joy. She cannot help herself.

"I'M A SERAPH!" she screams jubilantly. "I'M A SERAPH!"

At this moment, she wishes her Nana were around. She wants to share this moment with someone. She looks up at the ceiling, as if gazing into the heavens.

"Thank you." She sobs softly. "Thank you God."

She jumps from her chair and runs upstairs. She races to the second story of the house, into the master bedroom and grabs her Nana's credit card case. She knows it is not an emergency, but she wants to go to the school's website and buy all sorts of WSU merchandise. Surely, Nana will understand. She will make sure the products were cute sweaters and such so Nana will not mind. She runs back to her bedroom and jumps back on her laptop. She types in the web address, but stops.

"I have to add my name to the college wall!" she exclaims.

Natalie's high school set up a web page where seniors can add their name when they are accepted to college. Natalie types in her school's website, clicks on the college wall link, and registers her name. The page turns scarlet and gold, and gives Natalie a list of items she will need to succeed her first year. She prints the list and clicks the completed link. The website goes to a congratulations page.

"Congratulations! You are a Seraph! You will be joining the following students at Westin State University."

The site shows a list of 12 students from her school who were also accepted to WSU. She begins to read the list and stops on the second name.

Bennett, Lynn

Natalie reads the third name.

Bynes, Monica

Natalie feels dread build in the pit of her stomach. She is stunned. Her dream of attending WSU is staring her in the face, but if she wants it, she will have to deal with Lynn and Monica. Natalie's name is fourth on the list. As she reads down the list, her worst fears are realized.

Fifth name: Haynesworth, Howard

Sixth name: Long, Heather

Ninth name: Ruiz, Marco

Tweleth name; Tyler, Ashley

"NO!" she screams. "FUCK! NO!" She slams her fists on the table and puts her head down in tears. She cries. Life has just played the cruelest joke it could. She can have her dream, but only if she deals with four more years of torment and grief.

Giggle!

Her head shoots up. She has heard that voice before. That meek, high-pitched voice is giggling, and she can hear it loud and clear.

This is perfect!

"What?" Natalie asks. "How is this perfect?"

Two birds, one stone!

Two birds, one stone. Natalie has heard this expression before, but she does not understand its significance at this very moment.

"What does that mean?" she demands and bangs her left hand on the table, causing great pain.

She clutches her hand to her chest, trying to ease the pain. She opens her fist and undresses the wound. The impact causes the gash to bleed again. The sight of her blood triggers her memories. She remembers the beating she received earlier that day. She remembers the physical and emotional pain it caused her. She flashes back to her dream afterwards, and the joy she felt when she killed her tormentors.

The final stage!

She now fully understood. This is perfect. The six are sticking together, making them easier to find. Two birds, one stone. By going to WSU, she can live her dream of attending college and have her chance at revenge. This will be the final stage. Heather, Howard, Lynn, Ashley, Marco and Monica, all will arrive at Westin as freshmen, but they would leave as carrion. She looks at the ceiling again, this time with a sinister grin.

"I will be a Searph." She says softly. "Thank you."

Natalie stays out of school the rest of the week. She wants some time to heal from her injuries and plan her next move. She knows that in order to have a chance for revenge, she needs to change who she is, inside and out. She does not want her six targets to recognize her. She needs a plan of action and spends the time to develop one.

First, she will have to change her physique. She weighs her self and takes body measurement. She stands at five feet, eight inches tall, and weighs 133 lbs. Not overweight, but Natalie thinks she can do better. She downloads different meal plans and exercise programs. She wants to lose about 15 lbs before she starts college. She decides on a rigorous routine of daily exercise and five small meals a day. She goes to the grocery store to buy the proper foods that she can eat.

Second, she will need a new wardrobe. If her body changes, she needs to have nice clothes at the ready. She never feels attractive or sexy in life, and knows that this is the route she needs to take. No more sundresses or cute little sweaters. She goes online to check the major designers, Donna Karin, Dolce & Gabbana, Louis Vutton, etc. She orders skirts, low cut tops, coulture blouses, chic headware, fashionable shoes, etc. She wore a size six, so she orders all the clothing in a size four. She is especially careful to pick clothes that accentuates her curvy backside, long legs, and size C breast.

Finally, she has to change her attitude. Natalie has very low self-sesteem and a pessimistic outlook on life. That needs to change. This will be her most drastic step. She knows she needs self-confidence and knows she will have to interact with others to get it. She is not sure what she will do but she gives herself until after graduation to decide.

Natalie returns to school during Finals Week. She misses the preparatory exams, but she is smart enough to pass her finals without difficulty. She keeps to herself during the week. Since the school days are shorter, she leaves as soon as her tests were complete. By Wednesday, her finals are finished and she stays home on Thursday. Friday is graduation day. Natalie takes her seat with the rest of her classmates and anticipates getting her diploma. Sitting in front of her is Lynn Bennet. Next to Lynn is one of her teammates from the tennis team, Stacy Davis. Those two are very close, so this is nothing new. Natalie does notice however, that Stacy places her hand on Lynn's leg, on the inside of her upper thigh. As Natalie studies the scene, Lynn slowly moves her own hand and places it on top of Stacy's. The two young girls also steal glances and shy smiles at each other throughout the ceremony.

Oh my God! Natalie thinks to herself. *Lynn might be a lesbian!*

After all students receive their diplomas, they walk out of the auditorium. Natalie keeps a close eye on Lynn and Stacy. While leaving the stage, the girls walk together, and briefly lock fingers with each other. They nervously release when they are out in the open.

A closet lesbian. Natalie makes a mental note.

Natalie goes straight home after the graduation and begins her summer routine. The next day, she begins running and doing yoga. She cooks all five of her meals and sticks to the strict guidelines of her selected diet. Every morning of the first week, she wakes up very sore. She begins to use her Nana's hot tub every night to relax her sore muscles. She also invests in tubes of muscle relaxing cream. She weights herself after the first week and discovers she has lost three pounds. She is on track to hitting her mark.

As she works her body, she keeps her mind focused on her goals. Every night, she dreams of Heather, and how she would love to kill her friends with her watching and knowing there is nothing she can do. With each passing night, her dreams become more violent. For her tormentors to die is not enough. They have to suffer. She wants them to realize they are being murdered. They need to feel the anxiety before the execution, to feel their hearts beat for the final time.

When she can, she will devert time to research, to find out information about her targets. In the yearbook, Monica mentions a time she went to little league game. Her dad gave her a bag of peanuts and she ate one. The next thing she remembered was waking up in a hospital. The doctors told her and her parents that she had a severe peanut allergy. Although she only had one peanut, it almost killed her. Natalie keeps this information handy.

The yearbook also awarded titles to certain graduating seniors, such as most likely to succeed, or most likely to be president. She noticed that Marco was voted class flirt, information that can be useful.

Natalie begins to delve into pop culture trends of people her age. She has to fit in and not stick out to anyone. The key to her success is to remain incognito. She surfs the net and looks up the popular website 'MySpace.' Out of curiousity, Natalie searchs for Heather Long. Her search returns 4,581 results with 27 in Washington State. She narrows her search to the two Heathers in Marion County. She finds her Heather and studies the page. Her interests are baseball, acting and spending time with friends. She has over 300 friends listed nationwide and has music playing in the background. Nothing Natalie finds on this page is of any use, however; she does agree with Heather's favorite quote.

"Keep your friends close, and your enemies closer."

She cannot agree more.

Natalie's packages begin arriving midsummer. Clothes, shoes, and accessories, they all arrive in bunches. As the deliveries arrive, Natalie tries them on. Most are slightly too tight in the hips and shoulders, but she does not mind. She can see that she is making progress with her workouts. As she packs them away, she is careful to keep the receipts organized, as she knows she will have to explain these purchases to Nana.

As the summer comes to an end, Natalie has her work cut out for her. She hits her weight goal and all her clothes fit, but she does not yet feel beautiful. She is not ready. It is time for her to take her final step. She goes downtown on a Saturday morning and gets a manicure, pedicure and her hair done. She returns home and lays out some of her new clothes and shoes. She picks out what she believes is a stunning arraignment and puts it on. That evening, she hits the town.

She takes the bus to downtown Seattle and begins to walk around. She has no destination in mind, she just wants to be in the open and gauge the public's reaction. She notices a gathering a young people her age inside a fast food restaurant and decides to act.

She walks in and gets in line at the counter. She keeps an eye on her surrondings, trying to see if anyone will notice her. She reaches the counter and orders a salad. The cashier takes her order and gives her a claim check. Natalie finds a table, sits down and waits. She takes quick glances over at the group and watches. They consist of two females and five males. One of those males, roughly six feet tall with blonde hair and brown eyes, keeps looking at her. The two lock eyes and Natalie flashes him a quick smile and looks away bashfully. After a few minutes, the young man walks over to Natalie and sits at her table, much to her surprise.

"I don't think I've seen you around before." he says.

"I'm new in town." she answers shyly. That is a lie. She does not know why she lied, but she just said the first thing that came to mind.

"New huh?" he asks. "Well, maybe you could use a local to show you around."

"I could," she answers, "if a certain local was willing."

"Well, who knows when that will be, but maybe I could fill in until that local shows up." he quips.

"I don't know." she shoots back. "I don't even know your name sir." He laughs lightly at her remark.

"The name's Shepard." He extends his hand. "Jackson Shepard." Natalie extends her hand as well.

"Rolle." She says. "Gloria Rolle." Another lie. Jackson accepts her hand and kisses it.

Natalie blushes as Jackson turns on the charm. As he leans forward, Natalie can see an insignia on his jacket. She presses further.

"Tell me Mr. Shepard," she begins, "do all you local boys wear Posrche jackets?"

"Only when we got the goods to back it up." He answers. He reached into his coat pocket and pulls out his car keys. "Wanna take a ride?"

She calmly answers, "Sure."

Jackson takes Natalie by the hand, leads her away from her table and towards the door. As he walks out, one of his male friends yells out, "You hit that, baby boy!"

They walk out of the restaurant and head towards the parking lot arm in arm. They make their way towards the back and Natalie sees his car. It is a brand new 911 Turbo, yellow with a wing in the back. Natalie walks up to the car and leans against it.

"Very nice." She remarks.

"So are you." he shoots back. He presses the keyless entry and the car unlocks.

"Let's ride." She heads for the passenger side of the car.

"Wait, hold up a minute." He walks up to her. He reaches into his pocket and pulls out his wallet.

"How much is this going to cost me?" he asks.

Natalie is puzzled. "Cost you?"

"Yeah." He answers. "When I saw you, I was like 'Man she's fine. She's gotta be expensive!' So fine."

"Oh my god!" she utters. He thinks that she is a prostitute.

"So how's this?" he continues. "We start slow, you know, you give me some head, and if it's all good from there, we do the whole damn thing."

Natalie gives nervous chuckle.

"No, no. I'm not like that." She replies.

"Right, right." He answers. "I get it. You're going decide what we do." He reaches behind her swiftly and places both hands on her backside. He squeezes hard. "I like that."

Natalie gasps and shoves him away.

"No, no!" she repeats. She can barely put her thoughts together. "No. I…I….no!" She turns to walk away. He angrily grabs her by the arm and throws her against the side of the car.

"Fuck that no shit!" he sounds upset. "I aint never been told no by a street walker, and it aint starting tonight."

"I'm not a street walker!" she yells back.

"Well what the fuck are you, an escort?" he mocks her. Natalie fears for her safety.

"A hooker's a hooker," he continues, "and pussy's pussy."

As if a reflex to his words, Natalie slaps him hard. She is very upset and angry, and she wants to leave the situation. As she tries to leave again, he grabs her and uses his body to pin her against the car. He puts one hand to her neck and quickly runs his other hand up her skirt. She struggles to break free but his hold is too strong. She is trapped.

"STOP!" Natalie screams. "HELP ME!"

"Hold still bitch!" he yelled back.

One of his hands is inside her skirt, pulling her panties aside. His other hand is on her neck, holding her down. Natalie tries punching on his back but it's no use. She cannot impede his advance. He presses his hips against hers as he withdraws his phallus. Natalie screams again, but no one is around who can help her.

No fear!

Natalie hears her thoughts again.

No fear! Only hate!

She feels her fear turn to anger.

Hate him!

Her anger and rage builds and turns to hate.

Make it end!

Her pulse quickens, her blood runs hot, her emotions harden, and she lets her hate consume her.

Make him pay!

Natalie stops screaming. She is now enraged, and waiting for her moment to strike. She feels his penis slide against her exposed vagina and reacts. She reaches inside his pants, grabs his genitalia and squeezes hard.

"UGH!" he yells, and pulls back a little bit.

She moves quickly. Using the additional space, she grabs ahold of his scrotum and squeezes again, using her fingernails to dig in. He screams in agony as she tightens her grip. She does not hesitate. Using her free hand, she grabs the back of his head, turns it sideways, takes his earlobe in her mouth and bites down hard. The sharp pain of her teeth piercing his skin shoots through his body. He tries to break loose, but his every movement only increases the pain. He falls to the ground, but she does not let go. She lands on top of him and increases the pressure in her grab and her bite. He writhes the entire time, trying to break free, but the possessed woman will not let go. She feels her nails break the skin of his groin and the warm blood coat her hand. Her teeth cut deep into his ear, leaving only a thin flap of skin connecting it to his head, and she can taste his blood run into her mouth. She knows he is in pain, and loves every moment of it. Everytime she hears him scream, she increases the pressure. She wants him to suffer for as long as she can.

Giving one last tug, she rips away with her jaw and tears the flesh off his ear. She lets go of his groin, stands up, and spits the detached lobe into his face. She can feel his blood draining from her mouth and his warmth covering her fingers. She looks down at him and chuckles. He is rolling on the ground, one hand holding his half ear, the other trying to soothe the pain and stop the bleeding from his groin. She turns to walk away again.

"You crazy fucking bitch!" he yells after her.

Natalie instantly stops in her tracks and reacts. She turns toward him, takes a big step and plants a full swing kick directly to his mouth. His head recoils, and he spits out four of his teeth. As she is watching him bleed from the mouth, she sees his car keys on the ground, and realizes his car is still unlocked. She opens the driver side door and pops the truck. She lifts the lid, looks under the spare tire and pulls out the tire iron. She walks back to her prey.

"CALL ME A BITCH?" she yells, and swings the tool at his head. She connects, knocking him unconscious. His head hits the ground and he lays motionless.

She goes back to the car and shatters all the windows, mirrors, healights and taillights. She sit in the driver seat and uses the tire itron to bust up the centor console, the stereo, the gauges and anything else she can find. She enjoys a hearty laugh. She gets out the car and heads back to the bloody and beaten Jackson Shepard. She sees his wallet on the ground, picks it up, and takes all his cash, about $680.

"Thanks for your patronage." She says as she flings wallet back down. "Call me sweetie." She walks away.

Natalie walks back to the bus stop, tire iron still in hand. Despite the traumatic events of the evening, she is quite pleased with herself. She was verbally abused and assaulted, and did not stand for it. Her only disappointment was her failure to rip his balls off. Sitting at the bus stop, she studies the tire iron. She smacked Jackson pretty badly and the tool is still wet with his blood. She figures his friends will soon find him, call the police and start a manhunt. She has to get rid of the evidence. She walks over to the curb and dumps the rod into a sewer drain. The bus arrives, she gets in and sits towards the back.

She stretches out on the bench and relaxes. Blood still on her shirt, hand, chin, and shoe, she sports a satisfied grin. The bus pulls into another stop and an older woman gets on. She makes her way to the back and stops when she sees Natalie.

"Oh my god!" she exclaims. "Are you okay dear?"

Natalie chuckles. She cannot help it.

"Grandma," she answers, "I'm fucking fantastic!"

The old woman stands in stunned silence, then sits down in the front of the bus. Natalie laughs the whole way home.

One week passes. A cab pulls up in front on the old house. Rebecca climbs out of the rear, followed by her lover Etienne. They take their bags out of the trunk, pay the driver and walk up to the front door giggling. Rebecca unlocks the door and Etienne brings in the luggage. As Rebecca enters the foyer, she is relieved to find everything remaining just as she left it, clean and spotless. She heads to the living and stops when she sees the fireplace lit and a young woman sitting in her chair, reading a book.

"Natalie?" she asks stunned.

Natalie looks up from her book and smiles at her Nana. She is naked, except for a black silk and lace robe. Her skin is tanned to a medium-dark tone, her legs are shaved, her nails are manicured, and her hair is straight and lightened to a golden hue.

"Welcome back Rebecca." She says softly.

She stands up and heads towards her. The robe is extremely short, stopping at her upper upper thigh. Her arms are covered up to halfway down her forearm. She walks up to her Nana and kisses her lightly on the cheek.

"How was Europe?" she asks.

Rebecca does not know what to say. Her mouth hangs open wide and she has not blinked in the past 20 seconds. Etienne loudly clears his throat. The scratchy sound brings Rebecca back to reality.

"Oh. Um…Europe," she fumbles her words. "Europe was good, very nice."

The young man approaches and stands next her.

"Etienne," she starts, "This is…um," she snaps her finger and waggles her hand as if she has lost her train of thought.

Natalie interrupts her. "I'm the housesitter. The name's Natalie." She extends her hand.

"Etienne." He responds and kisses her hand.

"Hmm." Natalie continues. "So, you're the insatiable wild man, huh? The one Rebecca raves about. The mighty young buck."

"Guilty as charged." He responds.

"Well, I hope you two are thirsty." She says. "I just put on a pot of coffee, or I can prepare and serve some congac, if that's more to your liking."

"Actually," Rebecca cuts in. "Etienne was just being a gentleman walking me to the door. He was just about to leave." Etienne looks surprised.

"I am?" He asks

"Oh," Natalie replies. "Oh well, what a shame. Well, it was pleasure meeting you." She turns and heads for the kitchen. Etienne is puzzled and looks quizzingly at his lady love.

"You want me to leave?" he asks.

"Just for now." She answers. "Natalie is one of my favorite girlfriends, and I was really looking forward to some girl talk." Etienne smiles and shakes his head.

"I'll never understand you American women." He quips.

"You're not supposed to." She shoots back.

She gives him a quick kiss on the lips and watches him as he walks down the street. When he is out of sight, she runs back into the house and into the kitchen. She can barely contain her exuberance.

"FINALLY!" she yells. "I KNEW YOU COULD DO IT!"

Natalie laughs and embraces her Nana tightly.

"Oh Nana." She speaks as she hugs. "I can't even begin to tell you how good this feels."

They break their embrace. Rebecca looks Natalie up and down.

"Let me look at you." She says. She spins Natalie around. "Oh my god, where did that ass come from?" Natalie has to laugh.

"I'm serious!" she continues and smacks Natalie's backside.

"Ow!" Natalie reacts,

"You could bounce a quarter off it." Rebecca continues. "Natalie, you're stunning!"

Natalie walks over to the coffee pot and pours two cups.

"Oh Nana." she says, "You would not believe what I had to go through to get here."

"Well I'm listening." Rebecca responds. "And we've got all night."

The two women walk into the living room, sit down and talk for hours, well into the night. Natalie tells her Nana about the workout routines, her cooking her own meals, and how often she visits the hair and nail salons. When asked about her motivation, Natalie just says she was sick of feeling like a doormat and wanted a better life for herself. Rebecca hangs on Natalie's every word.

"Wait a minute!" Rebecca interjects. "The clothes, the shoes, the food, how did you pay for all that?"

"With your credit cards Nana." Natalie responds reather matter-of-factly.

"My credit cards?!" Nana raises her voice slightly. "Those were only for emergencies!"

"Nana!" Natalie looks Rebecca right in the eyes and holds a straight face. "Look at me before you left, and look at me now! I was an emergency!"

Rebecca stares blankly at Natalie for a second before responding. "Snappy! I like that!"

They both giggle.

"Point taken." Rebecca concedes. "Besides, best money I've ever spent."

"Thank you." Natalie sounds slightly relieved.

"Ok, now we can move on." Rebecca continues. "You're out of the basement and up here with me. I'm gonna make some calls and get your cute ass in magazines and lingerie catalogs."

"Actually," Natalie interrupts. "I've got other plans."

Rebecca is puzzled. "What other plans?"

Natalie walks over to the coffee table, retrieves a sheet of paper and gives it to her Nana. Rebecca takes the paper and reads it. Her eyes get big with excitement.

"You got accepted?" she asks happily. "You're going to Westin?"

"Yes!" Natalie exclaims. The two embrace again.

"You know what this means Natalie?' Rebecca asks. "You get a second chance. Another opportunity to get it right. And this time, you know what you are doing."

"I know." Natalie answers.

"Make me proud." Rebecca demands.

"I will." Natalie responds. "I promise."

The women continue to chat until 3:45 in the morning. By this time, they are both very tired and need to get some sleep. They share one final hug and head to their respective bedrooms to retire for the night.

When Natlie reaches her bedroom, her attitude changes, from jubilance, to furious anger. Her joy from her reunion with her Nana was fake. Natalie feels no joy, no pride, only anger and resentment.

How dare this woman embrace me after treating me like shit for six years? How dare she kiss me when for past six years she would practically spit on me? What gives her the fucking right to think she had anything do to with my transformation.

Natalie controls her emotions, but remains angry. She got what she needed from her Nana. She got permission to attend Westin State. She looks at her left hand and reflects on the scar embedded deep within the palm. She knows her purpose, and now has the permission she needs to achieve her goal. Natalie goes to bed and falls asleep.

The next morning, Rebecca summons Natalie to the garage. Curious, Natalie meets her Nana there.

"Natalie," Rebecca begins, "I want to give you something. Something that may help you in college."

Rebecca opens the garage door and Natalie looks inside. After initial confusion, Natalie sees the gift. It is a pickup truck, metallic green with white interior and a camper shell. Natalie looks at her Nana.

"Your grandfather, Harold," Rebecca begins, "he was a good man. Made it possible for us to live a good life, since the pageants didn't pay all that great. He worked hard and he made our lives possible. One day, after a show, I saw this guy trying to sell his truck. He was desparate, and needed to feed his new baby. I bought it for $300 and gave it to Harold for our tenth anniversary. He loved these big heavy things, and wanted to restore this one."

Her eyes begin to well with emothion, but she continues.

"He changed his mind after a year, and decided he wanted to start his own food delivery service. To help feed the poor. He had a freezer installed in the back and put the shell over it. He got his business license, company name, 'Southern Hospitality Catering'; and even made me the company president. We were in it together. That was his dream."

She begins to cry and has trouble keeping her words together. She goes on.

"We did one job, a beauty pagent. The food was so good and the guests loved our service. The next day, he went to the doctor, and found out he got the cancer, in his liver. He died three years later. When he got the news, he just seemed to give up on things that didn't seem to matter no more. He didn't wanna work, didn't wanna play poker no more, he just gave up. He told me, the only joy he had, was that he had a beautiful wife that he could look at every morning and bring a smile to his face."

Natalie listens to every word. She does not care much for her Nana's emotional state, but she is interested in her family history. Rebecca continues the tale.

"This truck was his last bastion of freedom. From the day he was diagnosed, to the day he died, we would load up the truck and drive the countryside. Every weekend, it was just him, myself, your mother, and the truck. It deserves an owner that's a fighter. Natalie, I know that I'm not the typical grandmother. I don't bake cookies, I don't sew or knit, hell, I don't even cook. I couldn't raise you like I raised your mother. I didn't know how after I lost my Harold, but I did the best I could. Last night, you showed me how much of a fighter you are. You could have given up, you could have quit, but you didn't. You fought, and I want you to have Harold's truck."

Natalie perks up when her Nana gives her the truck. Despite her feeling towards her Nana, she wants to say something nice, but does not know how to repond. She tries to say something when Rebecca places her hands on her shoulders and cuts her off.

"Natalie," she says, "keep fighting. I don't know what your inspiration or motivation is, but keep focused on it. Promise me Natalie. Promise me, that whatever your desires are deep within your heart, you will not stop fighting until your reach them."

"I promise." Natalie smiles as she answers and Rebecca hugs her tight.

"Thank you." Nana replies.

"Nana?" Natalie askesas she pulls away. "I don't know how to drive."

Both women share a laugh.

"It's easy." Rebecca tells her. "Go get some real clothes on and I'll show you."

Natalie gets dressed and meets her Nana back at the garage. Rebecca is able to start the truck right up. She explains that Etienne also likes old trucks and keeps this one in top condition. She carefully goes over the controls, knobs and switches inside the cabin. The truck has a manual 4-speed transmition and Rebecca explains how to use the clutch and shift through the gears. When she is sure she has explained everything, she lets Natalie drive. She has her share of trouble, but after 30 minutes, she gets the hang of it. After two hours, she is doing well enough to drive through the city. When they get back home, Natalie has to clear one last obstacle.

"Nana," she starts, "you know I don't have my license. How am I supposed to drive this to school?"

"Simple." Rebecca answers. "Stay within the speed limit and keep an eye out for cops. If you get pulled over, no male cop in the world will give a pretty girl like you a ticket. Worst-case scenario, you may have to blow him, but you'll be home free."

"And if it's a female cop?" Natalie asks.

"You're fucked." A simple question requires a simple answer.

That night, Natalie ponders what her grandmother told her, and she has to laugh. She does not remember much of the story of her grandfather, but she thinks long and hard about the end of her speech.

Would Nana really want me to pursue my dreams and desires if she knew what they really were?

She reflects on those desires. She wonders how great the moment of judgement will feel, when she ends Heather's life. She ponders the many different ways she can do it. She thinks about slashing her throat, or beating her to death with a crowbar, or even strangling her. She relives the night when she beat Jackson Shepard, or as she likes to call him, 'Dress Rehersal.' She remembers feeling the crack of the tire iron as it crashed into his skull. She remembers seeing his teeth on the ground after she booted his mouth. She remembers smiling bright as she saw the news report of a young Seattle youth nearly beaten to death in a parking lot, and the poor boy could not remember a thing. These memories bring her pleasure, but not satisfaction. She wanted to kill him. She wishes she had remained latched to his penis and ripped it off. She wishes she could go back in time, and shove the tire iron down his throat. She wishes she had wailed on his head with the same tire iron, until she cold see the gray matter of his brain. She vows, when she has the chance at Westin, she will finish the job. She falls asleep and enjoys another deliciously brutal dream. Her moment is nearing, and she hungers for the hunt.

Saturday morning arrives. Natalie has finished packing her clothes and supplies, and loaded the truck the previous night. Her Nana surprises her with one last gift, a brand new laptop computer and Coach carrying bag. She slings her bag over her shoulder, grabs her truck keys and heads upstairs from her bedroom. She meets her Nana in the living room and stands for final inspection. She wears a tight, red, strapless halter-top that leaves her midriff exposed. Around her hips is a tiny black micro-skirt that barely covers her ample bottom. Adorning her legs are tall black leather boots that stop at her mid thigh. Her hair is laser straight and hangs down to her shoulders and on top of her head is a black beret.

"Damn." Nana replies. "You learn quickly."

"To notice me is to love me." Natalie shoots backs.

Rebecca gets up and walks Natalie to her truck. They load the last of her luggage and look at each other for one last time.

"Natalie," Rebecca begins, "you are so beautiful, and you make me so proud."

"Thank you." She says and gives her a big hug. "I won't let you down Nana. I promise to push for my desires, and not stop until I reach them."

"I love you, my dear." sobs Rebecca.

"I love you too Nana." Natalie answers.

They break their embrace and kiss each other on the cheeks. Natalie walks over to the driver side of the truck, gets in, buckles up, and startes the engine. She gives her Nana one last wave goodbye and drives away. She sheds a tear as she watches her Nana disappear in the rear view mirror. She blows a kiss to her former life, and looks ahead to the life ahead. If she desires a peaceful future, she will have to move forward with a violent present.

Natalie follows the directions she received in her email and makes the four hour drive to Westin State University. She pulls into the student parking lot and parks her truck. Getting out of her vehicle, she notices the dormitory rush has already begun. Student and parents pull up to the front of the dorms and drop their children off. The scene is packed.

Natalie walks over to the mob and waits in line at the check-in table set up outside. On her way there, she is complmented on her boots three times and is flirtatiously cat called by a group of males standing by a tree. She thanks the girls for the compliments and blows kisses to the boys. She reaches the front of the line and smiles at the young man sitting behind the table.

"Hi." he exclaims and extends his hand. "Welcome to Westin State, home of the Seraphs."

"Glad I could be here." She responds and shakes his hand.

"I'm Doug Winsor," he continues, "your resident advisor. May I have you name please?"

The moment of truth.

She takes a deep breath.

"Natalie Cordova." She answers.

"Ok, let me see here." He murmurs.

He flips through his manifest and stops when he finds her name.

"Ah, here you are." He says. "Alright, it looks like we have you staying in room 1284."

He gives her a quizzical look.

"1284?" He chuckles, "I don't know what you did, but it must have been good."

"What do you mean?" Natalie asks.

"Room 1284," he answers, "is a private dorm. No annoying roommate to hassle you, plus it's the only room with a dedicated T1 high-speed internet line, and it's cable ready."

"Oh!" She quips. "Must be my lucky day today."

He reaches into a lock box and pulls out a set of keys. He gives them to Natalie.

"He you are." He says. "Feel free to check the room out and see if it's to your liking before you move your belongings in."

"Thank you." She turns to walk away, but stops and looks back at Doug.

"You said it was a private room right?" she asks.

"Yes ma'am." He answers. "It's all your's and no one else's."

She puts her hand on his shoulder.

"Good." She says. "Then maybe up could stop by and 'advise' me sometime."

Doug coughs uncomfortably.

"Miss Cordova," he says with a chuckle, "I try not to fraternize with the student residents."

"Good." She replies. "I had no plans of fraternizing."

She slowly brushes her hand off his shoulder and struts away. She looks over her shoulder and sees him stealing a final glance of her as she walks. She smiles at him and walks into the dorm. She checks the directory for room 1284. She finds it on the 12th floor, second door to the right past the elevators. She heads to the elevator hall, gets on a car, and rides it to the 12th floor.

The elevator is packed with students, shoulder to shoulder, with no room to wiggle. The 12th floor was at the top, so she guesses she will be the last one out. It stops on each floor except four and seven, and one person gets off at at time. The elevator reaches the 12th and she unboards, takes a right at the hallway and finds her room. She unlocks the door and walks in.

She had read that most dorm rooms are ten feet by eight feet in size, so she is shocked to see that her room is considerably bigger. She guessed it was twice the size of her bedroom at home, and like her bedroom, has its own restroom. A full size bed is on the right of the door, unmade, but with a fresh set of sheets folded on top. To the left of the door is a desk, with three drawers on each side, allowing her plenty of space to hold her supplies. On the floor is a lovely scarlet colored carpet, freshly vacuumed. Next to her desk is a full size walk in closet, with more than enough room for her clothes and shoes. Against the wall opposite the front door, is a 37-inch television on top of a dresser. She marvels at the room and wonders how she managed to get this wonderful reward.

She walks over to the bed. She wants to make it now so she will not have to make it later. As she reaches for the sheets, she notices a letter sitting on top with her name on it. She opens it and reads.

Dear Miss Cordova,

Here at Westin State University, we want you to know that we value new arriving students who appreciate the power of education. Upon review of all academic records of all incoming freshmen, we have discovred that you have the highest grade point average. We would like to congratulate you by offering you the finest dorm on campus. We hope this dorm will provide you with the proper learning environment to continue your pursuit of academic excellence.

Take care, and welcome to Westin State University.

Natalie finishes reading the note, and silently thanks the university staff. She finishes making her bed and heads back downstairs to retrieve her luggage.

Back in the elevator, Natalie waits as she descends to the lobby. The elevator stops on the eighth floor and the doors open. Natalie steps aside to let another passenger inside. To her chagrin, the other passenger is Lynn Bennett.

"Excuse me." Lynn says softly as she steps inside the elevator.

Natalie is startled. She did not expect to interact with any of her targets this soon. She begins to feel tepid and slightly nervous. Lynn was never good at holding her tounge. Whenever she saw Natalie, she was quick to insult and humiliate. Natalie dreds this very moment, and she does not know how she will react if Lynn says something provacative. Will she revert back to her old ways and remain quiet or will she say something back, which can lead to retaliation from the others? She soon realizes that this situation is vastly different from anything she has ever experienced.

Natalie keeps queit as the elevator resumes its descent. She keeps an eye on Lynn but tries to ignore her. Lynn, however, does not ignore

Natalie. She glances quickly over her shoulder, and looks Natalie up and down. When she sees Natalie take notice, she quickly turns her head and nervously brushes her hair behind her ear.

"Crazy day huh?" she murmurs.

Natalie is caught off guard. She has been expecting an insult of some sorts, but instead receives a pleasant greeting. She has to respond in kind.

"Very." Natalie replies.

"So many new faces," Lynn goes on, "I feel like such an outsider."

Dear God, Natalie thinks to herself, *she doesn't even recognize me!*

Lynn turns slightly to face her elevator mate.

"Aren't you nervous?" she asks. "You know, about meeting new people, and trying new things?"

Natalie gives her a smile.

"Actually," she replies, "I'm looking forward to hooking up with old aquiantences. But I'm very excited about trying new things."

The elevator reaches the third floor and the door opens. Lynn gives one final thought.

"Lucky you." She says before blushing and walking away.

The elevator reached the lobby, and Natalie cannot help but smile. One her tormentors did not regonize her, and they were standing mere inches from each other. She knows she can use this to her advantage, if she can just figure out how. She exits the elevator and heads for the parking lot.

She reaches her truck, unlocks the back and begins to pull out her luggage. As she is unloading her bags, she hears some familiar voices.

"Once I get in, it's all good." A male voice states.

"Hell yeah." Says another male voice.

Natalie peers to her left, to the source of the conversation. Leaning on the trunk of a car, about 15 feet away, are Marco and Howard. Natalie listens to their chatter with much interest.

"I was talking to Malik," Howard goes on, "and her told me, like, 'For brothers majoring in entertainment law, Sigma will take care of you, but only if you pledge.' I can't walk away from that."

"You ain't pledging for support." Marco interjects, "You're doin' it cause you wanna get some pussy!"

"I ain't even thinking about the Zetas." Howard defends. "Besides, once I make things right with Lynn, I ain't gonna need them bitches."

"Man, she dropped your ass," Marco exclaims, "get over it!"

"Shut up, fool!" Howard responds. "I just wanna know why."

"I told you why dawg," Marco answers. "She likes the pink fish tacos."

"Fuck you." Howard shoots back. "Lynn ain't a dyke!"

"Then what is it?" Marco asks. "Did you cheat?"

"No." Howard answers.

"You lie to her?"

"No."

"You smack her?"

"What?! Hell no!"

"I know!" Marco perks. "You can't get it up!"

"Listen asshole, my shit is primed and ready to go." Howard is getting upset. "My fucking nuts are as blue as the ocean."

"Maybe your little blue nuts need some little blue pills chico!" Marco quips.

Howard responds by popping Marco in the back of his head.

"I ain't got time for this shit." Howard replies and gets off the car before storming away. Marco is close behind, pleading with him to lighten up.

Natalie watches them as they walk away. She knows what Marco is talking about, and thinks that maybe he is right; that maybe Lynn is a lesbian. She rememberes seeing Lynn at their graduation; how she and her friend held hands and gazed at each other. She flashes back to the elevator, how Lynn spoke softly, blushed, played with her hair and flashed a smile as she departed. At this point Natalie realizes that not only did Lynn not recognize her, she was flirting with her! She keeps this information in the back of her mind and resumes gathering her luggage.

Natalie spends most of that first day setting up her room. She hangs her clothes in her closet, places her undergarments and socks in ther dresser drawers and sets up her laptop and charger on her desk. In her bathroom, she carefully arranges her cosmetics on the countertop and places her towels in the cabinet. After she is done, she decides to watch some television while deciding what to do next. She turns on the T.V. and watchs a video tour of the campus on a closed-circuit channel.

The tour displays multiple fly-overs of the campus and points out the newer buildings just opened, such as the new gymnasium, the soccer field, the observatory, and the shooting/archery range.

Her interest is perked by the archery range. She does not care too much for guns, but she is fascinated by archery. She admires the discipline and control required to fire the arrow on a straight enough line to hit the bullseye. She decides she will check it out at some point.

She looks over at her alarm clock and checks the time. 5:15 p.m. She wants to check out more of the campus and map out her classes before they begin. She gets off the bed and changes her clothes. She puts on a black tank top, blue jeans and black Mary Janes. The air is chilly, so she throws on a heavy wool sweater. She heads downstairs and exits the building.

Despite the cool, late afternoon, the campus is still fairly busy. Natalie's dorm had been checked in and the table was cleared from the front. She walks out the dorm and heads west toward the quad. She does not have to wait long to see some action.

A crowd is gathering in the quad, cheering and listening to loud music. Natalie squeezes her way through and catches a glimpse of what is happening. Upon reaching the front, she sees a group of males, roughly eight, standing shoulder to shoulder, staring straight ahead, and wearing matching blue fraternity sweaters. It is the Sigma Tau Upsilon (ΣΤΥ) stomp crew.

She watches as the men perform their routines, doing spins and acrobatics Natalie had never experienced first hand. The crowd gets worked up into a frenzy. As she watchs the performance, she scans the crowd, trying to see if anyone looks familiar. Across the way, she spots Heather.

Heather has both her hands in the air cheering as the men dance. She is flanked by Monica and Ashley, both of whom are cheering. Behind them are Howard and Marco. Howard has his hands cupped over his mouth and is shouting encouragement to the dancers. Natalie assumes that these stompers are the "Sigmas" Howard had mentioned to Marco earlier in the day. She makes a mental note to find out all she can about this fraternity. Maybe she can find something to use to her advantage.

Natalie can see the euphoria in Howard's face; he is in heaven. He claps and stomps along with the rest of the stompers, then stops suddenly. Natalie watchs as he turns around and darts away from his friends. Intrigued, Natalie leaves to follow him and investigate.

She keeps her distance to avoid arousing suspicion. She follows him to the nearby library courtyard. When he stops walking, Natalie takes a seat on a courtyard bench.

"Lynn!" he calls out.

A young woman with chestnut hair turns around. It is Lynn. She seems surprised.

"Howard." She answers. "Um, what's up?

"I was hoping you would tell me." He replies.

Natalie's interest piques. She continues to listen.

"You avoid me all summer," he continues "and you barely say anything when I call. What's going on?"

"Nothing." She answers. "Just stressed I guess."

She keeps her head down as she speaks.

"Stress over what?" He asks.

"You know, the tennis team." she replies. "We have our first match against Seattle State in one week. I just wanna be ready and not distracted."

"That's bullshit." He shoots back. "You're the top prep tennis recruit in the country, and you could've gone pro. Stress doesn't shake you."

"Well, maybe things have changed." She answers strongly.

"Not your tennis." He replies. "Something else is going on."

She does not respond.

"What's wrong Lynn?" he goes on. "Why aren't you talking to me?"

"It's just..." she struggles with her words. "I've been thinking about things, and {sigh}, I just gotta figure things out."

"Figure what out?" he demands.

"You know," she answers, "figure out where I stand. With myself, with you, with my studies, with...." She trails off.

"Your sexual preference." He interrupts.

"What?" she looks up.

"Cut the crap Lynn!" he becomes irate. "I hear the rumors, and see you flounce around campus, talking to all the little mamas. Dressing like a whore and flipping your hair and shit!"

She opens her mouth to speak but he cuts her off.

"I saw you," he goes on, "holding that girl's hand at graduation, your team mate. Stacy was it?"

She keeps her gaze on him, tears running down her reddening face, speechless.

"Humph," he continues, "I didn't know snatch slurping was a team sport."

She reacts, and slaps him hard across the face, leaving a deep red mark. She removes a ring from her left had and throws it at his chest. She begins to sob.

"I was wrong about you." She finally says. She turns away from him and runs, covering her mouth as she escapes. Howard bends down and picks up the ring. After looking at it for a second, he puts it in his pocket and leaves the scene.

This is an interesting development. Howard and Lynn have been an item since they were 13 years old. Now that relationship is over. Natalie cannot help but giggle. She takes this argument as confirmation of Lynn's homosexual urges. She gets up from her bench and leaves the scene. She heads back to her dorm.

On her way back, she sees Monica, Heather, and Ashley walking past her. They are talking amoungst themselves, apparently excited by a yellow flyer that Monica is reading. As Natalie's curiousity grows, a frat boy runs up to her.

"Hey there sweet thing." He says and hands her a yellow flyer.

She takes a second to glance over it.

"Flyer party?" she asks

"Yeah." He replies. "The Kappas are blowing up big this year. All the beautiful people get in for free, if they bring their own beer."

"Small problem." She interjects "If I gotta pay for the beer, then admission ain't really free now is it?"

"Oh, that ain't shit." He answers. He reaches into his pocket, opens his wallet and gives Natalie ten dollars. "All you need is a six pack of long necks."

"Alright." She takes the money. "See you on Friday." She turns to walk away.

"I'll be waiting." He replies. She gives him a wink and walks away.

Upon reaching her dorm, she reflects back on Heather and her two cohorts reading the flyer.

If they'll be there, so will I!

She looks at her alarm clock, 8:46pm. Not late, but Natalie decides to turn in for the night. Her classes started in two days, on Monday, and she wants to be prepared. She will spend Sunday buying her books and supplies. On Monday, she decides, she will see where the day takes her.

Monday arrives and Natalie dresses for her first day as a college student. She wears a pink, form fitting body shaper, with an abundance of cleavage; black jeans and high-heeled sandals. She makes sure to bring her laptop, as her first class is sure to be a doozy, THL216: Theological Concepts in Modern Day Anthropology. She leaves her building and heads for the classroom.

She arrives at the designated classroom and has a seat. She smiles as she walks in and garners some whistles from male ooglers. The room is not very big, about the size of a small movie theater, and half-empty. As the professor arrives, the students sit and wait for the lecture to begin.

The professor is an anthropologist, Dr. Rachel Winters. She is a graduate of The University of California in Berkeley and has a double doctorate in anthropology and theology, which makes her a perfect fit to teach the class. As she begins her lecture, the students relax. She is very easy going and wants to have a lot of fun with the students. She gives her introduction and all the students pay attention, except for Natalie.

Natalie's attention is diverted elsewhere; to the girl sitting three rows down and four seats to the left, Lynn Bennett. She is dressed very modestly, looks to be in a poor mood, and only half-interested in the lecture.

Dr. Winters announces she wants the students to walk around and introduce themselves to each other. The students begin to move around and introduce themselves. Natalie stays in her seat and continues to watch Lynn. A young man approaches Natalie and tries to start a conversation, but she only feigns interest and keeps watching Lynn. She watches as Lynn stays by herself and no approaches her. Natalie decides to act and interruptes the rambling boy.

"Excuse me Jerry." She stands up from her chair.

"Um, it's Jericho." He responds.

"Whatever." She walks past him and heads towards Lynn.

As she makes her way to Lynn, she gets excited. This will be her first intiated contact. Lynn looks up and sees her approaching. She recognizes the girl from the elevator on Saturday, gives her a friendly smile and waves to her. She blushes nervously. Natalie takes a seat next to her.

"Small world, huh?" Natalie asks and smiles.

"Yeah." Lynn responds. She blushes and her right eye twinkles.

Rip it out!

Natalie remains composed.

"So," Lynn continues, "did you finish moving in?"

"Yes." Natalie answers. "It was a lot of work, but well worth it."

"Cool." Lynn replies. "What room did you get?"

"Room 1284." Natalie answers.

"1284?!" Lynn asks excitedly. "I've heard about that room. Is what they say about it true?"

"It's wonderful." Natalie replies. "A view of the campus, 37-inch T.V. with cable, private bathroom, it's incredible."

"How did you get it?" Lynn asks.

"I dunno." Natalie responds. "Maybe I slept with the right person over the summer."

The girls enjoy a laugh together

"Aw man," Lynn goes on, "I would love to see it sometime."

"Anytime." Natalie answers. "Just let me know."

"I'm sorry." Lynn interjects. "I'm being so rude. I'm Lynn. Lynn Bennett." She extends her hand.

Natalie takes her hand and shakes it. Instantly, she remembers seeing the other girls hanging around campus, without Lynn. Maybe, they had a falling out, and Lynn was no longer one of 'them.' Natalie could not be sure, so she decided to take a bold step.

"Hi Lynn." Natalie replies. "It's good to see you again."

"Again?" Lynn asks. "Did we know each other in a past life or something?" She gives a little giggle. Natalie stares her in the eyes.

"You know who I am Lynn." She says. "Think hard."

Natalie averts her gaze and leans back in her seat, forcing her breast to press suggestivly against her shirt. Afterward she crosses her legs. Lynn is intrigued and struggles to regain her focus.

"Um, no bells ringing." Lynn gives a nervous laugh.

"We interacted almost everyday in high school." Natalie goes on. "I think you actually looked forward to seeing me so we could 'chat' a little bit."

Lynn cannot hear very clearly. She is busy, mezmerised by how the light hit Natalie's cleavage. Her heart races and she startes to sweat. Natalie smiles.

"Why you staring so hard?" she asks.

Lynn shakes her head and brings herself back to reality.

"I...uh," she stammers. "Dammit! I'm sure I would remember you."

Natalie leans in towards Lynn and gives a sly smile.

Moment of truth.

"I'm Natalie." She states. "Natalie Cordova."

Lynn gasps and almost chokes on her spit. She covers her mouth and coughs. The revelation is shocking.

"Natalie?!" she finally says. "Holy shit!"

Natalie sits still, trying to gauge Lynn's reaction, trying to decide what to do next.

"Natalie," Lynn continues, "um...you look great! Very different."

"Normally, you wouldn't have said that." Natalie counters.

"Oh...yeah." Lynn stammers again. "About that, um...we were just...dumb kids and I didn't...."

"Don't even worry about it." Natalie interrupts. "The past is the past, and it's in the past."

Lynn cracks a relieved smile.

"You're right." She says. "It's in the past."

"You know Lynn," Natalie goes on, "I've always admired you."

Natalie makes a play to gain Lynn's trust. It works.

"Really?" Lynn is astonished and smiles in reply. "Why?"

"You always seemed to have everything together." Natalie answers." A bright future playing pro tennis, a great body, a hot ass boyfriend, all the things a girl could want."

"Well," Lynn replies, "I think you got me beat on the great body part."

"You definitely were not like the others." Natalie interjects

"What do you mean?" Lynn wonders.

Natalie turns up the manipulation.

"Let's face it," she says, "Heather was so domineering. She just had to be the big bitch in the yard, daddy's little princess syndrome; and Ashley's so damn fake. Never angry, always a fucking sugar coated sweetheart. Monica is a poddle. All she knows how to do is follow. She can't lead because she doesn't know how. You tell her to jump, and she won't even ask how high, she'll just jump. Don't tell me you didn't notice that."

Lynn looks perplexed at first, then leans in aand speaks quietly.

"Actually," she says, "I was afraid, that I was the only one who thought that way."

Both girls share a quick laugh, and Natalie has a revelation. Lynn resents her comrades. This is useful information. It means that she would separate rather easily from the others. They continue to chat until Dr. Winters excuses the class for the day. As the girls gather their books, Natalie has an idea. She turns to Lynn.

"Hey, you still wanna see the dorm?" she asks.

"Yeah!" Lynn replies.

The girls leave together and head for Natalie's dorm. Upon arrival, Lynn stares in amazment and jealousy. The open area, the red carpet, the private bathroom, all the luxuries she does not have in her dorm. She walks to the window and glances outside.

"This is awesome." She says. "I would kill, to have a dorm like this."

Kill!

The word reverberates in Natalie's mind. She seems to freeze and stop what she is doing. She has Lynn in her dorm and they are alone. This would be a perfect opportunity. She holds her laptop in her hands.

She knows it would be so easy, to walk up behind Lynn and beat her skull in with it. She slowly takes her steps. She wants to strike.

Not yet!

Natalie stops herself, as this is not the right moment. Lynn is a premier athlete, and could easily fight her off and get away. That is not what Natalie wants. She wants Lynn in a weakened and vulnerable state. She places her laptop down on her desk and collects herself.

"You don't have to kill anyone." She tells Lynn. "You're free to come up, anytime you like."

"I appreciate that." Lynn replies. She turns her gaze to Natalie. "I just might do that."

"With one condition." Natalie adds.

"What's that?" Lynn asks.

"Don't tell your friends I'm here." Natalie states.

"Why not?" Lynn asks. "Why is that so important?"

Natalie reaches up and begins to stroke Lynn's hair and face, lightly and softly. She longs to grab a fistful of hair and rip it out, but she remains composed. Lynn closes her eyes and enjoys Natalie's touch. The sensation gives her goosebumps.

"Because," Natalie answers. "I know who they are in their hearts, and I know who you are. You, I like. Them, not so much. You know how they see me, if they knew that we hung out, who's to say they won't add to that nasty llittle rumor."

Lynn opens her eyes and takes a sharp breath. She knows of the rumor Natalie refers. After graduation from high school, three of Lynn's teammates on the tennis team came out of the closet and admitted they were lesbians. The news spread rapidly, and soon afterwards, Lynn was questioned daily about her sexuality. She would deny every accusation, but she has been struggling with lesbian urges since she was 16 years old. She tried to write them off to curiosity, but the urges grew stronger as she grew older. She became distant from Howard, and her friends use the rumor to rip on her in playful jest on a daily basis.

"You know about that?" she asks. There was sorrow in her voice and her eyes began to well.

"That's all it is right?" Natalie asks in return. "Just a silly rumor?"

Lynn slowly turns and looks away from Natalie. She feels dred in the pit of her stomach. She wants to deny the rumor yet again, but as she opens her mouth, different words come out.

"I don't know." She says quietly. Her voice begins to crack. Natalie places a hand on her shoulder.

"Hey, hey." She says, trying to sound comforting. "Whether it's true or not, it doesn't change who you are, and it doesn't change how I see you. You are always welcome to be who you are when you're around me."

Lynn turns to face Natalie.

"Thank you." She says softly.

Slowly and gently, Natalie reaches out, wraps arms around Lynn's shoulders, and gives her a tight hug. Lynn reciprocates, wrapping her arms around Natalie's waist and squeezing. She is enraptured in the comfort Natalie has given her and sobs softly on her shoulder. Natalie; however, sports a large smile, jubilant that the manipulation is going so well. She holds Lynn for a few moments before releasing the embrace.

"I should go." Lynn says. "My next class starts pretty soon."

"Stop by anytime." Natalie replies.

"I won't tell them you're here." Lynn promises. "I won't tell anyone."

"Thank you." Natalie replies.

Natalie walks Lynn to the elevator and waits in the hall until Lynn makes her descent before returning to her room. Once in her room, she begins to turn red. She feels her anger and frustration build. Her blood begins to burn and her hands tremble.

So close! So fucking close!

She walks over to her desk and repeatedly pounds her fist on the furnature. She knows she played the scenario right, but is feeling greedy. She wants more. She knows she must be patient, but it infuriates her. She jumps up from her desk, begins to punch the wall and screams.

"SO FUCKING CLOSE!" she wails. "I couldv'e had her."

A loud knock on the door startles her.

"Go away!" she yells.

"Miss Cordova," It is a male's voice "It's me Doug Winsor, your R.A."

His name calms her down. She remembers Doug. She recalls how she flirted with him, and thought he was cute.

"Natalie, please open the door." He requests.

Natalie quickly gathers herself, slaps on a smile and opens the door.

"Hey Doug." She says with fake enthusiasm

"I heard all the commotion, is everything alright?" he asks.

"Yeah. Yeah." She answers. "Just…a rough morning I guess."

Her face is still red, making her smile an obvious fake.

"Must have been hellacious." He says. "I don't think that wall can take anymore punishment."

"Oh my God," she giggles, "I'm so sorry if that disturbed you. Guess I just gotta get used to the stress of college life. You know, haven't had time to find an outlet yet."

He looks her body over, from head to toe and back up. He suddenly has an idea.

"Put a coat on." He insists. "C'mon."

"What?" she asks; caught off-guard.

"I wanna show you something." He says. "Hurry up."

Natalie goes to her closet, grabs her leather jacket, and follows Doug to the elevator hall. The make idle chit-chat as they go down to the ground floor and into the parking lot. They get into Doug's car and head east. Ten minutes later, they arrive at a newly contructed building.

"Where are we?" she asks.

"Have you ever shot a bow and arrow?" he asks her back. "Archery?"

"No." she answers "Why?"

Doug extends his hand to her. "C'mon. Let's relieve that stress."

Natalie takes his hand and he leads her to the entrance. He pays a small entrance fee and they walk inside.

"Welcome to the WSU archery range." He says.

Natalie looks around and marvels at her surroundings. On her right are the different inventory stands, where different types of bows, from traditional, to sport, to crossbows; and ammunition are offered. On her left is a vast open field with targets spread out everywhere, allowing archers different distances and angles to aim and shoot. Doug rents two sport bows and four quivers, and leads Natalie to an open stall. He proceeds to give her a lesson in archery. Topics include how to load the arrow, aim, and fire. She learns quickly. After 30 minutes of misfires and arm chaffes, she actually hits a target. After 50 minutes, she hits her first bullseye. She jumps for joy and hugs Doug in jubilation.

"How do you feel?" he asks.

"Better." She replies. "Much better."

"Good." He goes on. "Try this." He points to the target directly in front of them. "Hit this target, dead center."

DEAD center. She thought to herself.

"Imagine that it's someone or something you dispise." He continues. "Go on, give it a name."

Natalie thinks for moment. She knows she wants to name the target Heather, and impale her fleshy center with the arrow. No one deserves an arrow to the heart more than Heather.

"Monica." She answers. Her response shocks her. She wanted to say Heather, but when she spoke, she said Monica. She loses her focus, her fingers slips and the arrow fires.

"Bullseye!" Doug exclaimed. He wraps his arms around Natalie in celebration, but her mind is somewhere else. Her focus was on Heather, but that arrow was meant for Monica.

It's time. She thinks to herself. *Monica's time!*

Friday morning, and Natalie rises from her bed. The week has gone by smoothly with no more frustration. Natalie and Lynn have grown closer and became teammates in their Theology class. Their flirtations continue, going as far as the girls regularly hugging and kissing on the cheeks. Natalie even offered to let Lynn stay the night on one occasion only to be reluctantly turned down. Lynn spoke freely about the other girls and Natalie took note. Through Lynn, she learned that Monica's peanut allergy had gotten worse since her near fatal childhood episope. This would be very useful.

On Fridays, Natalie has no classes scheduled. Today will be the day that the first one her tormentors meets their judgement, and that first one will be Monica Bynes.

To prepare, Natalie drives to a seedy liquor store, just down the highway, 15 minutes from campus. The place is pretty sleazy, but the clerk does not card her for her beer purchase. She buys a six-pack of a Japanese beer, one bag of peanuts, a bottle of peanut oil, and one bottle opener. Arriving back at her dorm, she opens each bottle and drinks a small amount from each bottle. She gags at the first sip, but persists. Using a washcloth and an empty glass for a rolling pin, she crushes six peanuts, and sprinkles the dust into each of the bottles. Afterwards, she drops one whole, unshelled peanut into eash bottle. Finally, she tops off each bottle with the peanut oil and reseals the caps.

She checks the yellow flyer. The party begins at 9:00pm. At 7:00pm, she puts the six-pack in the freezer of her truck, to allow it at least two hours to chill. She goes back to her dorm and changes clothes, brown leather mini-skirt with matching jacket, black tank top and open-toe four-inch stilettos. She heads to the hardware store where she buys a small funnel and three feet of plastic tubing. She coils the tubing, hides it in her jacket, places the funnel in her purse and heads to the party.

She arrives at the Kappa house and the soiree is in full swing. She leaves her beer in the truck and makes her way around the front yard, looking for a familiar face. She does not have to wait long. Peering through the window, she recognizes the frat boy who gave her the flyer, and he is flirting Ashley Tyler. She figures, if Ashley is there, Monica and Heather cannot be far behind. She decides to move.

She returns to her truck and retrieves her beer and flyer. Arriving back at the frat house, she shows her flyer and gains entry. She is not deprived attention, as frat boys at every turn notice her. She hears some catcalls, but mostly encourages the lookers. No females are jealous, as there are plenty of boys to go around. She goes into the kitchen, props herself on a counter and relaxes. She spots her frat boy and motions for him to join her. He does not hesitate to accept the invitation.

"What it be shawty?" he exclaims as he runs up to her. He leans on the counter and places his hand on her leg. She likes it and quivers at his touch. He will serve his purpose just fine.

"Hey you." She answers. "So this is where all the action is?"

"No doubt." He says. "Like I said, Kappas are blowing up big." He motions to her beer. "What you got there?"

"Nothing." She answers and holds up the six-pack. "Just my favorite brew. Not too strong, but if you drink enough, it'll fuck you up."

"Oh, that Chinese shit. I've heard of that." He replies. "How about you and I crack those open and get this party crackin?" He reaches for the bottles, breathing heavily. She pulls them away.

"No, not yet. First I…." she cuts herself off and sniffs the air. She looks at her frat boy.

"You bad boy," she says, "You've started your own little party without me."

"Nah, nah" he replies. "Just a family reunion from my Mexican side."

"Your Mexican side?" she asks.

"Yeah." He answers. "Had to welcome back my little cousin, Jose Cuervo, and his baby mama, Mary Juana."

Natalie understands. This boy will be a perfect pawn in her plan.

Natalie looks up from her pawn and surveys the party. After a few seconds, she finds her target, Monica. She is standing next to the D.J. booth and talking to Heather. Natalie thinks quickly and acts. She gently strokes the frat boy's face and turns his attention to Monica.

"You see that hot little number right there?" she asks. "The one in the red skirt and black top, by the D.J."

"Yeah." He answers. "She's fine as hell!"

"She and I used to party together in high school." Natalie continues. "Sometimes, we'd get so shitfaced wasted, that we would start making out in front of everyone."

The frat boy slips and almost hits his head on the countertop when she says that, but he picks himself back up.

"Do continue." He insists fully alert.

"I told her once," Natalie goes on, "if that happens again, we ain't gonna waste it. We're getting a guy with us and wearing his ass out."

"I humbly volunteer my services." He interrupts. Natalie has to giggle.

"But there is one small problem." She continues. "You see that redhead bitch in pink next to her?" She points to Heather. "She hates me, and swore to keep me away from her. So, I'd like you to do me a favor."

"Ask it," he says, "and it will be done."

"Get one of your friends to occupy the redhead." She says. "Take her away from my minx, and keep her busy. Then, you move in and give her all six of these." She hands him the six-pack. "Have her drink them from this." She pulls the tubing from her jacket and the funnel from her purse. He takes the items.

"Give her an hour for the shit to take effect." She continues. "Dance with her until then, keep her body moving and her heart pumping. Do this for me and I swear to you, she and I will wear your fucking ass out!"

"Say no more." He blurts out. He turns to leave but Natalie stops him. She grabs the strange pendant around his neck.

"What's this?" she asks.

"Oh, that's just the skeleton key to the frat house." He answers.

"Okay. Why don't you let me hold on to it?" she asks. "As sign of good faith that you'll get the job done."

He takes off the pendant and hands it to Natalie.

"Find me in an hour." He whispers, and leaves the kitchen with the items in his hands.

Natalie smiles for her little pawn. He will do all the leg-work and all she has to do is watch. She goes to the fridge, grabs a beer, heads to the living room and gets comfortable. This is going to be a good show.

Heather and Monica are enjoying their first college party. They both came to the party dressed to kill and are looking to hookup with some frat boys.

"Oh my god!" Heather exclaims. "These guys are crazy. Two guys just offered to take me the Paris."

"Going for the gangbang?" Monica asks. "Nice!"

Both girls laugh. They have been drinking for the past 30 minutes and are feeling the effects of the alcohol.

"I don't care what happens." Monica speaks loudly "If a fine man approaches me tonight, I'm gonna fuck him."

"Save some for me!" Heather yells back.

"Every woman for herself." Monica replies.

"Excuse Miss?" A male voice asks.

Heather turns around and stares into the deep brown eyes of a blonde haired adonis.

"I'd like to see how you work that beautiful body." He continues.

"Oh!" Both girls exclaim.

The young man takes Heather by the hand and leads her away so they can dance.

"Get some for me!" Monica yells behind her.

"Every woman for herself!" Heather shoots back.

As Monica watches her friend disappear in to the crowd, a frat boy approaches her. She thinks he is cute so she smiles to greet him.

"Your girl would just up and leave you like that?" He asks.

"Yeah," she awnswers in jest, "she's a horny little slut."

"But that's not right." He goes on. "Now you're by yourself and lonely."

"I'm very lonely." She smiles as she replies. "Maybe you can make me feel better and cheer me up."

"Well I got just what you need." He holds up his hands. In his right, he has a beerbong and in his left, he has imported Asian beer.

"Just what I needed." She replies.

She follows him away from the D.J. A crowd starts to gather as murmurs of a beerbong spread. The frat boy takes one beer and gives the rest to other partygoers to pour in the funnel. Monica gets on her knees and puts the tube in her mouth. Chants of 'Chug, Chug, Chug' roar from the crowd as the beer is poured in to the funnel. Monica is not a beerbong rookie, and had put down three bottles once before. During this session, she gets four bottles down before she has to quit. She throws her arms in the air and gives a joyous shout as she stops drinking. She grabs one of the Asian beers and splashes it on herself and other onlookers. More beer is sprayed around and poured on people as the frat is whipped into a frenzy. Monica grabs her frat boy.

"Dance with me, now!" she yells.

She leads her frat boy to the middle of the floor and they dance. She is smooth and sensual, grinding up against him, and touching him in sensitive areas. He, in turn, makes no attempt to hide his advances. He fondles her backside and ample breast at will, with no fear of reprocussion. After two upbeat songs, the D.J. plays a slow jam. The two dancers get close to each other and slow dance, while maintaining their physical advances with one another. He leans in close to kiss and lick her earlobe. She moans in pleasure as the sensation is driving her crazy.

"You like that baby?" he asks.

"Fuck yeah." she answers.

"Why don't we go somewhere, where I can lick you in other places." he goes on.

"Absolutely." she replies.

He separates slightly to gaze into her eyes and convey his lust. Instead, what he sees sparks other emotions.

Monica's nose had begun to bleed heavily, and the blood was running down her face, over her mouth and began to drip onto her chest. He composed himself and let her know.

"Baby, your nose." he says quickly. "Something's wrong with your nose."

She reaches up and feels her nose and upper lip. She notices they feel warm and slick. She looks at her hands and sees them covered in blood. She begins to panic.

"Oh my god!" she says. "Oh shit."

"C'mon, this way." He puts his arm around her shoulder, lowers her head and leads her to the bathroom.

Natalie can see the scene from her vantage point. Once she sees Monica's nose start to bleed, she heads for the D.J. booth. Just as she suspects, both Monica and Heather's purses are sitting there unattended. She picks them both up and heads for the kitchen. She drops both purses in the trash compactor and turns it on. The machine roars to life, crushing the contents. Before the crush is complete, she sets the switch to lock. She gathers her own purse and heads back to the D.J. booth. Once there, she tells the D.J. to turn the music all the way up. He complies and Natalie heads to the hallway with the bathroom.

Heather is in heaven, dancing with her blonde haired, brown-eyed Adonis. They slow grind and touch each other playfully. As a slow song begins, Heather looks deep into his eyes. She wants to kiss him, but something catches her attention. In the background, she sees a frat boy hurriedly rushing Monica away. She does not have a good feeling about this, so she excuses herself and heads in that direction.

Reaching the bathroom, Heather sees Monica with her head in the sink and the frat boy standing over her, scratching her shoulders.

'Oh my god, what happened?" she asks.

"Heather?" Monica pants. "Heather is….that you?" She reaches out with her hand and Heather grabs it.

Monica is breathing hard. Her shoulders are red from the scratching and bumpy from a rapidly developing rash. Her arms and legs are shaking and she is cold to the touch. She is wheezing and struggling to breathe. The bathroom sink is a dark crimson from her severely bleeding nose.

"Moni, what happened?" Heather asks, trying not to panic.

"I…dunno." Monica answers. "Bad reac…tion….to…beer." she pants between her syllables.

"Okay." Heather says. "Don't talk. Save your strength." Heather looks at the frat boy. "You, our purses are by the the D.J. booth. Hers has an inhaler in it. It's a small black clutch bag. Please get it."

"Okay." the frat boy answers. "I'll be right back." He runs out the bathrrom, closing the door behind him.

Natalie stands in the hallway and watches as her frat boy pawn leads Monica into the bathroom, followed soon after by Heather. After less than two minutes, she sees her frat boy dart out and head to the D.J. booth. She does not stop him. She actually gets out of his way. She then calmly walks to the bathroom, pulls out the frat boy's skeleton key, inserts into the lock, and slowly locks the door.

Tonight the bitch dies. And Heather, you get to watch!

Natalie walks away from the restroom and deposits the skeleton key in her purse, as a memento of this occasion, her first kill.

The frat boy runs frantically to the D.J. booth and looks all around. There is no black clutch bag in sight. There are two other purses, one black shoulder bag and one red tote. He grabs them both and heads to the kitchen. He sees two more purses and grabs them. He makes a mad dash throughout the house, grabbing any purse he could find. When he can find no more, he heads back to the bathroom.

Monica worsens with every passing second. Her breathing tightens and her rash spreads to her entire body. Heather frantically scratches the rashes, desparate to provide her friend some comfort.

"I…can't…breathe." Monica pants.

"Just hold on." Heather pleads. "Please hold on. He'll be back soon. Please be back soon."

Heather is beginning to panic.

"Oh…god." Monica exclaims. She tries to turn from the sink.

"No Moni." Heather says. "Save your strength, please." Tears are streaming down her face.

Monica suddenly lunges, and vomits all over the floor. Her body convulses and she falls to one knee. Heather recoils in disgust, but tries to remain strong for her friend.

"Please…get…help." Monica begs Heather.

"I'm not leaving you hun." Heather cries. "Just hang on." She takes her fading friend into her arms and holds her tight, but she was starting to lose control.

Monica gets worse. The bleeding from her nose intensifies. She feels dizzy and her ears begin to ring. She vomits again and her eyes start to bleed. Heather is horrified. She does not know what she can do. She decides she has to get help and call an ambulance.

"Just stay here and keep breathing." she pleads. "I'll be right back."

She gets up and runs into the door. She grabs the knob and twists hard. The door will not budge. She jerks a few times to know avail.

"What the fuck?" She utters.

She pulls with all her strength, but the door is locked tight. She pounds on the door with her fists, trying to get anyone's attention.

"HELP!" she screams. "PLEASE HELP US! SHE'S DYING!"

She screams and keeps pounding on the door, trying to break it free. Monica continues to deteriorate. She vomits again and her breathing is no more than a shallow whisper. She begins to shake and her body convulses. Her eyes roll up in her head and she begins to foam at the mouth.

"NO! MONI!" Heather screams and drops to the floor to hold her friend.

"Talk to me!" she pleads. "Please say something." She is crying uncontrollably.

Monica says nothing. Her body continues to twitch and the foam turns bloody. Open sores have long formed all over her body and her bowels loosens, spilling stool and urine all over the floor. She twitches for a couple more seconds, then stops. Her mouth gives one last gasp and her head slumps in Heather's lap. She lays motionless, and dies in her friend's arms.

"Moni?" Heather struggles to speak through her tears. "Monica? Please say something."

Heather sits on the floor and cries as she holds her dead friend.

The frat boy returns to the bathroom, covered in purses. He grabs the doorknob and turns, but the door will not open. He yanks a few more times with the same result. He drops the purses, steps back and kicks the door open. Inside the bathroom, he finds the redhead on the ground in tears, holding a bloody carcass that was once her friend. He stares for a few seconds before she sees him. She says nothing, just puts her head down and continues to cry. He runs out of the bathroom, screaming for someone to call 911. Some curious partiers venture to the restroom to check out the commotion. Within minutes, the party is over.

Natalie has already left the party. She is sitting on a sidewalk bench two blocks away. After waiting for 20 minutes, she witnesses an ambulance racing down the street towards the party, sirens blazing.

"My work is done." she says to herself.

She reaches into her purse and pulls out a bag of peanuts. She begins to eat her snacks as she calmly walks back to her truck.

Driving home after a tough day at work, Detective Katrina Olivarez is exhausted. She had testitied in court for three separate cases and was part of a sting to bring down a local gang's gun running operation. She cannot wait to get home to relax with her husband. She is about to pickup her call phone to call him, when she hears sirens behind her.

She pulls to the right and sees two squad cars dart past her. She wonders what caused all the commotion. Her workday was over 13 minutes ago, but she has a strong sense of duty. She calls her husband, tells him she will be home late and follows the squad cars.

She follows the cars to the Westin State University campus and parks in front of a frat house. She remembers this particular house, home of the Kappas, as she had atteneded many parties here when she was a student. She gets out of the car and surveys the front yard. Something major must have happened. Students are huddled in small groups, hugging each other for support. One redheaded girl in particular, is breaking down, sobbing loudly, and leaning on her friend, a young black girl, for support. Katrina notices that the redhead's clothing is wet and soiled in patches, and as she gets closer, she smells like vomit or something worse. Katrina decides to leave them alone. Instead, she pulls out her badge and shows it to a patrol man.

"Detective Kat Olivarez." She says. "What happened here?"

"Detective," he replies, "it looks like we got a case a party 'till you drop."

"What do you mean?" she asks.

"I haven't got much detail yet," he replies, "but Sargent Colt is inside, you could try asking him."

She goes insinde to find the sergeant. The house is a disaster area. Broken beer bottles litter the floors, vomit stains are in the carpet, a beerbong is laying in the corner, and DVDs are knocked off the shelf.

"Kat?" a male says. She looks to her right and finds the sergeant.

"Hey Lou." She replies. "Looks like we missed the annual Kappa orientation fiesta."

"I wish we had." He says. "We got a call about 30 minutes ago, some frat boy in a panic. He said a girl was choking in the bathroom."

"Just choking?" she asks. "Didn't he use the heimlic?"

"It wasn't food." He answers. "Some kind of allergic reaction."

"Did the EMTs make it in time?" she asks.

"Judging by the restroom, I think not." He answers. "Take a look."

He points to the hallway leading to the restroom. Kat wades through the investing officers and reaches the hallway. She recoils her head in disgust, as the odor is nauseating. She puts her mouth and nose in her sleeve and presses on. She peers into the bathrrom and beholds the gruesome sight.

A desceased female student is sprawled on her back. Her face, arms and legs are swollen and covered in open sores. Her skin is red and bumpy, as if covered by a rash. Blood had streamed from her eyes and nose, and had since dried. The body is laying in a pool of vomit, urine, feces, and blood. Kat races out of the hallway, unable to stand the sight or the smell. She reaches the living and sucks heavily on the fresh air.

"What kind of allergy does that to someone?" she asks in between breaths.

"Guess I should have warned you." Lou replies.

As she leans over and pants, her mind flashes back to the victim's body. She knows that people who are aware of there allergies take great steps to avoid harmful reactions. She cannot understand how someone could be so far off.

Maybe she was drunk and lost her self-control, she thinks to herself.

She stares at a pile of bottles and notices something interesting. An empty beer bottle lays on the floor directly in front of her. It is empty except for a small nugget on the inside.

"Hey Lou," she calls out, "is there a CSI on site?"

"Yeah. Bassett!" he calls out. An older man comes over and goes to Kat.

"CSI Bassett," she begins, "can you tell me what this is?" She points to the bottle.

"Yeah," he answers, "That is Takeshi brand Kyoto lager. Not very popular with the college crowd, but not an exotic brand. You can get it at any grocery store."

"Okay," she goes on, "but what's that thing, inside the bottle?"

He picks up the bottle with his gloved right hand and shakes it around. The object bounces around inside the bottle. It is small and round, about the size of a molar. He turns the bottle upside down and the object falls out, into his gloved left hand. He examines it closely. It is covered in an oily substance.

"A peanut?" he asks. "Takeshi doesn't come with peanuts."

"You don't say." She replies. "CSI Bassett, I'd like you to run trace on all the Takeshi bottles here as well as a controlled sample of the other brands of beer here at your discretion. Also, I'd like a tox screen on the vic as well as her medical records."

"Tox and trace I can do," he replies. "But I can't get medical records until we identify her."

"She's not I.D.'ed yet?" Kat asks.

"Her hands are too swollen to take prints." He answers. "But there was another student with her when we arrived. She must have been her best friend. The poor girl was holding the corpse and crying her eyes out when we arrived."

"Is the girl still here?" she asks.

"She won't talk." Sargent Colt interrupts. "She hasn't been able to stop bawling since we got here. She resisted and screamed when we pulled her away from the vic."

"Where is she?" she asks.

"Hey sarge!" a male voice calls out from the kitchen. "We got something over here."

Kat, Lou, and Bassett go to the kitchen. A young policeman points to the open trash compactor, Inside are two purses, a small black clutch bag and a pink tote. Both had been crushed inside the compactor. Bassett take out the pink tote and starts to finger through the contents. He pulls out a wallet and looks through it. He finds cash, credit cards, and a photo I.D. He hands the I.D. to Kat.

"This is your witness." He says. "Looks like her name's Heather Long." Kat takes the I.D.

"Where is she?" Kat asks.

"She's outside." He answers.

Kat takes the I.D. and the black clutch and heads outside. She sees much of the same students crying and chattering. She finds Heather, the redhead she noticed was wet and smelled bad. Kat now knows the reason why.

"Heather Long.?" Kat asks.

Heather says and does nothing. She continues to hug her best friend tightly. Ashley looks up and acknowledges Kat.

"I told you guys, she's not ready to talk." Ashley says through choking tears.

"I'm sorry," Kat replies, "but we need her account so we can narrow down what happened."

"Can't you give her some more time?" Ashley pleads. "Just a little more time."

"I think your friend was murdered." Kat blurts.

"What?" Ashley and Heather simultaneously ask. Heather raises her head from Ashley's chest.

"I know it's really early to say," Kat continues, "but things just aren't adding up to equal an accident"

Both girls let go of each other and stand at full attention before the Detective. Katrina flips through the black clutch bag and looks at the credit cards.

"Was her name Monica," she asks.

"Yes," Ashley answers, "Monica Bynes."

"That's her purse." Heather stammers.

"Please try to remember," Kat pleads, "what happened in the bathroom?"

"She was in so much pain." Heather's voice is weak. "Her nose bled, she puked so much. I tried, to get her to stay calm, to stay strong. She got worse so fast. I tried to get help, but we couldn't get out."

"Couldn't get out?" Kat asks. "Out of the bathroom?"

"The fucking door was locked!" Heather yells, her tears returning. "She died in my arms!"

She breaks down and crumbles to the ground. Ashley squats down to catch and hold her as they weep. Kat takes a step back. She is not going to get anymore information from them. She goes back into the house and heads for the bathroom. She inspects the lock and the door jam. It is an antique lock that needs a skeleton key to lock and unlock. She darts out and heads for the CSI.

"The vic's name is Monica Bynes." She hands him the clutch bag.

"Alright, I'll get you your requested info." He replies.

"Thanks. Lou!" she calls out. He comes over.

"What did you find out?" ha asks.

"Those girls were locked in the bathroom." She states. "They couldn't get out while the vic was dying. That door can only be locked by a skeleton key. One of these frat boys has to know something."

"I'll have my men round them up for questioning." He replies.

"When do we start?" she asks.

"You are going home Kat." he answers.

"But we have a murder here." She shoots back.

"We might," he replies, "but we cannot confirm that tonight. Once we do, I will need a well rested detective to formally assign to the case." She lowers her resistance.

"Still looking out for me after all these years." She gives him a smile. "Alright, but I want those result on my desk by morning."

"And you shall have them." He replies. "Good night Detective." He turns and walks back to the bathroom.

Kat walks outside and heads towards her car. She notices that Heather and Ashley were gone. She understands. They are in pain and need time to grieve. She gets in her car and drives home.

The sun rises on Saturday, and Natalie sleeps late. The previous night, she had gone to sleep is a good mood. She felt satisfied, fulfilled and jubilant. When she awakes, she looks at her alarm clock. 9:47 am.

She rarely sleeps so late. Her nights are usually restless as she tosses and turns, and fights off nightmares, yet last night she was at peace. She dreamed of bright flowery landscapces, bird singing, and a cool breeze blowing, as if encouraging her to dance. So she did, and it was joyous dance, on Monica's grave.

She turns on the television as she heads to the bathroom. Although she does not watch, she feels comfortable listening to ambient noise in the background. She does not know what station the T.V. is set to, nor does she care. As she brushes her teeth, a news bulletin gives the local headlines. One particular story catches her attention.

"We have tragic news to report from Westin State University this morning. A young female student was found dead in the bathroom of a fraternity house last night. Police have very little to go on, but it appears she suffered some sort of allergic reaction to alcohol. This looks to be completely accidental, but the police have not ruled out fowl play. It has been reported the girl was locked inside the bathroom during her reaction, and was unable to get help or her inhaler. Authorities have detained all members of the fraternity for questioning, but at this time, no charges have been filed. The police are asking anyone with any information to please step forward, and assist with the investigation."

Natalie cannot help but laugh at the report. She remembers as a child that Monica wanted to be a T.V. star. Now, she will get her 15 minutes of fame. Natalie finishes brushing her teeth and takes a shower.

Hot water is much more plentiful in her dorm than at her home. This results in Natalie taking longer showers. She stays in the shower for an hour on this morning. She wants to wash herself clean of the pain and torment Monica had caused her. As the water goes down the drain, Natalie says goodbye to her past life with Monica in it.

Out of the shower, she puts on her black robe, thong panties, nothing else, and sits down at her computer. She has nothing at all to do today and just wants to relax. Before she can start some real web surfing, a knock comes from her door.

"Who is it?" she asks.

"It's me, Lynn." A voice answers. She sounds bubbly.

Oh, better get sexy!

She opens her robe a little bit to show more cleveage, takes her panties off, and throws them on the bed. She opens the door and leans suggestively on the doorframe.

"Hey Lynn." She says cheerfully.

"Hi…umm" Lynn stammers. "Wow!" She cracks a big smile and looks Natalie up and down. Natalie giggles in return.

"Come on in." she says, and steps aside so Lynn can enter. Lynn enters and stands in the middle of the room.

"How'd your match go yesterday?" Natalie asks.

"Oh, it was awesome." Lynn answers. "I won my match 6-1, 6-0. This girl was a beast. She jumped on me hard in the first set, but then she got cooky. I figured her out and wiped the court with her."

"When'd you get back to campus?" Natalie follows.

"About 20 minutes ago." Lynn answers. "Our flight got delayed by bad weather. We were supposed to be back late last night. I should be tired, but I'm so pumped. It was my first collegiate match and I dominated. Can you believe it?"

"Well I'm proud of you." Natalie says. She smiled and gives Lynn a big hug, making sure to press her chest into her. Lynn holds on tight and squeezes a little harder.

"Hey," Lynn interjects, "a new coffee shop just opened in town, just a few minutes away. You wanna check it out?"

"Sure," Natalie answers, "let me get some clothes on."

Natalie goes to her closet and pulls out some garments. She begins undoing her robe as she heads to the bathroom. Before she disappears, she drops her robe to the floor, giving Lynn a microsecond glimpse of her naked body. That microsecond becomes a vivid snapshot in Lynn's mind. Everytime she blinks, she sees Natalie naked. She sits on the bed to gather her thoughts. She tried to relax; however, she sees Natalie's panties sitting on the bed. She stops and stares at them. She knows that she should not, but she cannot help herself. They are so close to her, tempting her to grab them, and she does.

She moves the fabric around in her hands, stroking it and feeling the texture. Her breathing increases and she knew she should stop, yet she does not want to. She finds the gusset of the undergarment and strokes it lightly with her thumb. She holds it up, not knowing what she is looking for, but unable to stop staring. She can no longer hold back, she holds the panties to her nose and inhales deeply. She can smell Natalie's essence, and she wants more. She breathes her sent over and over. Her tounge protrudes from her mouth and she tastes the scent. She grows warm between her legs and becomes wet. She feels dirty, perverted, depraived, and she loves every second of it. She wants to touch herself, but the bathroom door slowly begins to open. She quickly throws the panties to the floor and tries to compose herself. Natalie exits the very next second.

"Okay I'm ready." She says. She sees Lynn on the bed breathing hard and sweating. "My god, are you alright?"

"I'm fine." Lynn shoots back. "Just…um…an emotional high. That's all."

"I understand." Natalie replied. "So, you ready?"

"Yeah, let's go." Lynn answers.

She helps Lynn off the bed and they head to the door. She holds it open and Lynn walks out. As Natalie is leaving the dorm, she sees that her panties are no longer on the bed, but on the floor. She laughs to herself and leaves the dorm.

They reach the ground floor and Lynn's cell phone rings. She looks at the screen and curses under breathe.

"Fuck." She utters

"What is it?" Natalie asks.

"It's Howard." she answers. "He hasn't stopped bugging me since we broke up. He knows that I can't NOT talk to him, so he always calls me."

"Gimmie the phone." Natalie insists and holds her hand out.

"What?" Lynn asks.

"I'm gonna help you out. Gimmie the phone." She says again.

Lynn nervously hands her the phone. Natalie clears her throat and answers the call.

"Hello?" she says. Her voice changes. She sounds just like Lynn.

"What do you want?" she asks. Lynn begins to laugh.

"You always wanna talk, but there ain't nothing to talk about."

"I don't care abou that. You should've thought before you spoke huh?"

"Why are making me waste my time with you? I'm with my man right now. I ain't got time for this shit."

"I know what you thought, you made that clear, but you're a stupid muthafucker for thinking that."

"Look, I gotta go. I'll think about calling you back. Bye."

"Bye."

"BYE!" she hangs up the phone.

Lynn doubles over with laughter. Her face is turning red, her eyes are watering, and she holds her stomach.

"Oh my god!" she exclaims. "That was great!"

"Glad I could help." Natalie replies.

The two girls resume their walk to Lynn's car. Upon reaching the car, Natalie looks up and sees Heather Long running towards them. She becomes nervous but is able to keep her cool as Heather approaches.

"Looks like we got company." Natalie says to Lynn and motions to Heather.

Heather arrives out of breathe. She leans on the car, barely able to stand. She looks tired, weak, and haggard. Her face is red and puffy, as if she has been crying all night. She looks up at Natalie. Her eyes are red and full of tears.

"I'm sorry," she says "but I need to talk to Lynn privately for a second."

She is not rude or pushy. She is actually polite for once. Natalie figures that Heather does not recognize her. She decides to reply in kind.

"Sure," she says, "go right ahead."

"Heather," Lynn interjects, "now's not a good time."

"Lynn it's important!" she yells.

"It's ok Lynn." Natalie says. "I'll just wait on the bench over there." Natalie walks to a nearby oak tree and sits on a bench underneath.

"Heather!" Lynn shouts. "That was so rude!"

"She's dead!" Heather yells. "Monica's dead!"

"What?" Lynn asks. "When?"

"Last night." Heather answers.

Lynn's legs become weak and she can barely stand. She leans on Heather and cries. She weeps loudly and hugs Heather tightly. Overcome by grief, she cannot think. Heather puts her arm around her and leads her away. The girls cry as they leave.

Natalie witnesses the whole scene and watches as Heather and Lynn run away. She feels neither remorse, sadness, nor grief. She feels like laughing. She wants to jump and scream out her joy. She resists the urge to run over to Heather and Lynn, knock them to the ground and foreshadow them of their pending demise. Instead, she calmly walks to her truck, climbs inside, and starts the engine. The coffee shop sounds like a good idea, and she is thirsty.

Detective Olivarez sits at her desk, going over the results of the trace on the beer bottles. They show the standard fare of ingredients in most of the bottles, but six of the eight open bottles of the Asian beer show large amounts of palmitic, linoleic, and arachidic acid. The other two open bottles of the exact same beer show no trace of theses ingredients. The small nugget she found is confirmed to be a peanut. After doing research on the three ingredients, she discovers they are the main components of peanut oil.

After reviewing the trace results, she focuses on the toxicology tests done on the victim, Monica Bynes. She tested positive for alcohol, marijuana, and large quanities of peanut oil. Along with these results, the coroner finds three whole peanuts in her stomach. The coroner determines the cause of death as a fatal reaction to a peanut allergy, most likely unknown to the victim. There is a knock on her door. A patrolman enters and hands her Monica Bynes' medical records. She eagerly opens and reviews them. After reading for a few minutes, her boss, the Chief of Police Grant Foster, walks in.

"You wanna tell me what you were doing at the frat after you were off duty?" he asks.

"You know me chief, my work is never done." She answers.

"On this case, it is." He says. "The coroner has ruled this, an accidental death due to an unknown allergy, and ingestion of the allergen."

"Accident?" she asks and holds up the records. "Have you read her medical records?" She hands them to him. He takes the records and begins to flip through them.

"This girl has had anaphylaxia since she was five years old." Kat continues

"Anaphylaxia?" he asks.

"It's a form of peanut allergy." She answers. "Anaphylaxia is the most severe form. Ingesting any type of peanut or other nut, can be fatal within hours if not treated. In her case, mere minutes. She's been in and out of hospitals at least three times a year from her fifth to her fourteenth birthday, and each time the reactions have gotten worse."

"But if she knew about it, why would she drink so much of it?" he asks. "Maybe she was suicidal."

"I had CSI Bassett and his team inspect her dorm." She answers. "Not a single food product contained any peanut ingredients or components. They found lists of dangerous products and books of peanut free diet plans. Her records show no signs of clinical depression and no prescriptions for those kinds of meds. Plus, suicides are typically done in seclusion, with a suicide note left."

Kat's door opens and CSI Bassett walks in.

"Hey Kat," he says, "I just spoke to a representative for Takeshi Lager. They don't use any peanut oil in their beer, nor do they put peanuts in the bottle."

"Thank you." She replies.

The chief looks bewildered and somewhat resigned.

"Let me have this case chief." She pleads. "I know this girl was murdered. Just give time and I can prove it. I've never let you down before."

He slowly heads back over to the door.

"Do what you have to do detective," he answers, "but leave the media out of it. I don't want to cause a panic on campus."

"No problem chief." She answers.

The chief leaves her office and Kat goes back to work.

Natalie returns to campus with a small café mocha in her hand. On her way back to her dorm, she notices the campus bookstore is open. She had visited the shop the previous week but never looked around. She decides to make a side trip and explore the store.

As she walks in, she notices the store is much bigger than she remembers, larger than any of her classrooms. The shelves are lined with classroom textbooks and non-fiction novels. There is a periodical section with newspapers and magazines. As she ventures to the back, she passes a shelf with small computer peripherals and sees a cute little webcam she likes. She just has to have it so she grabs it.

She ventures further to the back of the store a catches an unexpected sight. Marco Ruiz is leaning against the wall, hugging Heather. Natalie ducks behind a shelf and decides to listen.

"Hey, hey," Marco says, "it's not your fault."

"I should have done more." She replies. "I should have had her inhaler with me."

"Listen," he interrupts, "we've all been out drinking before, and this never happened. How were you supposed to know this would be different?"

"A cop told me, that she may have been murdered." She says. "She sounded so sure of it."

Natalie's ears pique.

"Think about chica." He says, "She probably just said that to get your attention. Ashley said you were pretty torn up."

"We both were." She replies.

"Tell you what." He says. "Wednesday, the day after the service, you and me, we'll go out. We don't have to do nothing special, we'll just relax, remember Monica, and try to move forward. It'll just be you and me."

"I'd like that." She gives him a little smile.

They break their embrace and walk out of the store hand in hand.

Natalie is disturbed. A cop thought Monica's death was murder. She knew that police would get involved, but she has to be more careful. She puts her stress out her mind, purchases the webcam and leaves the store.

Outside the store, she reads a flyer for the men's basketball team. It is an advertisement and schedule of the upcoming exhibition tournament schedule. She scans the games and one particular contest grabs her attention. It is the seventh annual Seraph Invitational and the opening round is against Duke University.

Duke Blue Devils. Zack plays for Duke!

She fondly remembers Zachary Flood from their previous interaction in Mrs. Schoval's math class. She likes him. She wonders if he is still dating Ashley. The game is scheduled for next week, so she had until then to find out.

Tuesday morning comes, and Monica is laid to rest in her hometown. She is reveared as one of the social elite, and most of the town shows to pay their respects. News of her death makes national headlines as a tragic accident, and some of her friends are interviewed on television. Heather rides to the funeral with her friends and they spend the day in Salem with Monica's family.

Back at WSU, Natalie attends her classes as usual, and plans her next move. She spends some time at the archery range to clear her thoughts. She needs to figure out, what she can do next that will hurt Heather the most. Two people come to mind, Ashley and Marco. Ashley is her best friend and would give her emotional support through this process, Marco, however, is her boyfriend and would make her feel loved. In this situation, love trumps emotion. She reflects on her eavesdropped conversation in the bookstore between Heather and Marco. She makes her decision; Marco will not make the date.

Wednesday afternoon holds no surprises. Natalie chats with Lynn and consoles her when she speaks of her decreased friend.

"Thank you for being so kind during this whole thing." Lynn says, choked up on tears.

"It's the least I can do for you." Natalie responds

"How are you holding up?" Lynn asks. "I know that seems like an odd question, but wasn't Monica your best friend at one time?"

OUCH!

"Yeah," Natalie answers, "but she made her choice about that when we were younger. I cried for her, but I don't think it would have been very respectful of me to go to her funeral."

Considering I put her there!

"Well, there may be very few," Lynn goes on, "but at least you have some good times with her you can reflect on."

"Yeah, so do you." Natalie replies. "Hey, this may seem unusual for me to ask, but how is Heather doing?"

"She's doing better than yesterday, but she's really broken up." Lynn answers. "She tried to pull it all together. She even went with Monica's sister Tara yesterday after the service and got a tattoo!"

"A tattoo?!" Natalie asks in surpise.

"Yeah, a small one." Lynn answers. "About an inch or two big. Monica always called her 'The Queen Bee,' so Heather got a bee with a crown on its head, just behind her right shoulder."

"That was sweet of her." Natalie replies. "A nice little memorial."

"Yeah, but she was a hysterical wreck during the procedure." Lynn says. "Tara said she wouldn't stop crying and saying 'This is for you Monica.' It was insane."

"So she's still in bad shape then?" Natalie asks.

"Yeah." Lynn replies. "Marco's gonna try and cheer her up tonight. They're going to meet up around 9:00pm and he's gonna try to get her to move forward. I'm actually supposed to meet him in 10 minutes at his dorm to help him arrange something nice to wear."

"I'll walk you there." Natalie insists.

Natalie walks with Lynn to Marco's dormitory building. The girls hug one last time and agree to meet up Thursday night in Natalie's dorm to watch movies. As Natalie walks away, she is tempted to thank Lynn. Not only has she given her the information she needs about Heather and Marco's date, she shows her were he lives. Marco is set to leave to meet Heather around 8:45pm. Natalie prepares to intercept.

She heads to the same seedy liquor stor as before and purchase a bottle of strong tequila and a couple of hangover prevention pills. After returning to her dorm, she changes into a very skimpy, suggestive, and provocative outfit; a black microskirt, white boy beater top, and white heels. Looking in the mirror, she feels incomplete. She knows she looks sexy, but wants validation, as Marco might be difficult to persuade on this night. She puts the tequila in her purse and heads for the exit. Outside, she searches for a man. Any man will be fine. She finds one, a rookie security guard on patrol in the quad.

"Excuse me." She says as she approaches him.

"Yes ma'am," he replies, "can I help you?"

"Yes." She answers. "I was just wondering were the blue lights were."

"Blue lights?" he asks. "I don't follow."

Natalie steps in closer.

"I heard that most colleges and universities have blue lights lining the walkways at night. So when a young lady is in trouble, she can follow them and get to safety." She says.

He can smell the sweet scent of her perfume. It intoxicates him, and brings a smile to his lips.

"Unfortunately, we don't have that system in place right now." He starts to stammer his words.

She steps closer, pushing her chest into his.

"But how is a girl supposed to feel safe at night?" she asks.

"W..well, I suppose, I could escort you to you destination, if you feel unsafe." He replies.

She presses closer to him and wraps her arms around his waist.

"You would?" she asks "You'd protect me" Keep me safe?"

He jumps a little as he feels her hands.

"Absolutely." He answers. He reaches down and moves her right hand from his hip to his back. "Just don't touch my gun." He says.

"Oh." She giggles, "No problem."

When he moved her havd, he inadvertently placed it from his gun to his handcuffs. Natalie realizes this and slowly begins to withdraw them. She leads him though the campus to Marco's dormitory entrance. She carefully slides out his handcuffs and places her hands behind her back.

"Well, thank you sir." She says.

"Anytime young lady." He replies.

He steps closer to her and looks into her eyes. She returns the stare and smiles back at him. She can see that he is starting to sweat. She thinks that maybe she should thank him for the handcuffs. She leans in slowly. He does the same. She hasd never kissed anyone before, so she has a small air of anticipation. She closes her eyes as his lips draw near.

"McDermott, where the hell are you?!" his radio screams.

"Oh fuck." He murmurs to himself and answers the raido.

"I'm in front of the southeast dormitory." He answers.

"Get your ass to the Zeta house. We've got reports of a panty raid." The raido yells.

"I'm on it." He answers and puts his radio away. He looks at Natalie. She is turning pink from giggling.

"I..uh…" he begins.

"Better go save those panties." She interrupts.

"Yeah." He says.

"I'll see you around." She says with a smile.

"Okay, bye." He leaves and runs towards Sorority Row.

Natalie checks the time on her watch, 8:40pm. She barely made it to Marco's in time. She tucks the handcuffs into the hem of her skirt and takes a seat on a bench outside the dorm. Two minutes later, Marco emerges. He is dressed rather nicely, purple button down shirt with black jeans and white sheakers. He walks out the door and descends the steps.

"Whoa, looking good!" Natalie calls out.

Marco looks over to the source of the catcall. He sees a blonde beauty sitting on a bench. Her hair is laser straight, clothing is tight and hugging, and her legs are long and perfectly tanned. She is a bombshell and he is intrigued. Marco may be commited to Heather, but old habits die hard.

"What's the occasion?" she asks.

"Oh, um," he answers, "just going to meet up with a friend."

"A friend?" she asks. "Would this be a special friend?"

"Uh…yeah, kind of." He answers. "We both just had a close friend of ours pass away, and I just wanna make her feel better."

"Oh, that's so tragic!" she replies. "You're really sweet to do this for her."

"Yeah." He replies. "But it's a little difficult to figure out what to say to her."

"You're in luck." She says. "I have just the thing you need."

She reaches into her purse and takes out the bottle of tequila. Marco cannot hold his alcohol very well, but he never refuses a drink. She removes the cork and hands him the bottle. He takes a quick swig, and coughs in reaction to the strength of the liquor.

"Careful!" the young woman admonishes. "I heard that was some strong stuff."

"Ooo, wee!" he exclaims. "That some strong shit. What is it?"

"Agave negro." She replies. "From the finest plants in Guadalajara."

"They didn't mess around on this bottle." He says and takes another drink. "I heard it's rude for a man to drink alone." He takes a seat next to her and hands her the bottle.

"Indeed it is." She replies.

She swallows a small sip of the liquor. It hits her throat like liquid fire. This is her first experience with hard liqueur and she finds it hard to take. Her first reflex is a gag, followed by heavy coughing. She fights to catch her breathe. Marco puts his hand on her back and rubs up and down.

"Relax chica," he says, "take it easy."

"Wow, that hits…pretty damn…hard." She pants between breaths. She places her head on his shoulder.

"You took it like a champ." He says and takes the bottle back.

He takes another sip and begins to relax, losing track of time. Natalie bids her time and makes idle chatter with him in between his multiple sips. She keeps track of the time. 30 minutes have passed and he is just settling in, so she huckers down for the long haul.

"And so I tell that bitch, to shut the fuck up." He rambles on. One quarter of the bottle is empty.

Natalie does not speak much during the encounter, only throwing in small tidbits to encourage his interest and prolong his drinking. She checks her watch again. 10:10pm. over one hour has passed and Marco is pretty wasted. She seems content she can now have her way with him. Ten more minutes pass when his cell phone rings.

"Who the fuck?" He belts out. Checking his phone, his eyes get big. "Oh, shit!" He yells. "I gotta go!"

He jumps off the bench and runs off, before Natalie can grab him. She curses herself. She let him ramble on for too long, and now found her moment wasted. She sits back down and has a sudden thought.

Follow him!

She jumps off the bench and gives chase. She has had only had one shot of the tequila, but her balance is now off. She thinks it could hinder her focus, but she chases anyway. After chasing for two minutes, she sees Marco run up to Heather. She sneaks up to be closer, then hides to listen in on the impending fireworks.

"Where the hell have you been?" she demands.

"Sorry babe," he answers breathing hard." I got caught up with a friend."

"With a friend?" she asks. "You make a promise to me and you…" she trails off and sniffs the air. "Have you been drinking?"

"Just a little." He answers. *'BURP'* Heather turns her head in disgust.

"I can't believe you!" she yells angrily. "You make a date for us, insinuating that maybe we can get back together, you promise to make me feel better, so we both can move forward, and you blow me off for a drink?"

"I didn't blow you." He answers. "I here right?"

"You're drunk!" she replies and turns to walk away. He grabs from behind.

"Where you going?" he asks.

"Don't touch me!" she screams.

"I thought you wanted me to spend time with you!" He yells back.

"I didn't just want to spend time with you," she answers. "I needed you Marco! I needed your strength! I needed your support, and maybe your love. Fuck, of all the times you could've pulled this shit, you choose now, after I lost, we lost, one of our best friends!" She begins to cry. "I didn't just want you, I needed you!"

"Well maybe you weren't so damn weak, you could stand on your own two feet!" he roars back.

She reacts on emotion and slaps him hard across the face, leaving an impression.

"I hate you!" she screams through tears. She turns and storms off into a nearby dormitory.

"Fuck you, jodienda puta!" he yells and walks off in the opposite direction.

Natalie is stunned. She had only seen Heather in a similar rage against other girls, never towards Marco. Heather adored Marco and never raised her voice to him.

Natalie clears her mind and focuses on a more important matter, Marco was once again alone and now very vulnerable. She follows him to the quad, where he sits down at a table and pounds his fist. She quietly walks up and puts the bottle down on the table next to him.

"Looks like you had it rough stranger." She says.

He turns his head in surprise and recognizes the familiar blonde bombshell from earlier in the evening. He also sees the bottle of tequila. He takes it and gulps a big swig.

"That was fucked up." She says.

"What?" he asks. "You saw that?"

"You were so sweet to offer your time to her." She answers. "She had no right to throw your generousity back in your face, just because she's weak."

"Damn straight!" He takes another swallow of tequila.

She steps behind him, places her hands on his shoulders and begins to rub. She squeezes firmly, yet gently and continues for a minute. He closes his eyes and throws his head back, enjoying the easing of his tensions. Natalie keeps him talking and drinking. The bottle is soon three-quarters empty within minutes.

"You know," she says, "it's kind of open and public out here. Why don't we go somewhere private and talk some more?"

"I got just the place." He says. "I volunteer with the construction crew on the new aquatic center. The security system's not working yet."

"Let's go." She replies.

Taking each other by the arm, they walk to the aquatic center. When they arrive, they go around the building to the east wall. There is an unsecured window they can crawl into. After prying the window open, Marco hoists his new blonde acquaintance into the building. She helps pull him through. He stumbles while climbing in and falls on top of her.

Natalie catches a whiff of Marco's drunkard breath and nearly gags. He lays on top of her and tries to look in her eyes. She fights to maintain composure amid his breath and his weight.

"Hey," he says, "why don't we forget about talking, and move on to something more interactive."

With that statement, he lightly presses his lips against her neck and begins to kiss. Natalie is disgusted. She wants to scream in her anguish of him kissing and laying on her. As he increases to the tempo of his kisses, he runs his hand up her skirt and begins to rub her mound. She is starting to sweat and about to panic, but she would not be afraid. She looks for a way out of her predicament and sees that they are not far from the swimming pool. She pats him on the back and tries to get his attention.

"Hey, hey!" she asserts. He stops and looks her in the face.

"I have a better idea for, interactivity." She continues.

"Oh yeah?" he asks.

"Yeah, help me up." She says.

He stands up and helps her off the ground. She takes him by the hand and leads him to the pool.

"You said the security system is not up yet, right?" she asks.

"Yeah." He answers. "No one would ever know we're here."

"Good." She replies.

She leads him to the deepest end of the pool. Without notice, she lifts her shirt and throws it to the ground. Marco stands there and stares, as the moonlight strikes this blonde angel. She undoes the hem of her skirt and slowly slides it down her legs, careful not to shake the handcuffs. She takes her shoes off and kicks them to the side. Marco marvels as she stands before him in only her bra and panties.

"Your turn." She says.

Marco wastes little time. He quickly rips open the front of his shirt, popping off all the buttons, and throwing it to the ground. He kicks off his shoes and drops his pants, leaving only his boxers and socks still on. He steps towards Natalie for an embrace when she stops him.

"No yet." She asserts.

With that, she reaches around to her back and pops the clasp of her bra. She shakes her arms downward and shimmies the undergarment to the ground, leaving her breast exposed. She then pulls down her thong underwear and kicks them at him. He catches them and sniffs deeply. He quickly throws them down and pulls off his boxers and socks. They both stand and stare at each other, naked as jaybirds.

"Come to papi!" he exclaims.

He lunges for her, desperate to hold that heavenly body against his. She thinks quickly and sidesteps his approach. As he lines up for another shot, she jumps into the pool.

She swims out for a short distance and then turns to face him.

"If you want some," she says, "You play by my rules." She flashes him a big smile to give off a playful demeanor.

"First rule?" he asks.

"Jump in!" she commands.

She does not have to tell him twice. Instantly, he is in the pool and swimming towards her. When he approaches, she shoves a hand full of water in his face.

"Catch me!" is her next rule, and she darts away.

He tries to follow and give chase, but she is quite a swimmer, and the effects of the tequila make it difficult to keep his head above water. She surfaces every few moments and playfully splashes him, egging him on to keep playing. As she swims closer to the edge of the pool, he is finaly able to grab her foot. She surfaces in front of him and looks into his eyes.

"Next rule?" he asks.

"You don't get to touch me, not just yet." She answers.

Natalie swallows hard. She knows this next step is goig to be difficult, but she has to keep him enticed. She grabs both sides of his head and kisses him hard on the lips. Marco returns the kiss, shoving his tongue deep into her mouth as he eagerly sucks on her's. Natalie feels sick to her stomach and fights the urge to vomit. She wants to stop, and force his head underwater, but he is too strong and would be able to fight her off. She needs to restrain him. She breaks the kiss.

"Okay, my puppet," she says, "out of the pool."

She hoists herself out and stands on the edge. He follows behind her and stands at attention. She positions him so he is standing over her skirt at the edge of the pool. She reaches down and begins to stroke his swollen manhood. He closes his eyes and sighs in relief and pleasure. She drops to her knees.

"Finally." He says and places his hands behind her head, trying to draw her forward.

"No," she says, "not yet." She shakes her head slightly and he removes his hands. As she pumps him at a steady pace with her left hend, she reaches down to her skirt with her right hand and finds her handcuffs. She releases her grip, stands up, and showed him the cuffs.

"Are you willing to let me have my say, and do as I please?" she asks, and flashed him a coy smile.

"Hell yeah!" he answers.

She reaches behind him and cuffs his hands behind his back. When the cuffs are secure, she reaches up and kisses his some more.

Oh Heather, if only you could see this!

She runs her hands up and down his chest, causing goosebumps. She wants him to be hot and bothered, to be worked up. She increases the pressure of the kiss. He tries to respond in kind, but she presses her mouth so hard, he is reeling backwards. She breaks the kiss and stares at him.

"You want more?" she asks.

"Si mami." He answers.

"Do you want to feel something, you never felt before?" she asks.

"Hell yeah." He replies. "Give it to me baby!"

"Good." She says.

She takes a small step backwards and looks at her prey, the smile gone from her face. She then takes and big step forward, lunges, and shoves Marco into pool. Marco is caught off guard as he falls in to the pool. As he sinks under the surface, he gulps in some of the water. He kicks hard to resurface and coughs out the water. He feels dizzy from the sudden change and the alcohol. He fights hard to stay above water, but with his hands cuffed, the task is almost impossible.

Natalie stands at the edge of the pool and watches Marco as he struggles to get air. She fights the urge to vomit and wipes her mouth hard, trying to get his taste off her tongue.

"Hey baby!" He fights to speak between breaths. "What the fuck gives?"

"Fuck you Marco!" She yells.

"What?' he asks when resurfacing. "You know…my…name?"

"When you get to hell," she continues, "tell Monica, that Natalie sent her there!"

"What?" he asks again resurfacing. "Who the fuck are you?"

She walks over to a switch on the side of the pool. On top of the switch are the words, 'Pool Cover.' She flips it and a motor roars to life. From the shallow end of the pool, a cover begins to extend, just above the surface. Natalie watches as the cover slowly moves from the far end towards Marco. He too sees the cover and tries to get to the edge of the pool. He kicks hard and tries to lunge out of the water. Each time he fails, he sinks deeper into the water, gagging for air whenever he manages to surface. Each time, he spends more time underwater.

On one lunge, he manages to get his head above water, and over the edge of the pool. Natalie sees this and acts quickly. On his next lunge, she is waiting. She rears her right leg back and times his lunge. As his head emerges, she kicks forward and nails Marco on his nose. He falls back underwater. Through the splash, Natalie can see the blood rush from his face. The cover nears the end of the pool, and Marco is out of space. He makes one last plea as the cover sails over him, trapping him in the pool.

Marco tries to lunge through the cover, but the material forces him to shoot right back under the water. His uses his mouth to spit out the water that rushes into his broken nose. Fatigue sets into his legs, and his kicks grow dramatically weaker. After a minute, he can no longer kick to the surface. He feels the water rush into his nose as he sinks deeper into the pool. He tries to spit the water out, but it rushes in too quickly. He has no more air in his lungs. His body twitches and begins to spasm. He feels his heartbeat in his ears and hears it slow. He can no longer move, or fight. He opens his eyes and stares into his watery grave.

Natalie stands at the edge of the pool and puts her clothes back on. She gathers Marco's clothes and takes them with her. On her way to her dorm, she passes a homeless man begging for change. She reaches into Marco's pants and pulls out his wallet. Along with all the cash inside, she gives the man the clothes. She keeps the wallet. It makes a nice memento.

Heather awakens Thursday morning in a foul mood. She has not slept well the previous night due to intense crying. She is still angry over Marco's attitude and still cannot believe that he would opt to have a drink over spending time with her. Although they had broken up before the school year started, he was very sweet to her and she hoped to re-ignite the flame. That hope died last night, and she wants to curse him one last time. She wants to sleep in, but she has an inportant class and cannot afford to be absent from it. She begrudgingly peels herself out of bed and heads to the bathroom to take a shower.

Natalie walks out of her first class with Lynn right behind her. They are making plans to get together that night when Heather approaches and speaks to Lynn.

"You will not believe what Marco did to me last night!" She asserts.

"Heather," Lynn begins, "can you hold up for just one second?"

"That's ok Lynn." Natalie interrupts. "Just meet me upstairs at around 6:45pm. The movie starts at 7:00."

"I'll be there." Lynn answers. The two girls hug and Natalie leaves. Lynn turns to speak to Heather.

"Understanding friend you got there." Heather remarks.

"Yeah," Lynn replies, "she's a sweetheart."

Natalie walks towards her truck. She hates how Heather would take liberties and interrupt her conversations. She also hates how Lynn is so weak to allow it to happen. She arrives at her truck and begins to relax. She wants some pleasant memories to reflect on. She grabs her necklace and fingers the skeleton key that dangles for it. She smiles for minute. She feels at ease, knowing that the key represents her life without Monica. She reaches inside her purse, and feels the texture off her new wallet, representative of her life without Marco. She knows those deeds are done, but she feels a small emptiness. Although they are dead, they did not die by her direct hand. An allergic reaction and drowning deprevie her of feeling her victims last breaths. She wants more power over her prey. She climbs into her truck and drives off. She needs to clear her mind.

Natalie drives around the city aimlessly. She needs a spot to clear her mind. One particular place looks interesting, and she pulls over. She gets out of her truck and walks inside. To her surprise, it is a combination of an internet café and a tattoo parlor. She watches as a young man takes a print out and runs it to an artist. The artist then makes a stencil and begins the tattoo on the man's calf.

Natalie's mind harkens back to the previous day, when Lynn told her of Heather's tattoo. See jumps on an open PC and begins surfing the net. After finding some interesting photos, she uses the computer's photo editing software to create a picture she becomes excited about. She prints the picture, brings it to the counter and waits for an artist. After a moment, someone comes to assist her.

"Who's working with you?" He asks.

"No one." She answers. "I just drove past and saw this place."

"Do you know how we operate?" he asks.

"No, but I think I got the gist of it." She answers and holds out the printout. The artist studies it for a moment.

"That's a pretty aggressive concept." He remarks. "Why would you want something like this inked on you?"

"One-ups manship." She answers. "Someone's gotta be knocked down a peg."

"So you're going after the queen bee?" he asks.

"Gotta aim high right?" she asks back. He cannot help but laugh at her arrogance.

"Alright." He says. "Come back tomorrow. I'll clean up the concept and have something real nice for you."

"See you tomorrow." She replies and walks out.

Climbing back into her truck, her cell phone rings. The caller ID shows "Tennis Bitch," meaning Lynn is calling.

What the fuck does she want?

"Hey hun!" Natalie answers.

"Hey Nat." Lynn replies. "Hey, maybe you can help me out."

"Sure. What's up?" Natalie asks.

"It's Heather." Lynn continues. "She's really pissed about Marco. He ditched her for some tequila last night."

"What?" Natalie yelps, trying to sound surprised. "That's horrible."

"Yeah I know." Lynn goes on. "Anyway, she wants me to hang out with her and Ashley tonight, but I don't know if I want to."

"Why wouldn't you?" Natalie asks.

"I don't know." Lynn answers. "I was hoping you could help me figure that out."

"Lynn," Natalie replies, "I can't tell you how to feel. I can only give you my input."

"That's why I called you." Lynn says. "What is your input?"

"My input?" Natalie answers. "Well, I don't know, but I was looking forward to hanging out with you. Just getting comfortable on the floor, watching a movie, and just chilling."

"Me too." Lynn replies.

"Well, it's whatever you decide," Natalie says, "but I hope you come over."

"Well," Lynn giggles, "maybe I'll see you tonight."

"Hopefully." Natalie shoots back, "Bye-bye." She hangs up her phone.

Fuck, this girl is weak!

Natalie has to act quickly. Lynn is a pawn in Heather's life and is always on a short leash. Natalie will need a little luck tonight. She has no choice but to let Lynn make her own decision. She decides to prepare, just in case fortune smiles on her again.

Natalie starts her truck and heads to a local grocery store. Inside the store, she buys six bags of ice. She drives around to a nearby alley, climbs into her trucks bed and fills the onboard freezer with the ice. Afterwards, she goes to a hardware store and purchases a padlock. Lynn is becoming weaker, and Natalie has to put her on ice, before she jeopardizes her plans.

Evening approaches and Natalie returns to her dorm. She places the padlock and its plastic bag in her purse. She changes her clothes to simple gymshorts and tank top. She sits on her bed, turns on her T.V. and waits. 6:45pm, Lynn does not show. 7:00pm. the movie starts and

Lynn has not arrived. Natalie figures she will not show up. She curses herself for not being more assertive with her, but now it is too late. The opening credits begin to role when Natalie hears a knock on her door.

"Who is it?" she yells

"It's me, Lynn." A female voice replies. "Open up please."

Fortune smiles again!

Natalie gets up, walks over to the door and opens it. Lynn is standing outside, red-faced and looking upset. She leans into Natalie and gives her a big hug.

"Hey, what's wrong?" Natalie asks.

"I never should have tried." Lynn states. "She can be so cruel."

"What happened sweety?" Natalie asks. She leads Lynn to the bed and they sit down.

"I go to Heather's dorm," Lynn begins, "and we start talking. She starts venting about how Marco did her wrong and how alone she feels. I tell her she still has two of her best friends in Ashley and me and just call when she wants to talk or something. She turns around and says that I've been distant from her cause I'm busy chasing tail!"

"Wow." Natalie exclaims.

"Yeah," Lynn continues, "and lambasted me for breaking up with Howard, despite what he said to me, and then she calls me a ragin lesbian!"

"But you don't know if you're a lesbian, right?" Natalie asks.

"Right!" Lynn shouts. "You'd think if she were one of may best friends, she'd give me the benefit of the doubt, let me make up my own mind, and then respect my decision. Dammit, I love that girl, but she just pisses me off!"

Natalie reaches over and gives Lynn a big hug. She presses Lynn's head to her chest and lightly strokes her hair.

"It's all right." Natalie says. "You're with a real friend now."

"I know." Lynn replies. "I should have just come here." She squeezes tighter and breathes in Natalie's scent.

"Did the movie start yet?" Lynn asks.

"Yeah." Natalie replies.

The settle in and watch the movie. It is a romantic comedy that they both like, and enjoy watching whenever it comes on T.V. The movie is followed by a classic horror film. They scream and cower in jest, and laugh about how chicken they were. The time is 11:35pm when the movies are finished.

"You're probably tired." Lynn says. "I'll see you tomorrow maybe?"

"I'm not tired." Natalie replies "Wait here a second."

Natalie disappears into her bathroom. She re-emerges after a few minutes, wearing blue jeans, sneakers and a loose top.

"Let's go!" She says.

"Go?" Lynn asks and laughs. "Go where?"

"Let's take a walk." Natalie answers. "Let's find some action on campus."

"Alright," Lynn says, "but understand, I think you're crazy."

"And you love me for it." Natalie replies and blows Lynn a kiss.

The girls head outside and head towards Fraternity Row. The talk and joke about random things and exchange catcalls with some of the boys they came across. They are having a great time until they reach the end of the row. They look at the stoop of one of the frat houses and see Howard. He is making out with a pretty girl and running his hands all over her body.

Howard grabs a handful of breast and squeezes hard. The young woman moans into his mouth and kisses him harder. Using his other hand, he grabs her backside and presses her hard against him. She hooks her leg around him and grinds her groin against his, dry humpimg him. She breaks the kiss, places her lips against his neck and begins to suck. He wraps his arms around her back and looks up. He notices two girls standing on the sidewalk, staring at him. He notices one of the girls is his ex-girlfriend, Lynn Bennett. He looks right back at her, smiles, and flips her off. He then runs his hand up the girl's skirt and clutchs a handful of bare bottom. The young woman leads Howard by the hand, back into the frat house.

Lynn is infuriated. She is hurt by his public display of affection, but for him to rub it in is the most hurtful gesture of all. She turns in the opposite direction, puts her hand over her mouth and runs off in tears.

Thank you Howard.

Natalie is close behind her. Once the reach the main campus, she reaches out, grabs Lynn by the shoulder and slows her down. Lynn turns around, furious.

"I HATE HIM!" She screams. "I HATE HIM, I FUCKING HATE HIM!"

She tries to run again, but Natalie grabs her, wraps her arms around her and holds her close. Lynn tries to break away, but soon breaks down in Natalie's grasp.

"I hate him." She repeats softly and cries loudly, her face buried in Natalie's bosom.

"Shhhh," Natalie whispers soothingly. "It's ok. It's ok to hate him. I leaned that a long time ago. Sometimes, all you can do is hate."

Lynn slowly lifts her head. Her face is red and wet, covered in tears.

"I'm so sorry Nat." Lynn cries. "For everything in the past, I'm so sorry."

"It's ok, really." Natalie replies. "You just move on, and don't look back."

"How do I do that?" Lynn asks. "How do I move on?"

Natalie releases her grasp and raises her hands to Lynn's face. She slowly brushes her hair back and gently strokes her cheeks, wiping her tears away. She lightly runs her thumb over Lynn's lips.

"Find something new," Natalie says quietly, "and exciting."

"Exciting," Lynn repeats, "and new."

Lynn raises her own hands and places them on Natalie's face. She grips lightly but firmly and stares into Natalie's eyes, slowly drawing her closer. Natalie does not resist. She leans in and brings her lips to Lynn's. They kiss.

I got you now.

The kiss lasts for a few seconds, but it feels like an eternity to Lynn. She feels the warmth of Natalie's mouth and tastes her tongue as it slides in. She returns in kind and feels their tongues dance together. Lynn is on fire and melts into Natalie's mouth.

They break the kiss and breathe hard. Their hands remain on each other's faces and they press their foreheads together. Lynn is breathless. She feels it was the most loving kiss she ever experienced. They look at each other and Lynn smiles.

"That was exciting." She says and giggles.

"I guess now you know." Natalie relies.

"Yeah. So, you wanna go back upstairs?" Lynn asks flirtatously.

"No." Natalie answers. "Too far. C'mon"

She takes Lynn by the hand and leads her away. They arrive at a large hedge next to a dormitory by the parking lot. They climb behind the hedge and sit on the ground. Lynn has to giggle.

"Well, this is defiantly exciting," she says, "but not new."

"You little freak!" Natalie shoots back and both girls laugh. Natalie leans in close.

"Hey, let me drive for a while." She says.

Both girls lean in and resume their kiss. They go at it with vigor and more passion, voraciously sucking on each other's mouth and tongues. Natalie runs her hands all over Lynn's upper body, squeezing her breasts and lighty pinching her nipples. Lynn moans periodically, as the pressure drives her crazy. Natalie's hands swoop under Lynn's shirt and bra, and fondle the bare skin of her breasts. Lynn is delirious with delight. Her head is spinning as euphoria rushes over her. Natalie breaks the kiss.

"Time to get you primed." She says.

Resuming the kiss, she takes one hand and places it on Lynn's leg. Slowly, she runs it up the full length, under her skirt, arriving at the waistband of her panties. Using her fingertips, she lightly traces over the fabric, across and down, and stops when she feels wetness. She extends two fingers and rubs the damp spot, feeling the moisture spread.

"Oh my, fuck!" Lynn squeals loudly.

Keep the bitch quiet!

Natalie locks her lips back onto Lynn's and sucks harder. She increases the pressure on Lynn's crotch, and is rewarded when she feels her legs spread wider apart, inviting her to probe further. Natalie shifts the gusset aside and runs her fingers up and down Lynn's slit. Natalie's fingers becomes soaked as she increases her tempo. She finds Lynn's clitoris and strokes faster. Lynn tries to moan, and catch her breath, but Natalie presses her mouth harder and will not allow it. Lynn begins to sweat profusely as her body temperature rises. She is at a fever pitch, and so close to the edge. Natalie senses this and plunges her fingers into the depths of Lynn's vagina.

Lynn goes willd and her body begins to jerk. She moans into Natalie's mouth and grinds her hips. Natalie works her fingers in and out at a steady, yet quick tempo. Lynn cannot think straight and lets her body react. Her hips push hard against the invading fingers, trying to bury them deeper. Natalie presses her thumb against Lynn's clit and sends her over the edge. Lynn's body jerks hard, her legs tighten, and she seizes up. She gushes in an explosive orgasm. Her breathing shallows and tears stream down her face. Natalie's hand is covered Lynn's juices.

After an eternity in orgasmic bliss, Lynn finally relaxes. Her breathing is shallow and her grin is wide. She turns her head and smiles at Natalie.

Take her now!

Natalie leans towards Lynn.

"I'm not done yet." She whispers. "Not even close. Close you eyes."

Lynn does as she is told. Her breathing is hard, but she is rife with anticipation and it prevents her from calming down. Natalie listens intensely to Lynn's breathing and slowly reaches into her purse. She takes out the plastic bag that holds the padlock. She dumps the lock and keeps the bag. Slowly, carefully, and intensely, she listens to Lynn breathe. She raises the bag purposely over Lynn's head. She just wants one last exhale. When Lynn breathes out, Natalie strikes.

Quickly, she pulls the bag over Lynn's head, tightens the opening over her neck and squeezes hard. Lynn's hands shoot up to her neck and her air is cut off. She frantically scratches and claws at her neck, trying to tear away at the restraint. The more she struggles, the tighter Natalie pulls. Lynn tried to scream, but has no air to scream with. Within seconds, her vision goes blurry and she feels dizzy; however, she continues to fight. Her arms begin to go limp and her throat burns as the pressure increases around her neck, crushing her jugular.

Natalie forces Lynn to turn over, then shoves her knee into her back and squeezes harder. She feels her victim begin to jerk as her body spasms. Lynn gives one last desperate attempt for air but she is too weak. Her hands and legs begin to turn blue from lack of oxygen. After two minutes of nonstop pressure, Lynn loses consciousness and her body goes limp.

Natalie knows she had won, but she wants to make sure. Using the bag as a hoist, she raises Lynn and slams her to the ground, crashing her head into the wall mounted sprinkler control. She repeats this multiple times before throwing her to the ground. She rolls her victim onto her back and peaks into the bag. Lynn's mouth is open and full of blood. The upper right corner of her head is crushed, looking like raw meat, and pooling blood into bag, surrounding her shattered teeth. Natalie checks around her wrist and neck, and feels no pulse. Lynn is dead.

Natalie smiles and smells the air, savoring the aroma of Lynn's blood. She pauses for a minute, just to bask in her success. This is her first real kill, not just a triggered event such as a drowning or allergic reaction. She has worked for this kill, hunted her prey, and earned her reward.

Natalie regains her composure and ties the bag around Lynn's neck, sealing it around the head. She has to move fast. She peaks out of the hedge and looks around. The parking lot is a ghost town, no one wthin eyeshot. Quickly, she darts out and runs to her truck. She backs the truck out of its spot and drives it to the nearby hedge. She backs in and hops the curb to get as close to the hedge as possible. She jumps out, runs to the back, and opens the tailgate. She goes back to the body, and using all her strength, she drags and dumps the corpse into the bed of the truck. She climbs in, bends Lynn's legs at the knees, places her into the freezer, on top of the still frozen ice and closes the lid. She closes her tailgate and gets back into the cab. She drives off the lot and heads to the same grocery store as before. There, she buys eight more bags of ice and drives back to the previous alley. Once there, she dumps the ice on top of Lynn's body and padlocks the freezer shut. She has future plans for the body and does not want it discovered just yet.

After climbing back behind the wheel, she takes a minute to relax. She reaches into her purse and pulls out her two new mementoes, Lynn's cell phone and panties, Natalie smiles as she balls the panties in her fist and smells them, remembering the moment of her kill.

At least she went out on a high note.

She examines the cell phone and discovers her newly obtained information; Heather's cell phone number, as well as Ashley's and their e-mail addresses. She puts her mementos back in her purse and drives back to campus.

Friday morning is christened by a chorus of power tools, as a crew of contractors work frantically to finish the wrirng of the WSU aquatic center. Thursday was a half day for most of the crew, so they work at a feverish pace to catch up. The foreman is sitting in the coaches office, and is reviewing a checklist of the new state of the art systems. The pool is equipped with such features as an Olympic filtration system and heater, sanitation monitors, and an automated cover for evenings. He has just finished testing the heater and is optimistic that all systems will pass inspection by the end of the day. He can then get started on the security system by Saturday morning. He is checking the sanitation sensors and becomes alarmed. He calls in his crew chief.

"Have we begun testing on the sanitation system on dirty water yet?" he asks.

"Not yet." The chief answers. "The pool was only filled on Tuesday."

"Well either the system is faulty," the foreman went on, "or you got some toxic water in that pool."

"The system is fine sir." The chief replies. "I finished the wiring and configuration myself only this morning."

"Then it's the water." The foreman says. "Open up that cover. Get about a quart of it and send it to the school's lab. Let's see what's setting those sensors off."

The chief walks outside and flips the cover switch. He goes to his workstation and gets a container to hold some water. He is curious as to what the sensors are detecting, and why they show the water is dangerous. He goes back to the pool, and notices a crowd gathered around the deep end. He wades through the crowd, telling people to get back to work. As he reaches to pool, he scooped some water and looks out upon the surface. He drops his container.

"CALL THE COPS!" He yells.

Natalie sleeps late on Friday, waking up around 11:00 am. Her smile is wide and her mood is calm. She slept in the nude the previous night, except for her newest pair of panties. She turns on her television and watches for an hour. At noon, she showers, dresses and heads to her truck. She drives off campus and heads to the tattoo parlor. On her way there, she sees a gathering of police squad cars outside the aquatic center. Her work must have been discovered.

Detective Olivarez stands on the edge of the WSU pool as the body of a young man is fished out. She is not assigned to this case, but she feels it could be connected to the earlier death of Monica Bynes. Two facts of this death pointed to murder, the victim is nude, suggesting a crime of passion; and he is handcuffed, preventing him from treading water for long. She finds the foreman and begins to question him.

"Call I have your name and position please?" she asks.

"Jake Saltzman." He answers. "Crew foreman."

"Mr. Saltzman," Kat replies, "I'm Detective Katrina Olivarez. Can you tell me when you discovered the body?"

"It was earlier this morning," he begins, "and I was checking out the sanitation system. It showed large quatntities of foreign compounds, so I sent my crew chief Aguilar to check it out. Next thing I hear is him yelling to call the cops."

"Why wasn't the body reported earlier this morning?" She asks.

"We didn't see nothing until that cover got retracted." He answers. "I think it was open when I left on Wednesday. Thursady morning we came in and it was closed. I assumed one of the last men to leave closed it."

"So the pool was covered all day yesterday?" She follows.

"Yes ma'am." He says.

"Has anybody I.D'ed the body?" she asks.

"I dunno." He answers. "I ain't asked any questions."

"Detective!" a voice shoots out. "We got an I.D."

Kat leaves the foreman and heads to the voice. She arrives at poolside and finds a rookie detective speaking to a worker. She steps in to ask her questions.

"You know who the victim is?" She asks.

"Yeah." He answers. "That's Marco Ruiz. He was one of the student volenteers. He's an engineering major, and those students could help out on school improvement projects."

"Are you positive?" She asks. "Could it be someone else?"

"Si, I'm sure." He says. "El Diablo, on his right shoulder. One of a kind."

Kat turns and heads to the body, which is now face up and laying on the side of the pool. He is swollen with pool water due his prolonged submersion and his nose is distorted, as if it is broken. The handcuffs have been removed and tagged as evidence. Kat kneels and examines his right shoulder. On it, she finds a tattoo of a devil raping a woman while stabbing her in the chest with his trident, very grotesque. He is naked, indicating his murder was a crime of passion. Kat stands up and walks back to the rookie detective.

"What do we know about Marco Ruiz?" she asks him.

"Not much." He answers. "He usually came in the morning, sometimes with a redhead on his arm."

Kat remembers the redhead witness in the Bynes murder. She wonders if she is the same one.

"Does the readhead have a name?" she asks.

"Um...Helen, or Heidi. Something like that." He answers. "No one here is really sure."

"Heather, maybe?" Kat interjects.

"Quite possibly." The rookie responds.

This cannot have been a coincidence.

"Detective," she says, "I think this has a connection to the Bynes frat party incident. Who's running this investigation?"

"I am." He answers.

"Well, we may be working together on this." She replies. "Gather whatever intel you can and be ready to meet with me tomorrow morning." She turns to leave.

"Where are you going Detetive?" he asks.

"I'm going try to link two dead people to a redhead." She answers.

"So you have a suspect?" he asks.

"Not yet." She answers. "But I might have a good lead." She leaves.

Natalie arrives at the tattoo shop and walks inside. She recognizes the artist who assisted her the previous day and heads right for him. He recognizes her as well and has a stencil ready for her to review.

"What do you think?" He asks.

"It's beautiful!" she replies. She marvels at the details.

"Where do you want it?" he asks.

"Lower back." She replies. "Can we do it now?"

"Right this way." He replies.

He leads Natalie to his chair and tells her to remove her shirt. As he begains to trace his stencil to her back, she gives her credit card to a clerk who charges her for the tattoo. Once the stencil is traced, he applies the ink. Natalie sucks and bites down on her lip as the needle pierces her virgin skin. The pain is incredible. She whimpers and a few tears run down her face. He asks on several occasions if she wants to stop. She refuses each time and insists that he finish. Three hours pass before the job is done.

"All set." He says. "Right over here." He takes Natalie by the hand.

Slowly, Natalie stirs from her seat. Her face is red and stained with tears. Her back throbs, and she cringes whenever she feels her skin move. The artist leads her to a double mirror, so she could she his work. Upon seeing her tattoo, she knows the almost unbearable pain was well worth the result.

Natalie drinks in every detail of her new art. On it, a queen bee is ripped in half, its body thrown to the ground, and its head cluthed in the jaws of a large black widow spider. Blood drips from the head and splatters on the entrails that cover its crown. Natalie forgets all about the pain.

"I fucking love it!" She exclaims.

Detective Olivarez makes her way to the Westin State University hall of records and gains admission from the staff. She begins digging through the student records. She easily finds Monica's records and puts them aside. She digs farther and finds Marco's records. She sits at a nearby table and begins to compare. She does not need long to discover the similarites.

Both victims are graduates of Salem West High School and both are Freshmen Seraphs. Both grew up in the same neighborhood and they listed the same person as a non-family emergency contact, Halem Long.

"Long?" she asks herself.

She heads back to the files and scuttles through until she finds the records of Heather Long. Sure enough, her father's name is Halem. Looking through the file, she sees that Heather also went to the same high school, grew up in the same neighborhood, and was a Freshman Seraph. She asks a clerk for a listing of all incoming freshmen from Salem West High School in attendance at Westin State. She gets her list and heads back to the records. Of the twelve students accepted, only seven attended. She grabs the files of Lynn Bennett, Natalie Cordova, Howard Haynesworth and Ashley Tyler. As she flips through, see notices that they all list either Halem or Cerise Long as their non-family emergency contact, except for Heather and Natalie. Heather listed Everett Tyler as her contact, the father of Ashely; and Natalie listed Etienne Devereux.

Katrina can understand Heather naming Everett Tyler as her contact. She figures Ashley and Heather are best friends and their families are close. Natalie's contact however, is completely foreign. She looks through the files one last time, but cannot find anyone named Devereux. She puts the files of Heather, Ashley, Lynn, Monica, Howard and Marco to one side, as they are connected to each other; and Natalie's to the other side.

"Six to one." She says to herself. "Why are you so different Ms. Cordova? Why are you the odd man out? What makes you so special?"

She gathers the seven files and takes them with her as she leaves the office.

Evening comes and Natalie returns to campus. She passes the aquatic center and sees a crowd gathering. The people are holding a candlelight vigil. Natalie parks her truck and walks over. Once there, she sees a pile of flowers laid at the entranceway and a handwritten sign that reads 'Rest in Peace Marco. You will be missed.'

Natalie scans the crowd and sees the sadness on everyones faces. Most hold their heads down and some are in a moment of prayer. Natalie feels no sadness or remorse, only joy. She reaches into her purse and fingers the wallet once more. She cannot help but wonder how would they all fell, if they knew the killer was standing amoungst them.

In the middle of the crowd comes loud sobbing from one female student. She emerges from the crowd and falls to her knees at the makeshift memorial. It is Heather. She cries loudly and is an emotional wreck.

"I'm so sorry Marco!" She bawls. "Please forgive me!"

She puts her face to the ground and wails. Howard and Ashley emerge and kneel next to Heather. They lift her up and Ashley hugs her tightly. Heather buries her face in Ashley's neck and cries. Howard wraps his arms around them both. They stay in that position for a few minutes before Heather looks up. For a quick second, Heather makes eye contact with Natalie. Startled, Natalie turns and walks away.

"Wait!" Heather calls out.

Natalie stops and turns. She stands face to face with Heather.

"You're Lynn's new friend right?" Heather asks through tears. "Where is she? I need her. I was so wrong, I need to apologize. I can't lose another friend."

"I don't know where Lynn is." Natalie answers. "I'm sorry."

"No," Heather screams. "Please tell me, where is she?" Heather grabs at Natalie's shirt.

Natalie gets angry. She loves to see Heather in pain, to watch her grovel, but how dare she touch her. She feels her skin grow hot, but she remains calm and tries to leave. Heather grabs more of her shirt.

"Where is she?" Heather demands, her voice growing loud. Ashley comes up behind her and pulls her off Natalie.

"C'mon hun, she doesn't know." She says and hugs Heather again. Ashley looks at Natalie and apologizes before taking Heather away. Howard stays behind and stands next to Natalie.

"I saw you that night." He says. "Please, tell Lynn I'm sorry, and that I know I was wrong." He turns and walks away.

Natalie is disguted and infuriated. Heather had no right to touch her, and Natalie feels tainted. She is able to find solstice in the fact that Heather is now hurting more than ever. She still loves Marco, but her last words to hime were 'I hate you' and his last words to her were 'Fucking bitch' in Spanish. After Natalie reflects for a second, she decides to send Lynn the message from Howard.

She walks back to her truck and sits in the driver seat. She turns her head so she is facing the freezer containing Lynn's freezing corpse.

"Hey hun." She begins. "Howard says fuck you, and he's glad you're dead." She laughs to herself.

Kat sits at her desk on Saturday morning. She is reviewing the student files from the previous night, still trying to figure out what separates Natalie from the others, yet what binds them all together. If she is going to crack this case, she will have to begin with these students. The rookie detective from the pool walks in, breaking her focus.

"Detective Rooks," she begins, "both of our vics attended the same high school and have a mutual friend in Heather Long. It looks like they were part of a close circle of friends with her and three other people: Lynn Bennett, Ashley Tyler, and Howard Haynesworth. What did you find out at the site?"

"The names Ashley, Monica, Heather, and Howard or 'Howie' are known by most of the rest of the crew." He answers. "No one mentioned a Lynn."

"What about a Natalie Cordova?" Kat asks

"Who's that?" He asks back.

"I don't know." She answers. "Maybe no one, maybe the one. Of the twelve kids accepted from that high school, only these seven ateended. All of them, expect for Natalie were part of some kind of clique."

"Coincedence?" He asks.

"More than likely," she answers, "but keep it in the back of your mind. She might have seen something about them. Anyway, I was able to get a yearbook from their senior year." She slides the yearbook over to Rooks and he begins to filp through it.

"Victim number one," Kat continues, "Monica Bynes. Found dead last Friday in the bathroom of a frat house after a party. Appeared to be an accidental ingestion of a severe allergen, in her case peanut oil. Trace showed elevated amounts of peanut oil in some beer bottles and three whole peanuts in her stomach. One peanut recovered from the bottom of a bottle."

"Exotic beer?" he asks.

"Yes and no." she answers. "Takeshi brand Kyoto Lager. Not really popular with the college crowd, but when have you known a group of frats to turn down a beer? Anyway, peanut oil is not an ingredient. Neither are whole peanuts. Look on page 56 of the yearbook."

He flips to the directed page and reads the highlighted caption.

"Monica let it be known, that she was fatally allergic to peanuts." Kat says.

"The beer was sabatoged?" he asks.

"Not only that," she explains, "but she was locked in the bathroom during her reaction, leaving her trapped and basically entombed between a sink and a toilet. Her purse was found crushed in a trash compactor, along with her emergency medication."

"So, you think this is a clear cut case of murder." He says.

"Someone went to that party intent on killing that girl." She replies. "We just need to know who brought the beer. Your turn."

"CSI Bassett ran a tox screen on Marco Ruiz." Rooks replies. "His blood alcohol was 0.09%. This was after he had been sumerged for over 24 hours. The coronoer's best estimation, his BAC was 0.18 at the time he drowned. Combine that with the handcuffs, he had no chance to get out of the pool. His nose was broken pre-mortem, suggesting he was beaten before he was thrown into the pool."

"Don't forget that he was naked," she interjects, "suggesting a crime of passion."

"Or intimidation." He responds. "Assuming that passion is more likely, we are looking for a female, unless Marco was gay."

"Not likely." She replies. "Page 42. Group photo with the same six people. Heather and Marco engaged in a liplock. Page 72. Marco was voted biggest flirt, aka lady killer."

"Closet homo maybe?" Rooks asks.

"No." Kat answers. "Three years back, he was the subject of a paternity suit. To prove his promiscuous ways, the prosecution called to witness four women he slept with the previous week. A player through and though."

"So we look for a female." He says.

"Natalie's a female." She shoots back.

"True." He replies. "Do we have anything else on her?"

"A little bit." She answers. "She's the daughter of former supermodel Raylene Cordova, and grand-daughter of 1940's pagent queen Rebecca Delmonte. Elementary records show that she has attended all levels, K – 12 with Heather, but that's it."

"Anything else of relevance?" He asks.

"Not right now." She answers. "I've spoken with the university president. She's going to grant me a group interview with these students on Monday."

"I'll be in Portland on Monday." He says.

"I'll get you some good info." She replies.

Natalie sits on her bed and watches the midday news. She decides to lay low this weekend and enjoy the fruits of her labor. A local news bulliten catches her attention and brings a smile her face.

"Breaking news out of Westin State University this morning. Only a week after the body of a female student was found dead in a frat house bathroom, a young male student was discovered murdered in the school's swimming pool. Workers found him stripped naked and handcuffed,

floating face down, and drowned. Police are reporting the victim as having been dead for over 24 hours prior to his discovery. As you can imagine, students still reeling over the previous death, are horrified by this latest turn of events. Many students have come forward with names and theories, but no leads have lead to the killer. Police believe this could be linked to last week's death."

Satisfied with her handy work, Natalie turns to the local sports station, where another headline gets her excited.

"Across the nation, basketball fans are rejoicing! Today marks the start of the College Basketball Preseason Tournament schedule. First on the docket, the defending champion Blue Devils of Duke University, travel to Westin State to take on last year's NIT Cinderella, the Seraphs. The Dukies are coming off a season in which they were undeafeated, and averaged a national best 104.7 points per game. They are lead by returning Junior, Lester "Tank" Battle in the starting lineup, and the Freshman sensation, Zack Flood off the bench. The Devils look to start this season just like they started last season, by destroying Westin State."

This is a spot of pleasant news. Natalie had forgotten about the game until this point. She goes to the athletics department's website and purchases tickets. She misses Zack and wants to see him again. She wants to share another laugh, and this time, more than just a high five. She wants to get from Zack, want Marco wanted to get from her. For once, she does not feel the need to dominate. For Zack, she will be submissive and let him have his way with her. She checks the time, 2:00pm. She has three hours until the game begins.

Ashley sits on Heather's bed, talking on a cell phone to Marco's mother. She is getting the details of the developing funeral arraignments and taking notes to share with Heather, Lynn, and Howard. After the conversation ends, she sits on the floor next to Heather and wraps her arm around her. Heather lets her head drop into Ashley's chest and she continues to cry softly.

"I shouldn't have screamed." Heather whispers. "I shouldn't have slapped him."

"You didn't know sweetie." Ashley assures her "This isn't your fault."

"If I didn't push him away," Heather goes on, "then no one would have gotten to him. He'd still be with me."

"You don't know that." Ashley replies. "As far as you know, had he stayed with you, you might have been killed too."

"At least I'd still be with him." Heather responds. "I miss him so much. I just wanna hear his voice, and feel his touch."

"Oh, hun." That is the only response Ashley can muster.

"Where's Lynn?" Heather asks.

"No one's heard from her since Thursday night." Ashley answers.

"I need to find her." Heather replies. "I need to apologize, for my attitude."

"Take it easy hun." Ashley says. "You know how Lynn gets when she's pissed off. She just goes off in her own world for a while. Isn't the tennis team in California right now? She's probably there. She'll be back soon, and y'all be just fine."

"I hope so." Heather replies. "Without you and her, I don't know what I would do now."

"Yes you do." Ashley shoots back. "You'd find some other bitches you could boss around."

Heather looks up slightly shocked. Ashley just smiles slyly.

"And they would love you just as much as we do." Ashley finishes.

Heather laughs a small chuckle and wraps her arms around Ashley's neck. The girls hug tightly. After a moment, Heather separates.

"Hey," she begins, "isn't Zack in town to play basketball today? When are you going to meet up with him?"

"I've already left him message saying him I can't make it." Ashley answers. "I can't leave you by yourself."

"Are you sure?" Heather asks and slightly smiles.

"Yeah I'm sure." Ashley replies. "He'll understand."

"Thank you." Heather says.

The time is 4:30pm in the afternoon, and Natalie heads to the gymnasium. She is dressed in a navy blue top, white mini skirt, and blue sneakers, the colors of Duke. She parks her truck in the visitor parking lot and heads to the entrance. She picks up her tickets from the will call window, and heads to her seat. Much to her relief, she is surrounded by Duke fans. She takes her seat and waits for the game to begin. The Blue Devils take the floor for warm-ups and she cheers with the rest of the section.

Five o'clock comes and the game tips off. To Natalie's chagrin, the Seraphs get off to a hot start, quickly jumping to a 12 – 4 lead, causing Duke to call a timeout. After the timeout, Zack takes the floor and leads Duke on its resurgence. With each basket he makes, each assist he dishes, each steal and rebound he grabs, Natalie is out of her seat cheering. She never realized that basketball is so exciting until this moment. By halftime, the Duke fans treat her like a fellow Dukie, slapping fives and reciting cheers with her, as if she were a Duke student.

After halftime, the game goes from competitive to ridiculous, as Duke roars for a 34 – 6 run. Westin State students are glum and despondent while the Duke fans go wild. With five minutes left in the game, Natalie heads towards the visitor tunnel. She waits to for the game end to act. As Duke leaves the floor after a 104 – 62 win, Natalie makes her move.

"Hey, 21!" she calls out.

Number 21, small forward Zack Flood, turns around and stares away from the entrance of the tunnel. After a second, he finds his summoner and approaches her. She is a striking blonde beauty, clad in Duke colors, showing off her curves, and giving him a seductive smile. He returns in kind. She reaches in for a handshake and he accepts. While shaking his hand, she passes him a note.

"Good game." She says. "Very exciting to watch."

Zack opens up the note and reads it.

9:30pm. North Dorm. Ste. 1284. Please don't make me beg!
He looks up at the young temptress with a devilish grin.
"You know," he begins, "I may not be single."
"I may not care." She replies. "Is she here?"
His smile broadens.
"Nah." He answers. "She cancelled on me."
"So, her loss is my gain then?" She asks.
He hands back the note.
"Alright." He answers. "Cool."
He gives her a wink, then walks back down the tunnel to join his team.

Perfect. Natalie walks away, having secured a secret rendezvous with Zack. She also finds out that Zack is still involved with Ashley, but she blew him off this one night. This is perfect. Natalie devises a plan to exploit this situation to her advantage. She has never been intimate with a man before and Zack will be her first. Tonight, she will be his toy, but he will be her pawn.

Ashley sits on the floor of Heather's dorm room, watching television while her best friend sleeps. Heather cried most of the day and was exhausted. Ashley promised her she would not leave her alone, so she stayed and decided to sleep over to keep her company. Ashley's cell phone rings. She checks the caller I.D. It is Zack. She excitedly answers the phone.

"Hey baby." She says.
"Hey girl." He replies, "What's going down?"
"Nothing much." She answers. "Heather just now fell asleep. The poor dear, she's been a wreck all day."
"Tell her I said what's up, and I'm gonna get my grandma to pray for her." He says.
"She'll appreciate that, thank you." She says. "I saw the game on T.V. You were great."

"I had some extra energy." He replies. "I had to use it up since I wasn't gonna see you."

"Well," she goes on, "maybe we can hookup later on this evening. I could sneak out ya know."

"No can do babe." He replies. "Coach changed the travel plans. We're flying back tonight, instead of tomorrow morning."

"What!" Ashley sounds shocked. "That's so fucking unfair!"

"Hey, take it easy baby." He says. "I'll be back. Remember, we come back later on, when the regular season starts."

"I know." She replies. "Just wish I didn't have to wait so long. I'm burning up for you baby."

"Well you know I have that effect on you." He says. "Hey, I have to finish repacking. I'll call you when we get back to North Carolina."

"Alright." She says. "I love you."

"You should." He replies. "Bye." He hangs up the phone.

Zack finishes changing his clothes after he hangs up with Ashley. He picks up his wallet and gives his roommate one hundred dollars as cover money. He then leaves the team motel and catches a cab back to the Westin State campus.

Natalie finishes installing her webcam, ten minutes before Zack is set to arrive. She turns it on and tests it with a quick fifteen second recording. She adjusts the position of the lens and the zoom. She wants to frame the bed perfectly. When the shot is perfect, she looks into the camera and starts another recording.

"Ashley," she says, "this one's for you!"

As if on cue, there is a knock on her door. Natalie darkens the computer monitor and hurries to answer the door.

Zack knocks on the door and waits for it to open. He does not have to wait long. The door opens, and before him stands his blonde siren. Her eyes are big and blue, just as he remembers from the game. Her hair is damp, as if she just emerged from the shower. She wears a tight, pink shirt, and butt-clutching light blue jeans, barefoot.

"Hey." She says sweetly. "Come in." She steps aside to let him in.

"Hey there." He replies. He walks inside and visually takes in the room.

"I'm glad you could come." She says and closes the door.

"So am I." he replies. "Don't I know you from somewhere?"

"I wouldn't know." She answers. "Do you?" She walks up to him and leans in close.

"I'm sure I would remember a sweet young thing like you." He replies. He smiles as she leaned in and holds her close.

"Can I get to know you?" He asks.

She puts her hand to his head and lightly runs her finger across the back of his scalp.

"Only if you're very gentle." She answers.

'Why, you like it nice and slow?" He asks.

"I don't know." She smirks. "Let's just say, the fruits of my garden are…unpicked, and untasted."

"I'll just have to change that." He replies and leads her to the bed.

Natalie feels giddy, as this is a new experience for her. After sitting on the bed, they begin to kiss, and Zack takes his liberties with her body. He runs his hands over her thighs and chest. He grabs her breast and squeezes firmly, causing her to moan softly. Wasting no time, he yanks her shirt off, and exposes her bare chest. He again grabs and rubs her feminine flesh, before breaking the kiss and sucking on her nipples.

She is delirious and drunk with passion. He more he grabs, squeezes, strokes, and sucks, the more she wants. His hand is in her pants and furiously petting her, to the point of mild pain. Her eyes are closed and her head is thrown back. She moans and squeals loudly, with no cares if anyone walking past her dorm can hear her. She feels the pressure build in her loins, and her energy rises. She is feeling tired, but cannot stop. She spreads her legs wider and feels the intrusion of his fingers. Her vision blurs and see begins to see double. She loses track of anything happening around her and her hearing muffles. All she could do is feel the sensations driving her wild, and her pants coming off.

In the next instant, Zack is no longer at her side, and she feels a warm moistness running up and down her vagina. She moans louder as her panting increases. She feels suction on her hotspot, and hands on her hips, forcing her towards that suction, increasing its pressure. Her legs spread even wider, as if acting on their own, and her hands try to force the suction deeper inside of her. She is riding and emotional and physical high, a high from which there is no returning.

Then everything goes black. Her senses of sight, sound, smell, and taste, instantly disappear. She can only feel, and all she felt was an explosion; starting at her clitoris and spreading throughout her entire body. She feels a fire from the top of her head to the tips of her toes and through all her extremities, and the burn lasts for an eternity.

The rest of the evening is a blur to Natalie. After her first orgasm, she gives of herself completely and does whatever Zack tells her to do. She strips him naked and uses her mouth to take him over the edge of pleasure, drinking of his essence. She lays still and lets him take her virginity. She surrenders her body, and any orifice that comes with it at his command. The mindblowing pleasures and experiences feel as if they will never end, as time seems to stand still. She has long lost track of time when the encounter finally ends.

Zack rolls out of Natalie's bed, thoroughly drained and satisfied. He puts his clothes back on and heads back to the blonde diva still prone on the mattress.

"I'll be back later on this year." He says.

"I'll be waiting." She responds.

He gives her one last kiss and smack on her backside. He then rushes out the door, knowing he has to get back to the motel before his coach discovers he is missing. Natalie peels herself off the bed and tries to stand. She has little strength in her legs and can barely stay upright. Fighting to prevent her knees from buckling, she stumbles towards her laptop. She re-lightens the monitor and readjusts the zoom. With a wide, satisfying grin, she looks into her webcam.

"You were right Ashley," she says, "better me than you."

She stops the recording and saves the file. Exhausted and still naked, she hobbles back to the bed and collapses. She enjoys her best night's sleep in years.

The bus carrying the WSU Women's Tennis Team arrives back on campus mid-morning Sunday. Still undeafeated, the women are jubilant after their latest defeat of San Diego State University. The doors of the bus open and the girls stream out with their equipment in hand.

Howard runs up to the bus as the women unload. He scans the crowd looking for Lynn, but is unable to spot her. He calls out her name to no avail. He calls again and gets a response from a middle-aged Russian woman. She is too old to be a team member, yet she wears the same garb as the rest of the girls. Howard figures she must be the coach.

"You look for Lynn Bennett?" she asks, her accent heavy.

"Yeah." He responds. "Where is she?"

"I hope you tell me." She replies. "She not show for plane. We forced to play without captain."

This is disturbing news for Howard. He knows that Lynn is very passionate about tennis. He watched a match two years ago when she won the league title playing with a 104 degree fever. After the match, she had to be iced down, hooked to an I.V. and rushed to the hospital. She would rather die than miss a match. He heads back to his dorm, more confused than ever.

Natalie spends her Sunday morning on the internet. She wants to get back to her goals after her night of passion, and is researching for her next target; Howard Haynesworth. She still has the scar on her left hand from when he kicked her locker door shut on it, and she wants to pay him back, with interest. He will be most vulnerable, as fraternity rush has started, and he is desparate to join Sigma Tau Upsilon. This fraternity has a loyal following nationwide, yet she has difficulty finding anything about them she can exploit. During their pledge rush, they are strict about not allowing females anywhere near the pledges. She is about to give up when she finds the one exception she needs, The Gideon Hunt.

The Gideon Hunt is a tradition almost as old as the fraternity itself. It is performed in conjuction with the Sigma Sister Soroity, Lambda Zeta. A Zeta will dress in dark, almost gothic garb, and prance around campus sometime during the hours between dusk and dawn. Attire is typically a short black dress or skirt with black and white striped stockings, high heels, a black beret, and black and white face-paint. All Sigma pledges are dispatched to find her. Once a pledge spots her, he must bow at her feet and comply with any and all of her wishes. The Gideon will not speak. Instead, she will mime all her commands, so the pledge must interpret carefully. Her wishes can range anywhere from embarrassing, ridiculous, sexual, to even dangerous. The pledge cannot contest, and must complete each task without question or objection. After completion of all tasks, which have no set number, the Gideon will escort the pledge back to the Sigma house, where she is finally able to speak. At that time, she will declare whether or not the pledge has completed the tasks to her satisfaction. The Gideon has all the power. Her yes or no declaration will determine if the pledge is inducted into the frat. If she declares yes, induction is automatic. If she declares no, the pledge is automatically rejected and dropped from consideration.

Natalie thinks this is a great idea. Anything that takes power from one person and gives it to another without question, she supports. This is her ticket to Howard. If she can pose as the Gideon and get to Howard, he will be her poodle. She can draw him away and do whatever she wants. Upon further reaserch, she discovers that the Zetas can have multiple Gideons. The decision is up to them, independent of the Sigmas. This plays to Natalie's advantage.

Natalie decides to shower and heads to the archery range to clear her mind so she can think straight. After her shower, she turns on the

T.V, so she can listen while getting dressed. A news bulletin comes on, grabbing her attention.

"Police investigating the murder of Marco Ruiz, a student at Westin State University, have reported that after responding to many leads in the case, they are no closer to finding the killer. In an exclusive interview with Cable News Television, lead investigator Detective Katrina Olivarez promised to step up the intensity and increase the police presence around campus to prevent further loss of life. The community is up-in-arms, and after two deaths in less than two weeks at the same campus, some parents have pulled their children from the school, and enrolled them elsewhere. The Governor's office has even received phone calls from concern faculty members, demanding FBI intervention. The Governor has refused to comment at this time."

This is cause for concern. Natalie cannot hope to achieve her objectives if the police are poking around campus. She goes back to her laptop to re-evaluate her plan. Looking at the posted website, she finds cause for hope. The Gideon Hunt is conducted on the third Monday, of the first month of autumn classes. She checks her calendar. Tomorrow will be the third Monday of this first month. She cancels her trip to the archery range and heads to the mall instead.

Howard is in his dorm room with Ashley. He tells her how he went looking for Lynn that morning, but was told she never showed for the matches in San Diego.

"This doesn't make any sense." Ashley says. "Lynn doesn't miss matches; and if she can't go somewhere, she doesn't just not show, she calls."

"Something doesn't feel right." Howard responds. "I don't wanna start conspiracies and shit, but first Monica has a quote-unquote accident, Marco's found handcuffed and drowned in the pool, and now Lynn's missing? This doesn't pass the smell test."

"What are you saying?" She asks. "You think someone's after us?"

"I'm saying watch your back." He answers. "We gotta look out for each other. You, me, Heather, we gotta be careful."

"So what should we do?" She asks. "I'm so scared." She begins to cry. Howard walks over and gives her a comforting hug.

"Don't be afraid." He answers. "Let's see what the police do. They've already questioned us. I'm sure they're watching out. We'll be alright." He breaks the hug.

"I'm gonna go check on Heather." She says.

"I'll go with you." He replies.

Natalie arrives at the shopping mall and makes haste for a costume shop. She finds one and purchases face paint, a black wig, a prostitue costume, and black and white striped stockings. Leaving the costume shop, she comes across a sporting goods outlet and walks in. She finds the expected standard fare, such as basketball and soccer equipment. Walking further towards the back, she comes across the outdoors section and browses around. This is more to her liking. Rifles, air guns, fishing poles, and other various items abound. She notices a display case on her right and comes to a stop. What she sees makes her jaw drop.

Inside the case are collegiate class competition bows and titanium tip arrows. Next to the bows, she finds an assortment of hunting knifes of different lengths. The knives are nice, but she is awe struck by the bow. She has developed quite a taste for archery and decides she needs to have this bow. A sales clerk comes by and Natalie grabs his attention.

"Excuse me sir," she begins, "can I see this bow please?"

"Sure." He answers.

He does not object. Sales are slow today, and he needs the volume to meet his daily sales goal. He opens the case, retrieves the weapon and hands it to her.

"This is a fine tool of marksmenhip." He begins. "The arms are made of a military strength iron alloy and the bow is a blend of copper, iron and silver. The blend is precise, giving the shooter the optimal tension for a quick strike. The sight is perfectly balanced, increasing your chance of a bullseye ten fold."

She holds up the bow, pulls the string and aims. As she releases, she feels the snap and imagines the velocity it would create. She has to have it.

"How much?" she asks.

"$749.99, plus tax." He answers.

"American Express?" she asks

"Visa/Mastercarrd." He replies.

"Done." She confirms.

"With purchase, you get a free quiver of arrows and $50.00 store credit." He replies.

She looks back at the case, trying to figure out how to spend her fifty dollars. She looks at the knives and finds one she likes.

"How much for the white handled seven-incher?" she asks.

"One large." He answers.

"Fifty with store credit?" she asks.

"Not a problem." He replies and retrieves the blade.

He walks back to the cash register and begins to ring up the purchase.

"Never figured you to be a hunter." He says.

Hunter, I like the sound of that!

"I'm not." She replies. "My dad is, and his birthday is next week. I think he'll like these."

"I think he will." He says. "May I interest you in one last thing?" He walks to a nearby shelf and pulls down a radio scanner.

"This here is the latest in hunter survival." He says. "Let's say your dad is planning on a weekend hunt. He could use this to find out about weather conditions and so forth. Also, if he gets hurt, he could radio in to local police and ambulance frequencies, and radio in for help. It's got built in GPS, so rescuers can find him easily, and today it's on sale for only $129.99."

Police. Intercept police radio, might keep me ahead of them!

"I'll take it." She says.

The clerk takes all the items and gives her a total of a little more than one thousand dollars. As usual, Natalie hands over her grandmother's credit card and finalizes the purchase. The clerk, desparate for a sale, neither checks for ID, nor does he record her customer information. With her purchases complete, she leaves the shop.

Outside the mall, Natalie heads to her truck. She puts her bags in the back and climbs in the driver seat. She is ready to leave, when she notices a flyer in her wiper blade. She exits the truck, grabs the flyer, and reads it.

> SAVE AMERICA! RECLAIM OUR LAND FOR THE WHITE MAN!
>
> *Everyday, we are forced to sit back and watch, as more and more niggers are on TV destroying our communities, raping our women, and killing our children. The war has begun, but we have yet to begin fighting. If you are tired of coons, chinks, and spics running your daily life and want to relegate them back to the shadows where they belong, then you must join us.*
>
> HAMMERSKINS UNITE!
>
> *(253)437-4755 – Loyalty@hammerskinnation.net*
>
> *It is your Aryan duty to join the fight. Will you stand with your brothers?*

Natalie despises racist and feels they serve no purpose. Angry for no reason, no common sense in their arguments, and no rhyme or reason to thier tactics. Natalie is convinced that people of all races have potential for evil and cruelty, so why would she limit herself to focusing on torturing just a few? She is about to dispose of the sheet, but decides to keep it. Ashley and Howard, after all, were black, and a hammerskin can become an easily accessible tool. She heads back to campus.

Kat Olivarez arrives on the WSU campus early Monday morning. She wants to personally configure the conference room with the appropriate chairs and recording devices. Everything these students say will be recorded and analyzed with a fine-toothed comb. The school administrators agree to have the five students called in by ten o'clock, and Kat wants to be ready.

Natalie sits in her first class of the day and works on her assignement alone. She has no partner and the professor asks if Lynn is out sick. Natalie replies that she does not know and has not seen Lynn since Thursday. At that moment, an office aide walks into class and hands two office summons' to the professor. After reading them for a moment, she calls Natalie to her desk and gives her one of them summons. Natalie is to report to the admissions office immeidatly regarding a private matter. Natalie gathers her things and leaves the classroom, curious as to the meaning of the request.

Kat sits quietly in the conference room and waits patiently. At 9:47 a.m., a young woman walks in; average height for her age, slender build, and fiery red hair. She looks depressed, as if she has experience a tramtic experience resently. The two women make eye contact and the student takes a seat.

"Good morning." Kat says with a smile. "May I see you summons please?"

As the student reaches into her purse, the door opens and two more students enter. One is a black female with log curly hair down to her back, and the other is a black male, bald with a muscular frame.

"Ash!" The redhead exclaims as the second female student enters.

"Heather, hey!" The second girl responds and gives the redhead a quick hug.

The redheaded student also gives the male a hug. All three seem to know each other very well and look to be close friends. Kat make a reasonable assumption to the identity of the man, but keeps it to herself. Instead, she clears her throat and gains their attention.

"Your summons, please." She reinterates.

All three students hand over the appropriate papers and take a seat. As Kat reviews the paperwork, the door opens once more and a third female student enters. She is slightly above average height, bright blonde hair and radiant skin. Her entrance is different from the previous pair. Instead of greeting the other students, she notices them and stops cold in her tracks. She stares for a few seconds, then sits down at the opposite end of the table. Kat again assumed her identity.

"Young lady," Kat begins, "may I have you summons please?"

The blonde does not move or speak.

"Your summons, young lady." Kat speaks more assertively. The blonde is still unmoved, but her hand begins to twitch nervously.

Kat does not ask again. Instead, she pulls out the student records she had held onto since the past Friday.

"Don't want to speak?" she asks. "That's fine. That's why God gave us the process of elimination."

She begins at the top of the stack and reads off a name.

"Heather Long." She says.

"Yes." The redhead answers.

"Thank you." Kat says. "Lynn Bennett?"

No one answers.

"Lynn Bennett?" Kat asks again. Still no answer.

"Heather, do you know Miss Bennett" Kat asks.

"Yeah." Heather answers. "She's one of our best friends."

"Is the student to your far right her?" Kat asks.

"No ma'am." Heather answers.

"Thank you Heather." Kat says. "Ashley Tyler."

"Yes, here." The black girl answers.

"Thank you Ashley." Kat replies. "Howard Haynesworth?"

"Yes ma'am." The male answers.

"Thank you Howard." Kat replies. "I'm Detective Katrina Olivarez, and I am the lead investigator into the deaths of your fellow students Monica Bynes and Marco Ruiz. Heather, I spoke to you briefly outside the frat house a little more than a week ago."

"Yeah," Heather replies. "I remember you now. You said that Monica may have been murdered,"

"I'm still trying to find out," Kat replies, "and I'm hoping that by talking to you students today, we can gain some traction."

Kat diverts her gaze back to the blonde student, who is still silent and quivering nervously.

"Why don't we start with you," Kat continues, "Miss Cordova."

The jaws of the other three students drop. They cannot believe this beautiful girl is the same Natalie Cordova they went to high school with. She looks completely different. Heather now recognizes her, as the girl Lynn was talking to, and cannot comprehend that Lynn would not have known and not told her about it.

"Natalie?" Heather asks quietly.

"What?" Natalie replies, her tone almost a whisper.

"You…um, you look good." Heather says.

"What do you care?" Natalie shoots back. Heather falls silent and does not respond.

Kat re-enters the conversation.

"Natalie," she says, "It seems that no one here recognizes you. Why is that?"

Natalie is reluctant to answer. Her hands are trembling, her face is pale, and her eyes begin to well with tears.

"I didn't want them to." She finally answers.

"Why not?" Kat asks.

'Because…I. was…they…" Natalie struggles to speak. She wants to remain strong, but being around those three at the same time makes her feel old emotions of fear. She feels trapped, with no way out. Kat turns to the other students.

"Why would she not want you guys to recognize her.?" Kat asks.

Heather, Ashley, and Howard looks at each other quizzingly.

'I'm not sure." Heather answers. "I don't know."

"Yes you do!" Natalie interjects. "You know damn well why!"

"Why is that?" Kat asks. "What is the reason?"

Natalie feels her anger grow, but so does her fear. Her anger allows her to speak, but her fear shows her emotions.

"They are the reason," Natalie answers, "that I've wanted to die, and never again live with what they put me through."

"Which was what?" Kat presses.

"Embarrasment." Natalie answers. "Humiliation. Torment. Emotional anguish. Physical torture."

Kat turns to Ashley.

"Is this true?" Kat asks.

"That was just kid stuff." Howard interrupts. "You know, schoolyard bullshit."

"Schoolyard bullshit?!" Natalie cuts in, her anger taking control. "You call that schoolyard bullshit? Closing me inside lockers, throwing me in mud puddles, ripping the clothes off my back, sticking my head inside a dirty toilet, beating the shit out of me, you call that schoolyard bullshit?"

Howard stays quiet. Kat repeats Natalie's question.

"Do you call that schoolyard bullshit?" she asks him.

Again he remains silent. Kat looks back at Natalie.

"Go on Natalie." She says. "Were they all involved?"

"They had their duties." Natalie answers, fighting her tears. "Heather gave the orders, Howard and Marco carried them out, Monica recruited people to the cause, and Ashley did nothing."

"Nothing?" Kat asks. "So why are you mad at her?"

"Because she did nothing." Natalie answers. "She did not stop it, she did not help me, she did nothing, just watched as it happened."

"You said Monica was involved." Kat continues. "How?"

"Monica was my best friend in grade school." Natalie answers. "Until fourth grade. She was the only one, who would help me, and stand up to Heather and her ilk."

"What happened in fourth grade?" Kat asks.

"I don't know." Natalie answered. "I was out for a week. When I came back, she turned against me, and joined up with Heather."

Kat turns to Heather. "What happened Heather?"

"Nothing." Heather answers. "I just invited her to my birthday party, and she made her choice."

"Bullshit!" Natalie mutters under her breathe.

Kat looks back at the crying blonde.

"What about Marco?" she asks. "What did he do?"

"My last contact with him," Natalie begins, "He held me down, so Heather could beat on me."

"Physically?" Kat asks. Natalie nods

"The last week of high school." Natalie says.

Kat glances at Heather, disgust in her eyes. Hether looks down, but does not speak in her defense, conceding her guilt. Kat looks back to Natalie.

"What about Lynn Bennett?" Kat asks "Was she part of this?"

"Yes." Natalie says tearfully. "Verbally, she was the worst one."

"What a minute!" Heather interrupts. "I saw you with Lynn on Thursady. You guys made plans to get together."

"She extended an olive branch!" Natalie shoots back. "She recognized me, but instead of continuing the cruelty of the past, she apologized, and said she was sorry for her actions. She showed she was sorry too. She took me to lunch and worked with me on class assignments. Against my better judgement, I gave her a chance, but only her. I thought we really had a chance at friendship, but then she called and said you wanted her that night, so she never showed. Shit Heather, even when you don't know I'm around, you still find a way to affect me."

"Natalie," Kat says softly, "why would you not transfer to another school, once you found out they were here?"

"Growing up," Natalie replies through her cries, "they made me feel like I was nobody, a worthless piss ant of a person. Attending college was the only dream I had left, and Westin was my ideal destination. Not too far from home, but far enough away from them. The day I got accepted was the happiest of my life. But then I found out that they would attend too. I was crushed, and heartbroken, but I was deteremined to not let them take the last bastion of hope that I had left. I changed everything about me; my hair, my body, my attitude, my look, everything. I almost lost hope when Lynn recognized me, but she changed as well, and she promised not to tell the others about me."

Kat looks at Heather.

"So you're the ringleader?" Kat ask.

Heather remains silent still, unable to reasonably defend herself against Natalie's tearful testimony. Ashley interjects.

"I'm sure, that had we known what effect this was having on her, then we would have stopped." She says.

"FUCK YOU ASHLEY!" Natalie shoots out. "I came to you! I begged and I pleaded with you. I spilled my heart out to you, and you cried with me. But then you said, better you than me, and left. You knew how I felt, and you continued to do nothing."

Ashley stands out of her seat and heads towards Natalie. She puts her hand on Natalie's shoulder, and the girl becomes unhinged. She jumps out of her seat.

"DON'T TOUCH ME!" she screams "DON'T FUCKING TOUCH ME!"

Ashley jumps back and Howard holds her from behind. Natalie is now hyperventilating, and loses all her composure. She falls to her knees, clutches her chest and tries to catch her breath. Tears pour from her bloodshot eyes and stream down her face. Her throat is hoarse and her skin is blood red. Kat stands up and regains control over the situation.

"Natalie." she begins, "Go to your dorm and relax. I'll contact you later on."

Natalie wastes no time. She gathers her backpack and runs out of the conference room, crying loudly. Kat calmly sits back down at her chair. She rubs her hand along the underside of her arms before resuming the interview. She finishes her questioning after an hour and dismisses the students. Using her radio, she puts out an APB on Lynn Bennet before returnig to her car.

Returning to her dorm, Natalie throws herself on the floor and cries. She covers and wipes her face, but the tears will not stop flowing and her sobs will not quell. She curls in a fetal position and holds herself tightly, slowly calming her anxieties and easing her fears.

Must work faster! Noose is tightening!

Time is running out, and Natalie is only halfway to her goal. She makes up her mind. She decides to forgo her studies, and focus solely on her revenge. She will give up her dream of being a Seraph, in favor of achieving her destiny. Coming to this decision is not easy, as she lays in that prone positon for hours. She wants to act, but her body is resistant. Her anger and fears are pent up, beyond her control. She only knows of one way to cope.

She crawls over to her dresser, opens the top drawer and pulls out a bag. She opens the bag and pulls out her brand new seven-inch hunting knife. She climbs onto the bed and rolls up her left sleeve. She reveals the blade and puts the sleath in her mouth, biting lightly. She settles on her bed, sitting in an upright position. Slowly she brings the blade to her exposed left arm and rests it against her skin, two-inches from the elbow. She closes her eyes, sucks in her breath, bites down on the sheath, and quickly slides the blade across her forearm.

Howard, Ashley, and Heather are huddled together on the floor of Heather's dorm room. The police interview had ended long ago, but they barely muttered any words since. Ashley is in a state of reflection, retracing all her past dealings with Natalie. She feels sick to her stomach, and wishes she had behaved differently. Howard is stoic, and shows no emotions. He focuses on trying to soothe his friends. Heather is a wreck. She misses her two dead friends, and feels no closer to resolving the situation.

"Had we known," Ashley breaks the silence, "that all this would happen, would we have acted differently?"

"What do you mean?" Howard asks.

"With Natalie," Ashley answers, "and other people. Would he have behaved the same way?"

"We couldn't predict the future." Howard answers. "Beside, I'm sure she's got nothing to do with this. We should just let her live her own life now. Let her have her dream."

"We have to make amends with her." Heather interrupts. "We have to right the past."

"Heather," Howard begins, "if I remember correctly, you were the one we rallied around against her. Why would you have a sudden change of heart now?"

"Look at our situation Howard." Heather answers. "Someone is after us, trying to kill us, possibly over something we did. Now, I know we weren't angels. Hell, I've been an outright bitch, but something from our past has caught up to us, and we have to make things right."

"Wait a minute!" Ashley cut in. "Do you think that Natalie is the one after us?"

"I doubt it," Heather answers, "but someone is, and we can't take any chances. I don't think it's her, but we are going to need as many allies as we can get. We have to look out for each other and four pairs of eyes are better than three, and when Lynn comes back around, we'll have five. Lynn's her friend too, so that should make it easier"

"Lynn may not be coming back." Howard interrupts.

"What?" Heather asks.

"I checked with her coach." Howarded replies. "She said Lynn didn't show up for the last road trip, and she hasn't been to a practice or team event since Wednesday afternoon. We have to prepare for the worst possible news and assu…."

Heather cuts him off by slapping him across the right cheek.

"Don't you dare say that!" Heather says.

Howard slowly strokes his cheek and stands up.

"I know you're under stress," he says, "so I won't think much of this. Tonight is the Gideon Hunt for the Sigmas. You guys, stay here, and stay close. As soon as it's done, I'll be back."

"Good luck." Ashley said.

"Yeah, good luck," Heather repeats, "and I'm sorry."

"Don't worry about it." He says as he walks out the door.

Natalie is in her bathroom applying her face paint. She goes all white, with a few black shapes; a star around her left eye, a black square around her right, and black lips. She puts on a white turtleneck sweater and slips on her black streetwalker dress over it. The final touches are black leather gloves, black wig, striped stockings, a black beret and black Mary Janes. After reviewing her look in the mirror, she adds the coup de grace, her sheathed seven-inch hunting knife. She throws a black trench coat over herself, grabs her truck keys, and heads to the parking lot.

Upon reaching her truck, she climbs into the driver side and take one last look in the mirror.

No turning back! Make him suffer!

She guns her engine and heads to the Signa house. Upon arriving, she turns off the engine, and waits patiently.

The Sigma house is full of life, as loud music plays and members of the brotherhood stomp, dance, and taunt the pledges as they stand in a still line and await their instructions. Howard is the seventh pledge from the left and was the first to arrive that night. The music dies and fraternity master Malik Blaylock enters the room.

"Sigma!" He yells. "Answer the call!"

"Honor, respect, leadership, duty!" The brotherhood yells back.

"Pledges!" He yells. "Know your place!"

Instantly all pledges drop to their knees and begin to recite loudly.

"Honor the tradition and might of the Sigma brotherhood. Respect our Sigma brother when we see him, and correct the disrespectful. Natural born leaders, Sigmas do not follow. Our duty, is to uphold the the dignity of the Sigmas, and prove our superiority. Now and forever, so help us noble Sigma!"

"Rise!" Malik yells. All pledges rise their feet.

"Pledges," Malik begins, "tonight is the Gideon Hunt. Tonight one, or some, or none of you, will live your dream and be inducted in the honorable order of Sigma Tau Upsilon. Tonight is symbolic, as this is your last night of submission. As a Sigma man, you are a natural leader, but as a human, you are weak and submissive. The Gideon will work that submission out of you. When she is done with you, you will never want to submit to anyone, ever again. This will be humiliating, dehumanizing, and possibly, very painful, but your duty is to not object. You must please her. Make her happy. In order to rid yourself of submissive behavoir, you must feel the ultimate lows it can bring you to, and the Gideon will take you there. If you please her, and she feels you cannot get any lower, she will bring you here for your immediate induction. If you fail her, she will bring you here for your immediate dismissal, and your consideration will be voided. Any begging or pleading for our reconsideration will only serve to validate our decision. Do I make myself clear?"

"Sir, yes sir!" The pledges yell back.

"Pledges," he goes on, "I'm looking at a bunch of stinking, infected, wet, sloppy pussies! Will one of you come back a Sigma man? We will soon find out. Get the hell out of my sight!"

With that order, the pledges scramble and bumrush the front door. Each is in a hurry to be the first to discover a Gideon and win her approval. Howard is the third pledge out and heads west. Natalie sees him take off and drives in that direction.

Natalie follows from afar, keeping a close eye on where Howard is going. After 20 minutes, he is a good distance away from the Sigma house and pretty secluded. This is her chance. She parks her truck and steps out. After closing her door, she looks behind her and is face to face with a young woman dressed similar to herself, face paint and all. Natalie is shocked and does not know how to react.

"Oh my God!" the other girl quietly exclaims. "You have this territory?"

Natalie thicks quickly.

"Uh, yeah!" Natalie responds. "I've been stalking it all night, waiting for a pledge to enter my web." She smiles coyly.

"Hey, help me out a second." The girl pleads. "Please. I really need a pledge. If I don't get to toy with at least one, I know that bitch Shiela will evict me from the process. She fucking hates me. I have to be a Zeta, I need it."

The girl sounds desperate. Natalie decides to help her out.

"I'll give you two." Natalie says. "Three blocks that way, there are two of them working in tandem. Better move quickly." Natalie points east.

"Oh my God, thank you!" she says. "You're a life saver. I'll see you back at the house."

She hurriedly scampers away. Natalie cannot help but chuckle. Despite her horrid intentions, she does a good deed. The irony is striking. Putting the incident behind her, she locks her truck and heads towards Howard.

Although only 20 minutes have passed, Howard is getting frustrated. He knows he has all night, but he does not want to risk missing a Gideon. He has wandered far from the house and is even farther from Sorority row. He feels the seconds tick away and loses his patience. He is about to change location when he notices a slender figure walking toward him. He guesses the person is female. She is dressed in all black, hands in her pocket and her hand down, letting her black hair hang. The figure stops and leans on a tree. She takes off her trench coat and raises her head. Her face is painted white, except for her black lips and black shapes around her eyes. Her arms are covered in a white sweater and she wears a black beret. It has to be a Gideon. Howard runs toward her trying to get her attention. When he reaches her, he falls to the ground and bows at her feet.

Natalie is pleased by the scene transpiring in front of her. Amazing, the man who commanded her to her knees for a beating just months ago, is now on his knees trying to please her. She wants to laugh, but remembers she has to remain silent.

"Zeta Gideon," Howard says, "How may I serve you?"

She slowly raises her foot to his face, but resists the urge to kick him. He looks up slightly confused. She purses her lips in a kissing motion and wiggles her foot. Howard acts quickly, grabs her foot and kisses it. She wiggles her toes and Howard kisses them. She places her hand on his head, stopping him, and guides him to his feet. She slows walks away and motions for him to follow. Howard obeys and follows closely.

They walk for about two minutes and are further away from the student population, in close proximity to a school fountain. Natalie has her first idea. She motions for him to stop, then motion as if unzipping her pants. She then reaches in as if pulling something out. Howard understands somewhat.

"You want me to whip it out?" He asks.

Natalie smacks her forehead and shakes her head no. She repeats the motion and points to the fountain. She then throws her head back and closes her eyes. She holds her hands as if holding a hose in front of her.

"I want me to piss in the fountain?" Howard asks.

She nods yes. Howard walks over to the fountain, and excuses himself by two female students that are sitting there. He then pulls out his penis and begins to urinate into the fountain. The two girls scream and run away, calling him a pervert and a freak. Howard does not care. He is pleasing the Gideon. When he finishes, he runs back to his Gideon. She claps and smiles in her approval.

Natalie then coaxes Howard into following her to a nearby light post. She points to him, then grabs the post, rears her head back and jerks it forward quickly, stopping just before she collides with the pole. Then using her palm, she smacks herself on the forehead. Then she points to Howard and steps away from the pole. Howard realizes his task and sighs in dred.

"You want me to smack my head against the post don't you?" He asks.

She nods yes and smiles.

"You want me to give myself a concussion?" He asks.

She claps her hands, smiles and bounces up and down.

Needing to please the Gideon, he takes a deep breathe and grabs the light post. He measures the distance carefully and closes his eyes. He takes three slow warmups and then thrusts his head full speed into the pole. The post reverberates with a loud "DONG" and Howard falls backwards, grabbing his head in obvious pain.

Natalie grabs her stomach and doubles over in jubilation. She desperately wants to laugh, but remains composed and silent. Howard is dizzy as he slowly rises from the ground and grabs his head, trying to slow the world from spinning. Natalie creeps behind him, wraps her arms around his chest and nuzzles his neck. He takes this as her approval and awaits her next command.

Natalie helps him stand and gives him a minute to compose himself. She then points to him and motions as if taking off a shirt. This command is simple, so he takes off his shirt. She quickly reaches out and twists his nipples, hard. He groans in agony but does not protest. She maintains the pressure for a minute then releases. He breathes hard in relief and waits for the pain to leave his chest. The Gideon pats him on the shoulder and points out to the fountain. There is a group of three female students standing and chatting. Natalie points to the girls and twists his nipples again, this time very quickly. After she lets go Howard responds.

"You want them to give me purple, nurples?" He asks.

She nods, and then points to herself and gives the quiet sign.

"Don't tell them about you," he says, "got it!"

Howard jogs out to the girls and they make catcalls as he approaches. After some general flirting and coaxing, the grils begin to torture him. He wants to yell in pain, but he resists, willing to deal with the pain in order to please the Gideon. The girls take liberties with his chest, twisting hard and taking multiple turns. He more he squirms, the harder they twist. He is in hell. His nipples are burning and his chest throbs. After ten minutes of what feels like forever, the girls stop. They giggle and squeal as they run off.

Natalie is on the ground, fighting hard to resist the urge to laugh out loud. She is enjoying his torment and cannot bear to bring it to an end. She feels a gas bubble build in her stomach and hatches an idea.

Howard approaches his Gideon and waits for his next command, all the while trying to rub the pain from his nipples. Natalie turns away from him and hikes her dress up to reveal her bottom. She turns her head to face him, purses her lips in the kissing motion, and pats her bum. Howard crawls over, eager to comply. He plants his lips on her cheek and kisses her backside. She pats her rump again, demanding another kiss. As he lays his lips this time, she shifts her rearend, tightens her stomach, and unleashes a flatus into his nose.

Howard falls backwards on his back, turns his head and gags loudly. He waves his hand and coughs hard, but cannot rid the scent of fart from his face. Natalie can barely contain her glee. She falls to the ground laughing silently, holding her stomach, and almost wets herself.

No more fucking around!

Natalie rises to her feet and motions for Howard to do the same. He is in pain and dizzy from the light post, his nipples still throb, and he is thouroughly humiliated from a faceful of flatulence. He watches as the Gideon begins to ballet dance, and urges him to join her. He is reaching the end of his rope, but he has come too far to quit. He puts his hands over his head and begins to spin and dance with her. She encourages him to leap and spin while he dances, and he complies. Natalie slows her spinning and brings her hand to her waist.

The rapid spinning is not helping Howard's head. He feels ready to pass out, but he forces himself to continue. He loses track of the Gideon, but knows she was still watching. He spins and leaps with all the energy he has left. He takes one final spinning leap and stops cold on the landing.

He haunches over and grabs his stomach as he feels a sharp pain in his abdomen. In the next instant, he feels a jerking reaction and stumbles to his left. His abdomen feels warm, wet and sticky. He looks at his hands and sees they are covered in blood. He tries to get his thoughts together, when he feels the same pain penetrate his lower back.

Natalie stands next to Howard holding her hunting knife, it's full seven inches buried in his back. She quickly withdraws the blade and watches him twitch as he grabs his back. She steps forward and lands a downward thrust into his right shoulder, impaling him. As the blood rushes out of the wound, she rips the knife down, slicng him open. His blood flows freely from the tear in his flesh, and splashes onto her white, clown-like face.

Howard comprehends his situation when his shoulder is ripped open. He jerks forward and falls to his knees. He needs help, but before he can scream, he is stabbed again in his back, penetrating his lungs. He gasps for air as it rapidly leaves his body. Next is a blunt strike to his neck, sending him to the ground face first.

With Howard lying on his face, Natalie jumps on his back, draws her blade, and tears at his back. Her strikes have no precision, as she slashes and rips at any piece of flesh she can see. His blood flows and splashes with every strike, covering her arms, hands, and face. Her strikes are fierce and unaimed, as the sight of his agony drives her rage and makes her bloodlust insatiable. Bones and mucle tissue are clearly visible, but she does not stop, until she can move her arms no longer. Breathing hard, she lines up the blade at the back of his neck, and drops all her weight on top of it. The pressure drives the knife through his spine and throat, and it emerges on the other side. Howard takes one last gasp as the blood rushes from throat and mouth. His eyes close and his head drops to the ground. He is dead.

Natalie holds her position after the final thrust. She admires the sight of Howard's ravaged body, and revels in the sensation of his blood, still warm on her skin. She issues her final command as Gideon, as she holds her hand to his dead face, extends her middle finger, and silently mouths the words, "fuck off!"

She climbs off the corpse and picks up her newest memento, Howard's shirt. She throws it on over her dress and puts her jacket back on over the shirt. She resheaths her knife and scans the area, making sure she is clear. When she is sure no one is around, she scampers back to her truck, climbs in, guns the engine, and leaves the scene.

Heather awakens late Tuesday morning. She fell asleep on her floor the previous night, and her face is red from lying on the carpet. Ashley lays next to her and is still asleep. She figures they fell asleep after Howard returned, yet she does not remember him coming back. She checks the bed, but it is empty. She scans the rest of the floor, but he is not there. She gets up and walks to her cell phone, wondering if he tried calling her. She checks the call log, but has no missed calls from last night. She thinks, maybe he came back while she was asleep and left earlier this morning. She heads over to Ashely and wakes her up.

"Hey Ashley," she begins and shakes her best friend, "wake up."

Ashley yawns and looks around the room groggly.

"What's up?" Ashley asks in a tired tone of voice.

"Hey, what time did Howard get back last night?" Heather asks.

"He got back…" Ashley starts then stops. Her eyes get big and she shoots up from the floor.

"I don't know." She says. "He didn't come back before I fell asleep."

"Check you phone." Heather says.

Ashley reaches over to her left, grabs her cell phone, and checks the call log.

"No missed calls." She says. "He didn't call me."

"Oh my God." Heather says and grabs her hair. "Oh, shit."

"Get up." Ashley commands. "We'll knock on his door. I'm sure he just forgot."

The girls get off the floor and put their shoes on.

"What if he's not there?" Heather asks.

"Then we'll check the Sigma house." Ashley answers. "Grab your phone. We'll call on the way."

The grils grab their phones and leave the dorm.

Natalie wakes, wearing her new shirt. She showered the previous night, washing away all evidence of her endeavor. She wants to take some time to enjoy her work, but knows she cannot afford it. She left Howard's body out in the open, and figures it has been discovered by now. She turns on CB radio and searches for a police frequency. After a few minutes, she hears some cops call in some traffic disturbances, but nothing about Howard. She searches for a few more minutes, with the same results. She turns off the radio when she hears sirens blaring in the background. She looks out the window and sees three police cars and an ambulance heading towards fraternity row. Her pledge has been discovered.

Katrina Olivarez is pissed off. She spent the previous night reviewing admissions and high school records of the interviewed students and her two victims, but she felt no closer to solving this mystery. All she knows is that the students are friends and know each other, and they are dropping like flies. She receives a call this morning telling her to get to the campus immediatly, and she feels her stomach turn. Upon reaching the campus and surveying the scene, her worst fears are confirmed.

She pulls her car to a stop and parks at a courtyard, about a mile away from fraternity row. She is led by a patrolman to a slightly wooded area, just off the courtyard, the fountain still in sight. A body is strewn face down on the ground. It is male, black, and fairly tall with a muscular frame. The flesh of his back is torn to shreds, resembling raw meat. His blood is splattered around the ground and some of the surrounding trees, as well as pooled under his face.

Kat walks over to the head of the corpse and using a gloved hand, she twists it and looks at the face. She curses under her breath and puts his head down. She gets off the ground, walks over to the nearby trashcan, kicks it hard and curses loudly.

"FUCK!" She yells and kicks the can again. "FUCK ME!"

An investingating officer runs over to her, and places his hand on her shoulder. She harshly shakes it off.

"Kat!" the officer says. "Get a grip!"

She looks up at the officer and quickly composes herself. It is Chief Foster.

"I know this kid." She says. "I interviewed him and his friends yesterday. They were friends of the other victims." Tears begin to run downs her face.

"What's his name?" the chief asks.

"Howard Haynesworth." She answers. "Close frined of our victims Monica and Marco, and ex-boyfriend of our missing, possibly dead, girl Lynn Bennett."

"So, all these murders are connected then." he says. "Any leads?"

"Only a hunch, but nothing concrete." She answers.

"What's the hunch?" He inquires.

"Howard and his friends were the big high school clique." She begins. "You know, bullies and the sort. They were tight knit and stuck together. Him, and his five best friends enrolled here, and now he's dead, as well as two of his friends and another is missing."

"That's your hunch?" He asks.

"No," she answers, "those are just facts. Not only did the clique enroll here, so did one of their targets, or a victim of their bullying. She was in the interview yesterday, and she barely held herself together. The poor girl lost it and lashed out verbally."

"Is she your hunch?" He asks.

"Possibly," she replies, "but I'm not sure. She's very small. Even if Marco was intoxicated, she couldn't have possibly gotten him handcuffed and thrown into a pool, and with the security cameras non-operational, we can't place her at the scene. We can't place her at the frat party, nor can we tell if she was here. There is nothing that links her anywhere."

"So we have no basis for a warrant?" the chief asks.

"No," she answers, "and I know we can't go forward with a hunch, especially a weak one. I'm stuck chief, and kids are dying."

She leans on a nearby tree and lets her head hang. She feels useless, and this killer is one-step ahead of her. Her frustrations are clouding her thinking and her focus stalls. The chief senses this and re-approaches her.

"Detective Oliverez," he begins, "Do you remember case file number 52879-2?"

She looks up at him.

"Yeah." She answers. "Deacon Adler. He was tried and convicted of raping and killing seven senior women in 2003. Two were hanged, two were drowned, one was decapitated, and the last two died at the hospital of their injuries."

"Do you remember the lead investigator?" He asks.

"Yeah." She answers. "It was you. Your last case before you became chief."

"Right." He replies. "What did I do when I became stalled in the investigation?"

She grins slightly.

"You punched every door in the mens locker room." She answers.

"Okay," he says, "what did I do after that?"

"You re-examined the bodies and the crime scenes, combing every single detail." She answers.

"Who helped me?" he asks.

"I did." She answers.

"And what did you do?" He asks.

She giggles. She knows where this is going.

"I found the clues you missed." She answers.

"After the case was closed, and the verdict was read, what happened to you?" He asks.

"You became chief," she answers, "and promoted me to detective. I was only in my second year on the force."

"Go back to the scenes Kat," he says, "and find what you may have missed."

"NO!" a female voice screams in the distance.

Kat and the chief look in the direction of the scream, and see a young woman, running towards the scene. The chief moves quickly and interceptes her, holding her away from the body while she screams and kicks, trying to get free. She is slender, with bright red hair. Kat recognizes her right away.

"Heather!" Kat says and grabs the girl." Heather, calm down!"

Heather does not calm down. She is in a frenzy and tries to reach her slain friend. Ashley runs out from behind her and wraps her arms around the screaming girl. They are both red faced, eyes bloodshot and covered in tears. Heather's knees buckle and they fall to the ground holding eash other and bawling.

Kat stands back as the girls cry, her fist and jaw clinch in anger. She knows she cannot give up and allow anyone else to die.

The hours pass and Natalie decides to try her radio out again. Scanning through the usual traffic calls, she finds a familiar voice and decides to listen.

"Dispatch, this is Detective Olivarez, come in dispatch, over."

"Detective Olivarez, this is dispatch. We read you, over."

"I need a progress report from Lieutenant Saunders about Lynn Bennet. Has she been found yet? Over."

"There has been no progress on the missing persons, over."

"Dammit. I need a CSI Bassett's team to meet me at the Kappa frat house, over."

"Detective, that is a negative. CSI Bassett and his team have been dispatched to Los Angeles to assist with a murder investigation. Relief will arrive by tomorrow morning, over."

"Fine. I'm gonna reprocess the frat house and aquatic center, over."

"Copy that Detective. Will you require additional units for assistance? Over"

"No. Dispatch available units to escort duty for three students at the University. I have names, over."

"Proceed with the names Detective, over."

"Long, Heather; Tyler, Ashley; Cordova, Natalie, over."

"Copy that Detective. Will you require more than 24-hour escort? Over."

'I'll check in with them after I check the scenes. If they don't hear from me by 2100, that means we got the killer and they can return to regular duty, over"

"Copy that Detective. Bodyguards will be in place by the top of the hour, over."

"Over and out."

Natalie checks her watch, 2:34 pm. She has 26 minutes to act before she is surrounded by bodyguards and police minders. She has to think fast. Quickly, she logs on to her computer and prints a sign to hang on her doorknob. After printing the sign, she hurriedly packs her bow and quiver of arrows. She grabs her items, leaves her dorm, locks the door, and hangs her sign.

Do Not Disturb. I am sleeping.

She races out of the building and throws her things into her truck. She checks her watch again, 2:56 pm. Looking up, she sees a police squad car park at the curb in front of the building. Two officers walk out and enter the building. She backs out of the parking spot and leaves.

Ashley is alone in her dorm room. She has spent the last few hours with Heather being interviewed by the police. She is exhausted and emotionally drained. She wants to sleep, yet everytime she closes her eyes, she flashes back to the horrible image of Howard's corpse. She knows she will have that image burned into her mind for the rest of her life. She begins to reflect on all the choices she made in her life. All her friends and her few enemies. She thinks about Natalie, and what she said yesterday, about Ashley never helping her and stopping Heather. She feels guilt building in the pit of her stomach and wants to vomit.

Silence equals consent. How could I be so cruel?

She rises from her bed and retrieves her laptop. Ashley has a passion for literature and poetry, and discovered at a young age that writing helped to relax her. She turns on the laptop and begins to type. She types about her life experiences, her times with her friends and family, her times alone, her greatest joys, her worst fears, her funny memories, and her saddest recollections. Her thoughts turn to Natalie, and she begins to write about her. She writes about the abuses she witnessed at the hands and words of Heather, Monica, Lynn, Marco, and Howard. She recounts how she blew Natalie off when she begged for her help and how she now regrets the decision. Her words become a heartfelt apology, and flow freely onto the screen. Hours pass before she reads what she has written. Her words are sincere, emotional, and beautiful. She pours her heart out and lays out everything that needs to be said.

She makes a decision. Tommorrow, she will deliver these words to Natalie personally, and make peace with her. Then she will convince Natalie and Heather, to leave school with her, for their lives are in danger. She makes it her goal, to look out for friends, and she will start with these two.

Natalie checks her watch again, 7:42pm. Natalie has been waiting in the aquatic center for hours, waiting for the good Detective to arrive.

This is not in her plan, but Detective Oliverez threatens to prevent her from achieving her goal. If she is to have her revenge, all obstacles will have to be eliminated, violently if necessary. She strokes her bow with her right hand, and clears her mind. She has no other choice.

Detective Olivarez arrives at the aquatic center and parks her car. She recaps her sweep of the frat house, angry that she found nothing new. She exits the car and enters the center. The pool has been closed to all persons since the discovery of Marco's body. She goes through every poolside detail, lifting fingerprints from the switches, using blacklight to look for blood, and checks the the trash cans for anything. She searches for over an hour and finds no additional details. Her frustrations grow even greater and she curses under her breath. She needs to get back to headquarters. She wants to review the testimony of the Sigma frat boys and the Zeta Sorotiy sisters, one of them has to know something. She turns around and heads back to the entrance.

ACHOO!

A sneeze sounds off in the distance and Kat freezes. The aquatic center is closed to all persons and she is supposed to be alone. She figures she must be hearing things.

ACHOO!

Another sneeze, and again she freezes. This is no hallucination, she is sure of that. Someone else is in the center with her.

"Hello?" She calls out.

No response, only silence. Kat becomes apprehensive. She draws her gun and heads to the source of the sneeze.

ACHOO!

A third sneeze sounds and Kat knows she is getting close. Everytime she calls out however, she gets no response. This makes her nervous. She does not know if she is close to the killer, or just approaching a stoner looking for a private place to smoke. She is not leaving until she finds out. She rounds a corner and faces a storage depot.

The storage area is full equipment ranging from lifesavers, to boogie boards, and other flotation devices. The left side of the room is sectioned off with a temporarily wooden wall, possibly until a permanent wall can be built. The room is dark, only lit by a few rays of moonlight permiating from the window. Holding her gun forward, Kat slowly enters the room.

Natalie hides behind a storage bin, opposite the wooden wall in the storage depot. The room is a little dusty, and it caused her to sneeze a couple times. She hears the detective call and braces herself. When the detective enters, Natalie knows this is now or never.

Kat enters the storage depot and scans the area. It is dark and full of shadows, almost ominous. She holds her gun out and looks around corners. The room is so dark, she would have trouble finding anyone. She stays close to the wooden wall and slowly slinks towards the moonlit windows. She reachs the left side of the room and it is secure. She turns her head to the right, and her cell phone beeps, startling her. She takes a deep breath trying to relax. She lowers her right hand from her gun to answer her phone, but never gets that far.

Kat hears a "thwip" sound and screams in pain as a sharp and intense pressure catches her left hand, causing her to drop her gun, and pinning her hand to the wooden wall. She looks in horror as she sees her hand pinned to the wall by an arrow. She tries to remain calm and use her free hand to reach the ground for her gun.

"Don't move!" a voice rings out.

Kat freezes in place. She is convinced she is with students' killer. She panics slightly as she realizes her predicament, but she complies and does not move.

"Put you other hand up!" the voice demands.

The voice is female and familiar. She has heard it before, she just cannot figure out where. She has to stall for time.

"I'm a detective, with the police department." She cries out.

"Shut the fuck up and raise your hand!" the voice demands.

Kat still cannot make out her assailant.

"If I do, you'll only impale it." She responds. The pain in her left hand is excruciating, and blood flows from the wound.

"I'll impale your chest if don't rasie your fucking hand." The girl replies.

"Okay!" Kat shouts. She has no other choice. She slowly raiss her hand, complying with her assailant.

Instantly, another arrow cuts through the air and impals her right hand to the wall. The pain is unbearable as Kat screams in agony.

"I said shut the fuck up!" The voice screams.

Kat grits her teeth, in a vain attempt to deal with the pain. Her face reddens as she struggles to kept silient, unable to hold back her groans. Her lanced hands keeps her in a vulnerable position, and she knows it.

Natalie knows that Kat cannot move, and relaxes a little on the bow. She steps out of the shadows and exposes herself to the moonlight. Kat stares into the eyes of her assaillant.

"Cordova." She says breathing heavily. "Why?"

"Because they deserved it," Natalie answers, "and I refuse to live in fear anymore."

"Why not…just go to…another school?" Kat asks, trying to stall for time and think of a way out, but with every passing second, her chances of survival become more grim.

"Why should I give up on my dream because of them?" Natalie asks back. "I was ready to, but they wouldn't let me. I tried hard to change my fortune, and what do I get in return? I get my ass beaten and knocked unconscious, that's what!"

"Natalie," Kat interjects, "this isn't…the way…to live your…dream."

"Oh yes it is!" Natalie replies. "After Heather, Marco, and Howard beat the shit out of me, I had a new dream, a wonderful dream. Their deaths, along with Ashely, Lynn and Monica, and so far, my dreams have been coming true. Everything was turning up roses, and four out of the six are pushing daisies. All was going great, unitl you showed. But now, that won't be a problem anymore. Goodbye Detective."

Natalie raises her bow for a final shot. Kat screams and tries to rip her hands away from the arrows, but does not have enough time. Natalie fires another arrow and it impales her target; right through her open mouth.

Kat feels her head slam against the wall, as the arrow slices through the meat of her throat, protrudes through the back of her neck and embeds into the wall. The whole situation is painfully surreal to Kat. She knows she is going to die, and she cannot stop it. Blood rushes down her throat from the wound. She coughs and swallows, desperate to keep her airways open, but her blood runs too quickly.

Natalie slowly walks up to the fading cop. Kat is starting to choke on her own blood, but Natalie feels no remorse.

"At least, you saw it coming." Natalie says. "May you rest in peace."

Natalie reaches into Kat's jacket and removes her badge. She claims it for her new memento. She is about to turn and leave Kat to her suffering when something catches her eye, a strange scar on Kat's right forearm. Natalie rolls back the sleeve and finds a plethora of slash-like scars. Natalie stares for a second, then rolls back her own left sleeve and looks at her own scars. Natalie realizes, that Kat is like her. Kat was once a cutter as well.

"You're just like me." She says.

At this point, Natalie begins to feel remoarse and sorrow. She grabs the sides of Kat's face, leans forward, and kisses her on the forehead.

"Don't worry." She says. "You won't suffer. My revenge will be your's as well. I promise."

With that statement, Natalie steps back, aims, and fires one last arrow, plunging it into Kat's throat; ending her suffering, and her life.

With the deed done, Natalie takes a second to consider her options. Surely, the police will be out looking for Olivarez within a few hours and would be sure to check the aquatic center. She has to stall for extra time. She fishes around the dead cop's jacket and purse and finds her car keys. She gathers her bow and remaining arrows and leaves the center. Outside the complex, she presses the locking button on the key control. A pair of headlights blinks in response. She finds Olivarez's car, a late ninties Mecedes-Benz convertible. She heads to her truck, unloads her equipment and returns to the Mercedes. She starts the car and drives off. She drives for 30 minutes, until she reaches the inner city portion of town. She parks the car, leaves the engine running, and walks away, leaving the vehicle for anyone who wants it. She reaches a payphone and calls a cab to pick her up. After ending her phone call, she sees the Mercedes charging down the street.

That didn't take long!

She does not feel completely at ease. Despite where the cops find the car, the body will be discovered within the next couple of days, possibly tommorrow. She has to step up her assault and finish the job. Returning to the aquatic center, she climbs into her truck, and drives back to her dormitory.

Arriving at her dorm, she checks her watch, 10:43 pm. She checks the building and sees the squad car still there. She begins to feel dread, until she sees the same two officers from earlier in the day leave the building. The cops climb into the squad car and drive away. Natalie waits until the vehicle is out of sight, then dashs out of the truck and runs back up to her dorm. There are no cops outside her door, and her sign is still on the doorknob. Her ploy has worked. She enters her dorm, sits at her desk and turns on her radio. She will listen to police transmissions and will not sleep the entire night. She clears her mind, and gives herself a final 24 hours to complete her objectives, Ashley and Heather.

Wednesday morning arrives, and neither Heather nor Ashley have slept a wink. They have not yet received any updates on the murder investigation, and were told Detective Olivarez had not been heard from since yesterday evening. The girls sit together in Ashley's dorm.

"Heather," Ashely begins, "we can't stay here. We aren't safe."

"Where would we go?" Heather asks. "Who ever this person is, if he's after us, he'll hunt us down."

"All the more reason for us to leave." Ashley responds. "You, me, and even Natalie."

"Natalie?" Heather asks. "You saw how she was the other day. Why would she even want to be anywhere around us, much less leave with us?"

"She's not an idiot." Ashley answers. "She has to know what is happening around her. Her life is in danger, and even though we haven't been right with her, in times of crisis, it's never too late to get things right."

"You and I can leave," Heather says, "but she'll never come with us. She'd probably have me killed before going anywhere with me."

Ashley takes a deep breath, then asks something she never had the guts to ask before.

"Heather" Ashley begins. "I've never questioned you or anything, nor have I dictated how you live you life. You're my best friend, and I love you too much to to second guess you, but why did you target her so much? Why did you want to crush her?"

Heather feels her eyes well up. This is a story she never told before, and it hurts her to think of it.

"When I was little," she begins "before you and I met, my dad was an executive for an advertising company. It fell on hard times, and needed good ideas, you know, to stay in the black. Dad normally was the one who came up with ideas that made a lot of money, and he was good at it. One day, he was talking to some employees, when one of them blurted out an idea. Dad thought it was dumb and paid it no mind. The next day, during a meeting with the board of directors, that same employee, burst in and forcefully gave his idea. The board loved it, and they promoted him to a high level executive. In order to make room for him, they had to fire someone, my dad."

She begins to cry.

"Oh Heather," Ashley sas, "I'm so sorry."

"He came home that day," Heather continues, "and he was different. He didn't smile, wasn't happy to see me or mom, he just wasn't himself. A week later, he called me and mom into the bedroom. When we got there, he had a gun in his hand. He said he was sorry for letting us down, and for failing us. We were so scared, we couldn't move. He raised the gun, put it in his mouth, and pulled the trigger. He killed himself, with us watching."

"What?" Ashley asks. "That's not possible. You were on the phone with him yesterday."

"That's my stepdad!" Heather yells through her tears. "Mom remarried. My real dad is dead! I just never told anyone."

"Oh my God!" Ashley replies. She reaches out to hug her, but Heather stops her.

"The employee," Heather continues, "the one that cost my dad his job and his life, his name was Vincent Cordova."

"Natalie's father?" Ashley asks.

"No." Heather answers. "No relation at all, but I never forgot that name. The name that destroyed my life, and cost me my father. When I got to school and heard Natalie's name, all I heard was Cordova, and that was all I needed. I hated her from the day I found out she existed. I didn't care that she wasn't related, but I wanted her to suffer. Everything I ever did, was to make her pay, for what that name did, and nothing was ever enough for me. Anytime I saw her cry or scream, I felt better, and pretty soon, it became an obsession. I just could not stop. Until one day, a week before finals, I finally got the chance to physically destroy her. All the rage and anger I pent up was unleashed. I swung and puched and kicked, until I had nothing left and she was unconscious. The next day, I felt absolved. No more anger, no more hate, it was as if I achieved everything I had to do."

"Heather," Ashley says, "I'm so sorry. I for everything you have lost, I'm sorry. Nothing can bring your father back."

"I know," Heather responds, "and I know that neither Natalie nor her family had anything to do with it, but I was how I was anyway. So how can I expect to make things right with her?"

"Let's try this." Ashley says. "Let's write it on a letter, and give it to her. I'll deliver it and convince her to meet us tonight. We'll settle this, and then leave. All three of us, we'll get to safety and put all of this, our past behind us."

"You think it'll work?" Heather asks.

"I don't know." Ashley answers. "We'll at least try it. Whether it works or not, we'll leave tonight, with or with out her."

The girls sign on to Ashely's computer a draft a heartfelt letter. When they are satisfied with the wording, they print it. Ashely turns to Heather.

"I'll walk you back to your dorm." She says. "Pack your things and wait for me to call you by this afternoon. After I deliver the letter, I'll come back and pack my stuff. Once I call, we'll meet up, all three of us, and we'll leave. We'll leave all this behind us, and not tell anyone."

Heather nods her head in solemn understanding and the girls leave the dorm together.

Natalie sits wide awake at her computer, looking at the clock, and listening to the CB radio. The police have recovered the detective's car, but have not yet found her body. During the morning hours, she packs her clothes and other belongings, and loads her truck. She knows that by the time the night is over, she has to disappear. She thinks hard about how to draw out Heather and Ashley, but she feels rushed and her mind is drawing a blank. A knock at her door interrupts her thoughts.

"Who is it?" she asks.

"Natalie," the voice responds, "it's me, Ashley. Please open the door."

What the fuck?

Natalie stands up from her desk, opens the door and stares down Ashley. Her stare is cold and hateful. To see Ashley so close her causes her anger to build. She wants to hurt her in the worst and most painful way.

"Hey, Natalie." Anshley stammers. "Can I come in?"

"No." Natalie responds. "What the do you want?"

"Ok." Ashley takes a deep breathe. "You've seen what's been going on around here. I can't explain it, and I don't know if you can, but that cop, Olivarez, she said our lives are in danger. And I don't know if you heard, but Howard was killed the other night."

Natalie feigns concern but remains enraged.

"I'm sorry." She says and begins to shut the door. Ashley puts her hand up to stop it.

"Wait Natalie." She says. "You were right about me. I did nothing when you were in trouble, and I'm not going to repeat the mistakes of the past. We are all in danger, our lives in jeopardy. Heather and I are leaving campus tonight, and we want you to come with us."

"What?" Natalie asks. "Fuck you!" She tries to close the door and again Ashley stops her.

"Natalie, wait!" Ashley says. She reaches into her purse and produces an envelope. She holds it up and hands it to Natalie.

"You want answers for the past?" She asks. "Here they are!"

Confused, Natalie takes the envelope and looks it over. Ashley returns to her purse and pulls out a USB flash drive. She hands it to Natalie.

"Read the letter, as soon as you can." She says. "Afterward, if you are as willing as we are, call or e-mail me. My info is on the stick."

Natalie takes the flash drive and shuts the door. Ashley does not stop her this time. She has done all she figures she can do. She heads back to her dorm room to await word.

Natalie stares at the envelope, unsure whether or not she wants to read what is inside. Can it really justify how they treated her, or is it a sincere attempt at an apology? Against her better judgement, she feels her heart soften as she opens the envelope and reads the letter.

Dear Natalie,

You have experienced tremendous suffering and pain the past few years, a pain that has followed you throughout you life. This pain was propagated by Ashley, Monica, Lynn, Howard, Marco and myself. We did horrible things to you, things that cannot be justified, and cannot be forgiven, but I do want you to know, that none of it was your fault.

When I was a little girl, my father was replaced at his job by a man named Cordova. This man was not related to you in any way, only carried the same name. My father was so distraught over this, he commited suicide in front of my mother and me. Shortly afterwards, I began school and met you. I tried to live my life normally after the incident, but after hearing your name, I lost all sense of reality. Whenever I saw you, I saw the man who took my father, and I took all my rage out on you. Once I started however, I could not stop. Seeing you in pain, or watching you cry was not enough to placate me, I wanted to make you suffer. I let the worst parts of human emotion control me because of my loss, and you took the brunt of it.

I cannot justify the actions of the others, but they acted under my orders. I trained them to see you the same way I did and just made the situation worse for you. Whenever they acted cruel towards you, or embarrassed you in front of crowd, it was not for their satisfaction, it was for mine. My shelfish and evil desires would not be satisfied, until that one fateful day, when I assaulted you. After that was done, I finally felt like I could move past my own hurt and pain.

Unbeknownst to me, my morally repugnant actions did not stop there. I caused you to live with this pain everyday of your life. It wasn't until I saw you the last time, in the conference room, that I understood the effects of my actions. It was not right nor was it fair, for me to force my pain upon you and make you experience something that should have belonged to me.

Despite what occurred in the conference room, I have seen how you have moved on. You have done it the right way. You went to college, made new friends and took steps to renew your life. You were doing so well until I re-entered your life and brought your joy to an end.

Natalie, I apologize for all that I have done, and I understand I do not deserve your forgiveness. I can only take steps to show you how remoarseful I am. Monica, Howard, and Marco are no longer with us and Lynn has disappered. We cannot afford to wait for this killer to come after us. Ashley and I are leaving campus, and we do not want to leave you behind. I am praying, that maybe this can be a fresh start for the both of us; a new change for us to live life the way it was meant to be lived. Please say that you will come with us. You are too good a person for someone to take from this earth.

Sincerely,
Heather Long.

Natalie puts the letter down and stares blankly into space. Her eyes are bloodshot, her face is red and wet with tears, and her mind is spinning.

This wasn't my fault!

Her grip on the letter begins to tighten and her jaw clenches.

She blamed his death on me!

Her rage builds as she sits.

She took it out on me!

Her fists are tightly clenched and her fingernails begin to dig into her palms.

She ruined my life for no reason!

Natalie slowly rises from her seat, still holding the letter. She closes her eyes as her breathing increases. Her rage continues to burn and her skin is hot to the touch. Her mind races faster and she feels a pain in the pit of her stomach. She doubles over to relieve the pain, but it only grows. She grabs her hair, rears back and screams at the top of her lungs. The news of the orgin of her torment drives her over the edge. She pounds her fist on her desk, then runs to her wall mirror and punches it, scattering broken pieces all over the floor. She collapses to the ground, amid the broken glass, and cries heartily. Her tears are not of sadness. Her fury builds to unprecedented highs, and her mind breaks. She will never be the same again.

After an hour on the floor, she slowly stands up. Shards of glass had pierced her body, but she feels no pain, nor does she pay any attention to her bleeding. She inserts Ashely's flash drive into her computer and obtains her e-mail address. She composes a simple message for Ashley.

Meet me @ 7:00 in front of the Seraph Gym, so we can talk.

Before she finalizes the message, she attaches the webcam recording of her night of sexual exhuberance with Zack Flood, Ashley's boyfriend. After attaching the file, she sends the e-mail.

Natalie grabs her purse and retrives the white supremist propaganda flyer she found on her car. She dials the telephone number and waits. After two rings, a gruff voice answers the phone.

"Who's this?" the voice asks. It was male.

Natalie uses a panicking and angry voice.

"You have to help me!" she speaks loudly. "Please!"

"Calm down." He replies. "Who is this?"

"You're an Aryan, right?" she asks. "A part of the nation?"

"Yes." He answers. "I give my life to the brotherhood."

"Please help me!" Natalie begs. "There is this black girl, and she won't stop harassing me! She's threatening me! Saying she's gonna have her bruthas rape me, and then she'll fucking kill me." She fakes some tears to sound more convincing.

"Are you in danger now?" he asks.

"No," Natalie answers, "but she hangs out in front of the WSU gym everyday, around seven o'clock, and she knows that I have to go there today at 7:15 p.m. She thinks I slept with her boyfriend. I swear to you, I don't fuck niggers."

"Don't worry sister." He responds. "I will personally guarantee your safety."

"She's beaten me before." Natalie says. "Her and a group of her black bitches, they ganged up on me!"

"Sister, relax." He says. "I promise you, my word as a white man, she will never bother you again."

"Thank you." She says. "Just do me one favor. Make sure, she remembers not to mess with me anymore. I want to see her afterwards, and see the fear in her eyes whenever she sees me. I want her a feel physical and emotional pain she has never known, and I want her to live with it for the rest of her life."

"You have my word." He replies.

"Thank you." Natalie repeats and hangs up the phone.

Gullible Neo-Nazi mutherfucker!

Natalie despises racists, but she finds a use for one on this occasion. When the conversation ends, she packs her laptop and takes it down to her truck. Checking the time on her watch, 5:15 p.m. she walks to the bus stop and rides into town.

Ashley rushes as she stuffs her clothes into her luggage. She has already packed her shoes and small electronics except her laptop. She wants to allow for as much time as possible for Natalie to respond to the letter from her and Heather. An hour has already passed and she is starting to lose hope. She figures that she and Heather will be leaving by themselves.

Another 30 minutes pass, and Ashley gives up. She feels fine with her results, she tried her best and Natalie rejected her. She is saddened, but not surprised. As she brings up the shut down menu, her web browser pings audibly. She has received an email. She opens her inbox and breathes a sign of relief. It is a response from Natalie. She reads the message and writes down the place and time Natalie wants to meet. She is about to close the message when she notices that a file titled "confession" is attached to the message. She is curious, but figured it is a recorded response to the letter. She feels she owes it to Natalie to watch it. She settles in and plays the file.

The video file shows the inside of a dorm room with someone toyng with the camera, trying to get the angle aimed at the bed.

"Ashley, this one's for you!" Natalie says into the camera.

Ashley thinks that is rather cryptic. She looks at the time/date stamp on the recording, and notices it is a few days old. She becomes confused. If this is a few days ago, then it cannot be a response to the letter. Ashley watchs the video and sees a young man enter the dorm. She is shocked and her eyes grow big.

"Zack?" She says to herself.

Ashley watches as the two youngster exchanged flirts with each other, then the action began. She grabs her mouth in shock as Zack and Natalie feverishly kissed and groped each other. She cannot believe her eyes. Zack tore Naralie's clothes off and ran his mouth and tongue all over her body. Her horror continues as she watches Natalie return the act in kind. Her eyes overflow with tears as she watches her boyfriend, the love her life, enjoy every second of pleasing another woman. Her face becomes flushed and red, but she cannot turn away. Natalie gave herself in every way possible and Zack took advantage. Ashley feels sick and wants to vomit. Her heart breaks with every moan that Natalie made, and every grunt from Zack, but she cannot turn away. She feels her shock and sadness turn to anger and rage.

After what seems like a torturous eternity, the event ends, and Natalie gives one last message. It is a moment from their shared past, and it hits Ashley like a ton of bricks.

"You were right Ashley, better me than you."

The video ends.

Ashley keeps staring at the screen, barley breathing. Her jaw is tightly clenched, her hands are balled into fist, and her body trembles. She never felt this kind of rage before, and without warning, it erupted. She screams a blood curldling scream and pounds her fist repeatedly onto her desk. She strikes the desk violently, brusing and cutting her hands, but she does not care, nor can she top herself.

Her cell phone rings, and brings her out of her state. It rings once then stops. She grabs it and checks the caller I.D. It was Heather, and she missed the call. She checks the time of the call. 6:45pm. She does not think twice. She grabs her jacket and runs out the door towards the Seraph gym. She is no longer the peaceful Ashley she grew up to be. She knows Natalie will be at the gym, and she is determined to beat the hell out of her.

At 6:00.p.m. Natalie unboards from the bus and walks down the block. She arrives at a bar, and puts her game face on. She walks towards the door and is stopped by a bouncer.

"I.D. please?" He asks.

"I'm not 21." She answers.

"No admittance to minors." He says.

"I don't need to go in." She responds. "My name is Gloria Rolle. I'm here from WSU, part of the Safe Streets Initiative started by the student union. I'm here to volunteer to take someone home who may be too intoxicated to drive."

"Are you serious kid?" He asks puzzled.

"I'm here to save a life," she replies, "maybe more if I can."

The bouncer has never heard of such a program, but the girl seems sincere. He decides not to ask questions and to take advantage of the program. He grabs his two-way radio and contacts a collegue.

"Hey Pete, come in." He says.

"What's up Jimbo?" is the response from the radio.

"Is Yuri at the bar?" Jimbo asks.

"Oh yeah." says the radio. "He's been drinking whiskey nonstop for the past two or three hours. His wife should be calling soon."

"Bring him to me." Jimbo replies. "We got a ride home for him."

"Alright, gimmie a minute." The radio says.

After a couple of minutes, another man comes to the door, lugging a drunk foreigner behind him. The foreigner is an older, slightly heavyset man with scruffy facial hair. He is so drunk, he can barely stand. The bar employee hands a set of car keys to the bouncer, who in turn gives them to Natalie.

"He drives that big Ford SUV over there." He says and points to a red Ford Excursion.

"We'll carry him to his car for you." He continues as they walk to the truck. "He lives on the Honey Wells Terrace cul-de-sac. Just go north on Buena Vista, past five intersections and turn right on Ventura. Go all the way up the hill and his cul-de-sac is the first on the left. His house is a big blue monstrosity at the back of the cul-de-sac. We'll call his wife. Hit the horn when you arrive and she'll help you get him inside. I'm sure she'll give you a ride back to campus as well."

They reach the truck and load Yuri into the passenger seat. Once they get him buckled in, Natalie thanks the two men and settles into the driver seat.

"Pretty girl," Yuri says "have asprin, you do?"

"I thought you might ask." Natalie replies. She reaches into her purse and pulls out a bottle of sleeping pills. She shakes out four pills onto her palm and hands them to him.

"Extra strength," she says, "here you go."

"Spaseebah." He thanks her in Russian. He reaches into his jacket and pulls out a flask. He pops the pills in his mouth and swigs from the flask.

Natalie starts the truck and leaves the parking lot. She heads north on Buena Vista and passes the first few intersections. Within minutes, the drunk is out cold and fast asleep. Natalie makes a u-turn and heads back to the WSU campus. She does not have much time left.

Ashely storms out of her dormitory and heads toward the gymnasium. Her heart is pounding, her ears are ringing and her blood is hot with rage. Her eyes are focused and she looks for Natalie. She does not know what she will do when she sees her, but I will be painful, she is sure of that. She reaches the front of the gym, but she does not see Natalie there.

"NATALIE!" She yells. "WHERE THE FUCK ARE YOU? GET OUT HERE NOW!"

Nearby, on the gymnasium steps, four white men with baldheads, watch as Ashley goes hysterical and starts screaming while looking for Natalie.

"That must be her." The one in front says.

He snaps his fingers and all four stand up and head over to the screaming black girl. Ashley does not see them. She continues to run around the front of the gym, searching for her target. She can barely focus. If she could, she would have noticed that no one was there. She leans forward and braces herself on her knees, trying to catch her breath and regain her composure. When she looks up, she notices that four men are surrounding her.

"What do we have here?" One of them asks.

"None of your fucking business!" Ashley shoots back.

She is enraged, but she is not dumb. She sees the baldheads, the black garb, and the red armbands. She knows they are white supremists, but she just does not care.

"Oh," he replies, "we have a feisty one brothers."

"This has nothing to do with you!" She replies. "NATALIE!"

She turns to leave, but one of the men sidesteps her and blocks her path.

"Where do you think you're going?" He demands.

WHAM!

Ashley does not think, just reacts, and punches the neo-nazi in his nose. The others strike quickly. One of the men grabs her from behind and covers her mouth. She bites down on his hand, but he resists the pain. Another one grabs her legs and they carry her away. She struggles against their grip and tries to scream, but she cannot break away. The hammerskins carry Ashley into a nearby white van, throw her in the back, climb in, close the door, and drive away.

Witnessing the scene from the red SUV, Natalie pulls out of the parking lot and keeps her distance as she follows the van.

Inside the van, the men throw Ashley to the floor. She screams, but is immediately struck across the mouth. She falls back to the floor and grabs her throbbing lower jaw. Her hair is pulled and she is hoisted off the floor. Without hesitation, she is thrown against the side of the van. She crashes head first into the steel and recoils on her back. She feels dizzy as her surroundings spun.

"Accuse a white woman of fucking niggers will you?" A voice yells out. "You got some fucking nerve!"

"What?" She stammers.

She is lifted off the ground and propped up, leaving her abdomen exposed. One of the Nazis land repeated blows to her midsection, and throws her back down. Her hearing is clear and she knows what they are saying. At that point, she knows she has been set-up. Then clarity strikes her.

The date on the video, the meeting place and time, this assault was planned. Natalie knew all along. Oh my God!

"HEATHER!" Ashley shoots up and yells.

She is immediately punched in the mouth. On the floor and reeling, she spits out blood, and some of her teeth.

"This black bitch is too hyper!" one of her attackers yells. "Shut her up!"

Ashley feels her shirt ripped off and the fabric thrown around her neck. A brute squeezes the shirt and cuts off her air supply. She claws at her neck, trying to rip the vice away, with no success. She is then slammed again head first into the side of the van.

The shirt loosens and Ashley lays on the floor gasping for air. She cannot get relief for long, as she soon feels blows slam against her back. Next, her skirt is torn away.

"Hold the bitch down!" One of them yells, she cannot tell which one. Despite the beating and extraordinary pain, Ashley never stops fighting. One of the men leans in close to her ear and holds her head face down to the floor.

"You were gonna have some brutish niggers gang rape our sister, huh?" He yells. "Maybe you'd want a taste of your own medicine!" He shucks her underwear off.

Two of her attackers hold her down, by pressing their full weight onto her arms and legs, almost breaking them. A third holds her backside in the air.

"Do it bro!" One of them yells. Ashley hears a belt buckle loosed and a zipper come down. She struggles harder, but cannot move her limbs.

She screams, and a hand is pressed against the back of her head, forcing her mouth to the floor of the van. She continues her muffled scream.

"Shut up you fucking black bitch!" One yells.

WHACK!

Ashley felt a stinging strike to her backside. Repeated blows land from an attacker's belt. She feels the fierce strikes pierce her skin and her blood drips on her legs. When the blows end, the real pain begins. She feels a shredding pain penetrate her rectum, and she screams. She does all she could to fight him off, but is unsuccessful. She claws the ground and breaks her fingernails while the rape commences. The attackers yell their encouragement and continue to punch her, leaving her body badly bruised.

The skinhead forcibly shoves his penis into Ashley's anus against her will, anally raping her. All the while, he yells obsenities and orders the others to hold her still. After a few minutes of thrusting, he ejaculates inside her. Panting, he withdraws and strikes her with the belt once again.

"Your turn!" he yells to one of his comrades.

Ashley feels the attackers switch, and the new one behind her rapes her vaginally. She is exhausted and can no longer fight or resist. All she could do is scream and cry from the pain and humiliation of the rape. The attackers take turns, taking her in different positions. One of them liked to choke her while having his turn.

Ashley is nearly unconscious when the ordeal ends. She can barely lift her arms, see around her, or hear what the men were saying. She bleeds heavily from her ears, nose and mouth; has lost numerous teeth, and broken seven of her fingernails. Her hair is tossled and some of it ripped out at the root. She is cold, naked, and her left arm and wrist are broken. Her body is covered in blood and semen, and the bruises leave her black and purple.

"Hey D, pull over." One man yells.

The van slows, pulls to the side of the road, and stops. The men opened the rear door and throw Ashley from the back of the van, into the street, and drive off.

Ashley can hardly move, but knows she is now free. Slowly she rolls to her stomach and cries. She feels so helpless, and thinks she will die out in the middle of nowhere. She tries to stay strong, but that is a difficult task. She knows she has to get help. She tries to get up slowly, but the pain in her arm brings her back to the ground.

Natalie sits in the red SUV and stops in the top of a hill. She sees the van pull over and waits to see what will happen. She sees Ashley fly fron the van and lay motionless, completely naked, in the middle of the street. Ashley lays there for a few minutes before she begins to stir. When she tries to get to her feet, Natalie slams on the accelerator.

Ashley is dizzy and woozy, but manages to sit upright. She does not know how she will get help, so she prays for a miracle. She then hears an engine roar in the background. A car is coming. She tries to get to her feet. If she can flag down the driver, she can get a ride to a police station. She waves her broken arm in the air as she sits up.

Natalie guns the SUV down the road, at speeds in excess of 85 mph. When she sees Ashely raise her arm, she drops the transmission into third gear, and gets a quick boost of speed. At 90 mph, she feels impact.

Natalie runs the grill of the truck into Ashley's face. Her skull explodes, and gray matter covers the front of the truck. Death is instantaneous.

Natalie glances in the rear view mirror as she drives away. Seeing Ashley's mangled corpse is enough for her. Five targets down with only one left. She is ready to take on Heather, but first, she has to get rid of Yuri, who is still sleeping in the passenger seat.

Natalie thinks quickly as to how she can rid herself of her drunken passenger. She remembers the directions to his house and gets an idea. Ventura Boulevard is a steep, straight hill that points to the train station.

All she has to do is make a right on the street after the cul-de-sac and she will be in perfect position. She makes a left and heads to the hill.

Upon reaching the top of the hill, she puts the car in neutral, sets the parking brake and gets out. She opens the back of the truck and looks for something heavy. She can only find a new laptop, still in its box. She grabs the box and returns to the driver side. She reaches over, and unbuckles Yuri's seatbelt, then places the laptop box on the gas pedal. The engine roars in response. Quickly, she slams the truck into drive, pops the brake and jumps from the truck as it screams down the hill.

The train station is quiet as usual during a late afternoon. Passengers line the terminal and wait for the train to arrive. On the street, the guardrails lower as the train approached. The train arrives and people pile on, ready to go home and relax after a hard day of working. No one sees the truck coming.

The red SUV slams into the train at full speed. The passenger car rocks and passengers on the impact side fly from their seats. In the truck, Yuri soars from the passenger seat, crashes through the windshield and lands face first onto the hood of the truck. The jagged edge at the rim of the windshield slices deeply into his belly. The combined effects of the alcohol, sleeping pills and impact keep him unconscious as he bleeds to death. The engine shuts off at impact and the gas tank ruptures. Gas spills all over the ground. Sparks fly from the side of the rail car. The spilled gas ignites and explodes. The firebell shoots inside train car, incinerating most of the passengers.

An hour later, police and paramedics are trying to come to grips with this tragedy. Local and national media have flocked to the scene and the police are working hard to get the cameras away. A cab drives past the scene and looks at all the chaos. The driver turns on the radio to catch a news report on the situation.

Details are sketchy at this time, but police suspect that this horrific accident was caused by a drunk driver speeding down the hill, and barreling into the train at over 90 miles per hour. Eyewitnesses say they never saw the truck coming. Survivors were rushed to the hospital with second and third degree burns cover 75% of their bodies. Including the driver, the death toll stands at 23 and climbimg.

"Can you believe that Miss?" he asks his passenger. "How terrible! Very tragic!"

"I know." She answers. "It's amazing what some people are capable of."

Natalie studies the scene from the back of the cab. She has no doubt the police will link the truck and the dead drunk to the mysterious corpse they will surely find. Natalie shifts all her focus to Heather. She has saved the best for last.

"Driver," she says, "the WSU campus please. North dormitory parking lot."

Heather is going crazy. The time is 9:52 pm and she has called Ashley no less than ten times, each call going unanswered. She panics, not knowing where her best friend is. Her bags and belongings are packed, but her and Ashley made a plan not to leave alone. They were supposed to speak at 8:00 pm, but Ashley stopped answering her phone and had not returned a single call. She cannot wait much longer. She grabs her coat and is ready to go to Ashley's dorm, when her room phone rings. She quickly answers it.

"Ashley," she begins, "where the hell are you?"

"Heather, this is Lynn. Ashley's with me." The caller replies.

"Lynn!" Heather shouts. "Oh my God, where have you been? Don't you know what's been going on around here?"

"I got attacked, but was able to escape." Lynn replies. "I've been in protective custody since. Heather, we don't have much time. I know who the killer is. I figured it out when he attacked Ashley."

"Oh my God." Heather says. "Is she okay, is she hurt?"

"No time to explain." Lynn shoots back. "He's after you! You have to get out of there!"

"Where do I go?" Heather asks in a panic.

"We were able to sneak out to a construction site," Lynn answers, "not too far from where the cops are holding us. It's on the 1900 block of Davinson Avenue. Get here now! We can only wait for you for so long."

"I'm on my way." Heather responds. She hangs up the phone and runs out the door.

Satisfied with herself, Natalie hangs up the phone. She has convinced Heather that she is Lynn and is leading her to her final resting place. Natalie leaves the phone booth, gets into her truck and heads for the construction site on Davinson Avenue.

Heather is torn between two emotions, relief and fear. She is relieved to hear that both Lynn and Ashley are okay, but is afraid of an unknown killer coming to end her life. She is not thinking clearly. All she knows is to find Davinson Avenue and get there as soon as possible. She gets in her car and brings up the street on her navigation system. Once she finds it, she speeds from the campus, vowing to leave this ordeal behind her.

Natalie reaches the consruction site and parks her truck behind the building. She climbs into the flatbed of the truck and unlocks the freezer.

If she's expecting to find Lynn, the she's gonna find her!

Some of the ice in the freezer is still intact. Most of it has melted and the liquid at the bottom is a reddish-brown color. Natalie shifts the top layer away and peers face to face with Lynn's corpse. Her skin has turned purple and blood has clotted in her mouth and on her forehead. Natalie scoops more ice out of the freezer and grabs Lynn's arm. The girl is stiff as a board from rigor mortis and feels heavy. Using all her strength, Natalie hoists Lynn out the freezer and throws her to the ground outside the truck. Lynn's body functions failed shortly after her death, and stool pours out of her as she falls to the ground.

After closing the truck, Natalie grabs the dead Lynn and drags her into the building under contruction. Adjusting her grip, she takes her upstairs and drops her in the center of the floor; not a moment to soon. Natalie hears a car pull outside and honk its horn. She glances over and sees Heather step out. This is it, Natalie's moment of victory, and she cannot wait.

Heather turns off her car and steps out the driver side door. She hits the horn again, but gets no response.

"Lynn!" She calls out.

"Heather?" A voice responds. It sounds like Lynn.

"Where are you?" Heather calls back.

"Upstaiars." The voice replies. "I need help, Ashley's hurt!"

Heather runs into the building and looks for a way to the second story. She heads up the stairs and stops. It is dark and she cannot see much around her. As her eyes adjusts to the moonlight, her vision clears up.

"Lynn?" She calls.

No response.

Walking towards the center of ther room, she sees someone lying on the floor. She cannot tell who it is, but sees the dark skin and thinks it as Ashely. The figure does not move and is completely silent.

"Ash?" She asks timidly.

No response.

She squats next to the young woman and places her hand on the girl's shoulder. The girl rolls over and Heather stares into the face of death.

The girl is Lynn. She is dead, her head is cracked open, mouth is frozen in the open position, teeth are broken, and her eyes are wide open, staring back at Heather.

Heather screams in horror and recoils backwards on her backside. She conintues to scream as her heart races. She brings her hand to her face and covers her mouth. She shuts her eyes and cries as she cowers next to a wall. She stops screaming and crawls back to the body. After taking a second heartwrenching glance, she regocnizes her friend.

"Lynn?" She asks.

A loud whistle echoes from the other end of the room behind her. As a reflex, Heather turns around to face the sound.

WHAM!

Heather feels a hard strike on her lower jaw and falls to the ground, hitting her head on the floor. She closes her eyes, grabs her throbbing mouth, and sucks on her bottom lip. She tastes blood. When she opens her eyes, she is face to face with her dead friend. She rears backwards away from the corpse and is grabbed from behind.

She feels herself being hoisted from the floor and flung into a nearby wall. She is held there as multiple blows are landed on her back. She cries in pain as each shot hits her spine. She is thrown back to the ground, where her mysterious attacker mounts her midsection, grabs her by the shirt and punches her repeatedly in the face. She puts her arms up in a futile attempt at defense, but most of the punches find their mark. After numerous punches, hands are wrapped around her neck and her airway is cut off. Heather claws at the grasp on her throat as she feels her air slip away. The grip tightens and Heather becomes dizzy. She feels her limbs go weak, when suddenly the clutch is released, and the attacker dismounts. Heather opens her eyes and places her hands on her neck as she feels the cold air rush into her lungs.

Heather's body throbs in pain. She is badly beaten, bleeding from her nose and eyes, and almost strangled to death, when her attacker relents. Heather is confused, but does not bother to find out why. She rolls over and tries to get up, but she is kicked in the gut. She collapses back to the ground, coughing and wheezing from getting her wind knocked out. Finally, her attacker speaks.

"Quit crying bitch!" The voice says.

It is a female voice that Heather recognizes. It sounds almost like Lynn, but she knows it is not. It is the voice that lured her to the site, but that is not the only thought in Heather's mind. She has heard this voice before, prior to this night. Heather looks up and sees a figure standing about five feet away from her. Judging by the voice and body shape, it is a female. Her face is covered in darkness, but her midsection is visible in the moonlight. Her back is turned, and Heather stares at a grotesque tattoo of a black widow spider killing a bee.

"WHAT DO YOU WANT FROM ME?" Heather screams.

"Not a single fucking thing!" the girl quietly responds.

"Who are you?" Heather asks.

"You're the first one to ask that question." The girl answers.

"What?" Heather is confused.

"Monica never asked that question." The girl continues. "But then again, being locked in a bathroom while choking on your own blood and vomit will always prevent questions."

Heather is shocked as she listens to this girl give an account of Monica's death.

"At least you got you say goodbye.' The girl continues. "Marco didn't get that chance. Funny thing is, he was still pissed at you while he drowned."

"Marco?" Heather gasps. "You?"

"Lynn was pissed at you too," she continues, "but don't worry. I put the bitch on ice for you."

As Heather hears the names of her friends, she is frozen with fear. She realizes that she is confronted with their killer, ans she is next on the list.

"Howard was easy." The girl says. "He chose to obey me. His death should be considered a suicide. Ashley had it rough though."

"Ashley?" Heather cries. "Please no."

"Oh yes!" The girl giggles. "After having her fill of four skinhead assholes, she kissed the front of an SUV as I rammed it down her throat!"

"Stop!" Heather screams as she cries. "Please stop!"

"Don't cry Heather!" The girl says. "Besides, you made me. You let all this happen. Maybe, I should thank you"

"You're crazy!" Heather shouts.

"Which is why," the girl continues, "I've decided, that you deserve to know who killed them, and who is going to kill you!"

The girl turns around and steps forward as she speaks. The moonlight creeps up her body as she moves, slowly revealing her face. Heather scampers backwards on her hands as her assailant moves towards her. At last, the murderer is revealed, and Heather freezes in shock and disbelief.

"Natalie?" she asks.

Natalie springs into action. She lunges forward and slams Heather's head on the ground. Grabbing Heather by the throat, she brings their faces together and stares Heather in the eyes.

"Beg me Heather." Natalie says softly. "Beg me to stop. Beg me to spare you. Beg me for mercy, and maybe I'll make your death a painless one."

She releases her grip on Heather's neck and stands up. Heather gasps for air, gagging and coughing. She knows she has little time, and she is marked for death. She has no time to think.

Natalie stands up and walks away from Heather. The time for toying with her is over and she wants to get this over with. She heads to a nearby table that contains an assortment of tools. As she reaches for a hammer, she is tackled from behind. She crashes into the table and the tools scatter.

Heather flips Natalie over and begins to punch her in the face. Natalie is able to deflect most of the blows, but is struck repeatedly. Heather gets up and tries to make a run for the stairs. Natalie gets off the floor and gives chase. Halfway down the stairs, Natalie jumps on Heather's back and the girls tumble down the rest of the way to the ground floor.

Natalie is the first off the floor and she kicks Heather as she tries to stand. Heather rolls as she recoils from the blow. She blocks a second kick attempt by grabbing Natalie's foot and tourqing her knee, sending her assailant to the ground. Heather again tries to get to her feet and get away, but she is tackled and mounted just like before. She uses one arm to defend herself and reaches out with her free hand to grab anything she could use. She finds a small pile of long nails. She grabs a handful and swings at Natalie's side.

Natalie yelps as four nails embed into her flesh, and she falls off Heather. Now free, Heather rolls over on top of Natalie and presses her knee into the nails, pushing them further into Natalie's side. Natalie grunts in pain as the nails push deeper, but still manages to reach up and strangle Heather.

The redhead continues to fight and begins to punch her attacker, but Natalie does not relent. Heather, in a desperate move, rears her knee back and drives it into Natalie's side, burying the nails completely into her skin. Natalie lets out a scream and releases Heather's throat. Heather goes on the attack and repeatedly punches Natalie in the face.

Natalie can only block a few of the strikes. She reaches up and presses two of her finger onto Heather's eyes. Heather stops punching and tries to shoo Natalie's hand away. Natalie is able to quickly glance her surroundings and finds a pile of sawdust. She grabs a handful and rubs it fiercely into Heather's eyes. The girl yells and falls off Natalie. Heather lays on the ground, trying to clear the sawdust from her face. Only a small amount gets into her eyes, but she feels a burn nonetheless. Natalie takes the second she has free and rips the nails out of her side. She screams as the nails are extracted. She gets to her feet and stomps Heather in her stomach and face. The pounding splits Heather's upper lip open and the blood pours.

Heather's vision is impaired by the sawdust, but she is able to see her attacker. She times Natalie's next strike and grabs her foot. She shoves the foot to the side and kicks Natalie in her open wound. This time, the pain is immense and Natalie falls to the ground. She cluthes her side and the fresh blood flows. Heather barely stirs as she lays on the floor. She is beaten, bloodied, and bruised, but she is still alive and has to take advantage. She glances to her right and sees her car outside. Natalie is still on the ground bleeding, and this may be her only chance to get away. She moves very slowly, her dizziness preventing faster movements, and gets to her feet. Her vision is blurry and she can hardly keep her balance, but she steps forward and slowly makes her way to the car.

Slowly, one-step at a time, Heather moves. Her throat is rugged and she coughs as she breathes. She wipes her mouth every few steps and catches the blood she is coughing. The world is silent, but she keeps moving. Slowly, the car is coming closer. Just outside the door, about 50 yards away, and she can leave, if she keeps moving. Suddenly the silence is broken, and Heather hears a heavy labored step right behind her. She reacts quickly, twisting and swinging her fist wildly behind her. She feels her punch connect, and sees Natalie fall back to the ground holding her mouth. Heather falls to her knees, turns back to her car, stands back up and resumes her pace to her escape.

Natalie rolls on the ground, and sees Heather reach the door of the building. She grows angrier, but her body aches all over, she bleeds profusely from her side, her bottom lip is busted open by the last punch, and her knee throbs from being twisted. She cannot give up, but fuctioning is not easy. She picks herself up and stumbles forward a few feet before falling over. She lifts her self again and freezes. In front of her is a hammer. It represents her last chance at redemption. She grabs it and stumbles forward, hurrying towards the door.

Heather is now outside. She is so close to freedom, she becomes excited. She moves slightly faster and reaches the car. She falls over and leans on the passenger door. She reaches into her pocket and fishes for her keys.

CRASH!

Heather falls backwards and looks up. Natalie stands next to the car, holding a hammer she just crashed through the window. She retracts her arm and reaches down for Heather. Heather reacts by grabbing Natalie's bloody shirt and squeezing the wound tightly. Natalie grunts and falls back, letting go of Heather. Both girls climb to their feet.

Heather swings her fist and catches Natalie in the eye. Natalie recoils, but stays on her feet. Heather swings again after Natalie recovers. This time, Natalie is ready.

Natalie falls to her knees, under Heather's swinging arm. She rears to the side, swings the hammer, and buries it into Heather's stomach. Heather doubles over and clutchs her belly, unable to breathe. Natalie stumbles to her feet, holding her side as she moves, and stands over the hunched Heather. The young target tries to regain her composure, but her fate is now sealed. Natalie reaches back and swings the hammer with all her might. The head of the hammer plows into the base of Heather's neck. The girl drops to the ground with an audible plop and lays motionless.

Natalie stands over her target and breathes heavily. Heather lays face down on the ground crying and wimpering. As the seconds pass, the cries get louder and her breathing increases. Very soon, she is in an all out panic. Natalie just stands over her with a deranged look. Her anger has reached an apex and she wants to finish the job, but she wants Heather to see it coming.

"Get up!" she demands.

Heather looks to her sides and continues to panic, but she does not move.

"Bitch, I said get up!" Natalie repeats.

Heather looks to her right and jerks her head hard, but does not move or say anything. Her panic increases.

"GET THE FUCK UP!" Natalie screams.

Heather screams in response, yet still does not move. She keeps looking to her right and jerking her head, as if willing herself to get up and move, but her body is non-responsive. Natalie is beyond pissed off and willl not repeat herself. She squats next to her victim and swings the hammer onto Heather's left hand, shattering the bones.

Nothing. No movement, no scream of pain, and no reaction in her hand in any way. Natalie freezes for a second, then begins to laugh.

As she laughs, Heather screams. She screams for help, begging anyone withing range to come to her aide, but she does not move. Natalie shifts on the ground and stares Heather in the face. The girl stops screaming.

"Tell you what." She says. "If you can lift your hand and flip me off, I'll let you go."

Heather stares at her hand and contorts her face in intense concentration. She grits her teeth and nods her head, but her hand will not respond. She screams in panic, and Natalie laughs.

Natalie springs to her feet, grabs Heather by one of her paralyzed legs and drags the girl towards the back of the contruction site. Heather screams as she is taken away. Once they reach the back of the building, Natalie drops the screaming girl. She stomps on Heather mouth in a successful attempt to shut her up.

"Please, stop." Heather begs after she spits away the blood coming from her lips. She is woozy, dizzy, and can hardly think straight.

Natalie ignores her and surveys the area. She finds a ditch that was dug and looks inside. The ditch leads to a hole where a large pipe is laid out. Next to the hole is a large pile of dirt. It looks to be the connection point to the sewer. Perfect.

Natalie returns to Heather, regrips her leg and drags her to the ditch. She lays her parallel to the trench, and pushes her in. Heather rolls clumsly into the hole, but cannot control herself. She stops laying face up looking at Natalie from the bottom of the ditch. She cries as she lays there, and gives up all hope. She cannot move her arms and legs, and therefore she cannot escape. Her breathing escalates as her panic builds. Natalie looks directly into Heather's eyes, and senses her impending triumph. She delivers a heartfelt eulogy.

"This is the end." She begins. "The end of my pain, the end of my torment, and the end of my past. A past that I did not want, but had forced upon me, by you. Your hatred, abuse, and treatment of me, led me to this, and while I may burn in hell for this, it was well worth it.

In honor this occasion, I will be true to to your word, and put you in the ground."

Natalie grabs a nearby wooden plank, and uses it to shovel the dirt into the ditch. Heather screams at the realization that she is being buried alive. She screams loud for someone to help her. Natalie welcomes the screams as shovels the dirt. Starting at Heather's feet, she moves her way upwards until she reaches Heather's face. She sweeps a large mound of dirt onto Heather's head, muffling her screams. Heather shakes her head to clear her airway, but the dirt keeps coming. Within minutes, she is covered.

Natalie does not take notice of when Heather falls silent. She continues to move the dirt into the hole, burying Heather alive, until no more dirt remains.

When the pile is cleared, Natalie falls to her knees. She feels a warmth and a joy in her heart she has never experienced before. Her tormentors are dead, killed one by one by her hand, and will never abuse her again. She feels the years of fear lift from her shoulders in that one instant, and feels like a new woman. It is a sudden rush of euphoria that she does not know how to handle. She looks up into the sky and cries.

With each tear she sheds, she feels the years of pent up pain, hurt, and anger release from her soul. Her memories of her torment flood her minded, and as each tear runs down her cheek, she sees them vanish. She stays on the ground and cries for hours, knowing her journey is complete.

Friday morning arrives, and the weather is perfect. The sky is clear, the morning dew glistens on the neighborhood lawns and birds are singing. Looking out the window, Rebecca thinks of Natalie, and wishes she were there with her. Although her grand daughter is away at college, Rebecca still makes phone calls, trying to find a way to get Natalie into the world of high fashion. She feels Natalie is too good for college and needs to be in a world were her looks will be appreciated and get her all the things she wants in life.

A honking horn brings Rebecca out of her daydream. She walks to the front of her house, to see what the commotion is about. She looks out the front window, and nearly drops her coffee. Her husband's old pickup truck is parked outside with the engine turned off, and the driver is leaning on the hood. Rebecca runs outside to greet the surprise visitor.

"Natalie!" She exclaims in excitement and hugs her grand daughter. Natalie winches slightly from the pressure on her wounds, but does not let on to her injuries.

"Hey Nana." Natalie replies.

"Oh dear child," Rebecca begins, "I've been watching the news, it's a madhouse up there. Did they close the campus while they investigate?"

"No." Natalie answers. "I just, um, decided to leave. You were right. I belong in a different world, not college."

"I wish I knew you were coming back so soon," Rebecca says, "I would have had your room ready and so forth."

"It's okay, it was a last minute decision." Natalie replies. "Nana, I'm ready to follow in my mother's footsteps, and in yours."

"I'm so glad to hear that." Rebecca again embraces Natalie. "Well, come inside. We've got so much to go over." She leads Natalie inside the house. "We need to discuss locations, photographers, designers, and of course, how much you'll get paid."

"Nana," Natalie interrupts. "If it's okay with you, I would just like to take today to rest and chill out."

"Oh, of course." Rebecca replies. "You must be emotionally drained from all that's happened."

"Yeah, it's been traumatic." Natalie responds. "I'll worry about the upstairs room later; my regular room will be fine."

"Sure," Rebecca begins, "that's no problem. I was about to head out and run some errands in town. Would you like to go?"

"I'd love to, but I think it's best I stay home for right now." Natalie answers.

Natalie gathers her luggage and makes her way downstairs to her basement bedroom. It is unchanged and exactly how she left it. The lamp is still dim, the paint is still peeling, and the furnace is still loud. The only change is Natalie. No longer is she the same unsecure, scared, and timid little girl she was when she first arrived six long years ago. She no longer cares about being intelligent or getting good grades. Though indirectly and not true to the exact words, she finally learned the lesson her mother tried to teach her so long ago. She used her natural gifts to get what she wanted; her murderous mind and cunning.

She sits down at the foot of the bed and spreads out her six mementos: a skeleton key, a leather wallet, a pair of white lace panties, a scarlet "SIGMA" button down shirt, a police badge and a small USB flash drive. She stands up and removes her blouse, revealing her black widow tattoo on her back, the seventh and final memento. She falls onto her bed, laying on top of the items and faces the ceiling.

Her mission is complete, the deeds are done, her enemies suffered, and were murdered by her hand. No obstacle, including the good Detective Olivarez, could prevent her. She feels a level of satisfaction, but not contentment. As she looks up, she stares and does not blink. Her conviction runs deep and her mind is focused, but her thoughts are very clear. The 24 hours between Heather's murder and Natalie's homecoming gave her time to reflect. While the original six tomented her, she realized that they were not the only ones guilty of her misery. Her battle is won, but the war rages on.

Six down, two more to go!

www.ingramcontent.com/pod-product-compliance
Lightning Source LLC
LaVergne TN
LVHW041807060526
838201LV00046B/1166